The Romantics

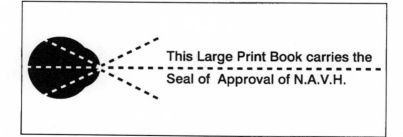
This Large Print Book carries the
Seal of Approval of N.A.V.H.

THE ROMANTICS

Pankaj Mishra

Thorndike Press • Thorndike, Maine

L P

Published in 2000 by arrangement with Random House, Inc.

Thorndike Press Large Print Basic Series.

The tree indicium is a trademark of Thorndike Press.

The text of this Large Print edition is unabridged.
Other aspects of the book may vary from the original edition.

Set in 16 pt. Plantin by Rick Gundberg.

Printed in the United States on permanent paper.

Library of Congress Cataloging-in-Publication Data

Mishra, Pankaj.
   The romantics : a novel / Pankaj Mishra.
    p. cm.
   ISBN 0-7862-3001-0 (lg. print : hc : alk. paper)
   1. Vårånasi (India) — Fiction. 2. College students — Fiction. 3. East and West — Fiction. 4. Young men — Fiction. 5. Large type books. I. Title.
   PR9499.3.M538 R66   2000b
   813'.914—dc21   00-064866

ACKNOWLEDGMENTS

My foremost debt is to Barbara Epstein. It would be hard to imagine this book without her support. Jason Epstein's early confidence in *The Romantics* was as crucial as his later suggestions. Mary Mount at Picador was a brilliant, ever-helpful editor, and I was fortunate in having such a conscientious publisher as Peter Straus. Sanjeev Saith at IndiaInk offered a very sensitive reading of the book. Hilton Als, John H. Bowles, Ulf Buchholz, Robyn Davidson, Helen Epstein, Arvind Krishna Mehrotra, Vandana Mehrotra, Judith Miller, Nicholas Pearson, and Tarun Tejpal offered valuable suggestions. I am grateful to Gillon Aitken for his encouragement through all the past few years. It has been a pleasure to work with Emma Parry and Sally Riley. I am also indebted to people who encouraged and assisted me in different ways: Robyn, Julie, William and Olivia, Norma, John, Patrick, Stuart, Chris and Sarah, Christina, the Sharmas at Mashobra, Paul, and my parents and sisters.

PART I

1

When I first came to Benares in the severe winter of 1989 I stayed in a crumbling riverside house. It is not the kind of place you can easily find anymore. Cut-price "Guest Houses" for Japanese tourists and German pastry shops now line the riverfront; touts at the railway station and airport are likely to lead you to the modern concrete-and-glass hotels in the newer parts of the city. The new middle-class prosperity of India has at last come to Benares. This holiest of pilgrimage sites that Hindus for millennia have visited in order to attain liberation from the cycle of rebirths has grown into a noisy little commercial town.

This is as it should be; one can't feel too sad about such changes. Benares — destroyed and rebuilt so many times during centuries of Muslim and British rule — is, the Hindus say, the abode of Shiva, the god of perpetual creation and destruction. The world constantly renews itself, and when you look at it that way, regret and nostalgia seem equally futile.

The past does live on, in people as well as

cities. I have only to look back on that winter in Benares to realize how hard it is to let go of it.

It was pure luck that I should ask the pujari at the riverside temple about cheap places to rent at the very moment Panditji came in with his offering of crushed withered marigolds. Panditji, a tiny, frail, courteous old musician, overheard our conversation. He saw me as a fellow Brahmin who had fallen on hard times and he offered to help. With his oversized rubber flip-flops slapping loudly against the cobblestone paving, he led me through narrow winding alleys, past large-eyed cows and innumerable little shrines to Hanuman, to his house. We went up steep stairs, past two identical enclosed courtyards on the ground and first floors, on which opened a series of dark bare rooms, to a tiny room on the roof. Panditji, his white wrinkled hands fumbling with the large padlock and the even larger bolt, unlocked the door. I saw: sunlight streaming in through a small iron-barred window that looked out onto a temple courtyard; whitewashed walls, a cot with bare wooden boards, a writing table and straight-backed wicker chair; fluffs of dust on the rough stone floor. The room, Panditji said, could be mine for just Rs. 150, what he called "Indian" rent, meals not included.

Oddly, I hardly ever spoke to Panditji again. He spent his days in a haze of opium under a pile of coarse wool blankets. In the evenings he would awaken sufficiently to give sitar lessons to American and European students — all identical with their long hair, tie-dyed shirts, and stubbly, emaciated, sunken-eyed look. I saw him occasionally, wearing a muslin dhoti and white Gandhi cap, carrying a pail of milk back to the house from the corner sweetshop, the skin on his exposed bony legs shriveled and slack, his sacred thread dangling from under his woolen vest. We nodded at each other, but never exchanged more than a word or two. All my dealings were confined to his arthritic wife, Mrs. Pandey, who lived in one of the dark bare rooms on the first floor with her family retainer, Shyam; she had long cut off all contact with her husband and claimed not to have gone downstairs for over fifteen years. The tenants lived in two small bedsitters on the roof, and I shared the view of the river, the sandy expanses beyond it, and the brooding city toward the north, the looming cupolas and minarets, the decaying palaces and pillared pavilions, with Miss West.

Miss West (as she was called by the local shopkeepers — it was weeks later that I discovered her first name was Diana) was En-

11

glish, middle-aged, and, from what I could tell, well-to-do — she presumably paid the "foreign" rent for her room. The perception that Miss West with her clean high forehead, hazel eyes, slender neck, and straight blond hair, now flecked with gray, had been very beautiful at one time came to me only later, when I was more accustomed to the physiognomies of white Europeans. Her presence in Benares, in a tiny room on the roof, where she appeared to do nothing all day except read and listen to Western classical music, was a mystery to me. I thought it had to do with some great sadness in her past. It was a large judgment to make on someone I didn't know at all. But the impression — seemingly confirmed by the serene melancholy she gave off as she sat on the roof, a Pashmina shawl draped around her shoulders, and gazed at the river for long hours — this impression came out of the mood I lived with for those first few exceptionally cold days in Benares, the thick mists rising from the river and shrouding the city in gray, the once-hectic bathing ghats now desolate, the sad-sweet old film songs from an unseen transistor radio in the neighborhood reaching me weakened and diffused as I lay huddled under multiple quilts in my chilly damp room, trying to read *The World as Will and Idea*.

It was the kind of big book that idleness made attractive. So many long hours of wisdom and knowledge it promised! It was why I had come to Benares after three years in the nearby provincial town of Allahabad, where I had been an undergraduate student at a decaying old university. In Benares, I wanted to read, and do as little as possible besides that. The city, its antiquity, its special pleasures, held little attraction for me.

But the weather made for a special kind of gloom. It brought back memories of an earlier visit to Benares. I was seventeen years old then. Hastily summoned from Allahabad, I had come with my father to perform the last rites for my mother. It was then I'd had, tinged with my confused grief and sense of loss, my first impression of the city. The thick river mists through which we rowed one cold early morning to scatter my mother's ashes; the priest with the tonsured head reciting Sanskrit mantras in a booming voice and waving incense sticks over the rose petals bobbing on the ash-smeared water; the temple bells and conches ringing out in unison from the great mass of the city — these were the memories, almost phantasmagoric, I had of that visit, and they kept coming back to me in those first few days in Benares.

I read slowly but understood little of *The*

World as Will and Idea. Nevertheless, I soldiered on. Other big books awaited their turn in the small octagonal niches in the whitewashed walls of my room where, when I first arrived, vermilion-spattered clay idols of Krishna and Vishnu had stood; and frequently, in the middle of reading, I would look up and let my eyes wander over the thick multicolored spines and grow impatient at the slow progress I was making, at the long interval that separated me from those other books.

Then the mists lifted and a succession of cloudless days followed. The river gleamed and glinted in the midafternoon sun. Bright red and yellow kites hung high in the clean blue sky. Children appeared on the bathing ghats; the uneven cobblestone steps came to be chalk-marked with hopscotch rectangles; scrawny drug pushers lurked on temple porches where chess players sat hunched over tattered cardboards; pilgrims dressed and undressed all day long in a slowly turning kaleidoscope of Indian colors: the South Indians in their purple Kanjeevaram silk saris, the visitors from Rajasthan unwinding the spools of yellow and crimson turbans, the widows from Bengal in their austere white cotton. In the evenings, the funeral pyres in the distant north of the city were like glowworms in the gathering dusk.

I abandoned Schopenhauer and started on Turgenev's *Torrents of Spring.* Miss West, who put on the first of the flowery summer dresses I was to see her in, said, "What wonderful weather! We must celebrate, we must have a party." This sudden familiarity puzzled me. Did the "we" include me? I had exchanged only a few words with her. One of the very first things she said to me was: "Where did you learn to speak such charming English?" I hadn't known what to make of this remark. Was she being complimentary or condescending? One sunny morning on the roof, as she lay in her sagging charpoy, her legs partially exposed in a way I thought immodest, her oval sunglass frames accentuating the whiteness of her skin, a mysterious haunting melody floating out of her room — Beethoven's *Archduke Trio,* I later came to know — one morning, she had asked me about my undergraduate years in Allahabad. "You see, Rudyard Kipling wrote for a newspaper published from Allahabad — how do you pronounce it?" she said. "But tell me: did you enjoy yourself there? And why did you choose Allahabad of all places?" She spoke with a sharp emphasis, in short rapid sentences, her voice demanding a similarly precise and brief response.

There wasn't much I could tell her. These things couldn't be explained. Just as my father, when he announced to me his decision to move to an ashram in Pondicherry after my mother's death, hadn't needed to explain anything. His decision was in accordance with an old rite of passage: the withdrawal from the active world in late middle age, the retreat into the self. We instinctively understood these ancestral obligations; we rarely ever questioned them and never asked for explanations. It had been so when, after an indifferent education in a number of nondescript small-town schools across India, the time came for me to go to university. Three generations of my mother's family had gone to the university in Allahabad, a sister city of Benares, and it was to Allahabad that I had gone.

On the face of it, it wasn't a bad choice. Set up in 1887, the university was once known as the Oxford of the East. To seekers of jobs and careers in the colonial dispensation it offered an attractive pedigree. But unbeknownst to those of us who still set store by its old reputation, the university had suffered a steep decline in the years since independence. Anarchy reigned behind the still-impressive façade of its domes and towers. Academic sessions were in total disarray: examinations due in April were more likely to be held in December, if at all. Everyone was locked in conflict: students against students, teachers against teachers, teachers against students, students against the management, teachers against the management, students against the police. Often these conflicts turned violent. Students shot at each other on the streets with country-made revolvers. Late at night, you were hurled out of your sleep by the sound of a crude bomb going off somewhere in the vicinity. In the morning, you read the details in the crime pages of the local Hindi papers: political rivalry, ambush, instant death, investigation ordered, no arrests so far.

Miss West appeared shocked by the few things I told her. "How extraordinary!" she exclaimed. "How absolutely awful! You must have been very brave to have survived all that." Then, in a calmer tone, she added, "You know I never went to university. My father belonged to a generation where people didn't bother with educating their daughters."

I thought this odd. Prejudices against female education were a feature of poor societies; I didn't associate them with England. Could it be that her father couldn't afford to send her to university? I wasn't sure, and didn't think it was the sort of question I could ask. Then she mentioned the party and confused me further.

I was nineteen years old but hadn't ever been to a "party." The word itself brought to mind noisy, half-naked revelers; it suggested the kind of empty frivolity and moral laxity I had been brought up to disapprove. My view of Miss West altered; I now saw her as an organizer of parties.

At the same time I felt myself corralled into her preparations. I bought the welcoming garlands for the musicians who Miss West said would perform after dinner; I went out to the bazaar and looked at the various kinds of Bengali sweets available; and, overcoming an innate aversion to intoxicants and stimulants, I even arranged for the bhang-flavored thandai that I'd heard was the staple item at such occasions in Benares.

Miss West fretted over her guest list. After five years in the city, she knew a great many people. In the end, she invited only a handful of them. "Can't possibly have them all over. It's frightfully small, this place," she said, her pencil stabbing at the list of scribbled names. "Mrs. Pandey might object to that many people trooping in and out of her house."

Mrs. Pandey and Shyam, her retainer, did look askance at our preparations. Sitting close together on low wooden stools, they would look up from a brass plate of finely chopped tomatoes, ginger, and garlic to exchange muttered remarks as people came up and down the stairs carrying logs of rolled-up dhurries and bolsters. The general drift of these remarks — some of which I overheard — was that Miss West's party was a poor approximation of similar events in their own past. One evening before the party when I had gone to eat with them — as I did each alternate day, sitting cross-legged on the floor in their dark, sooty windowless kitchen, awkwardly inhaling smoke from the chulha fire over which Shyam rotated slowly inflating chapatis with a pair of rusty iron tongs — Mrs. Pandey spoke pointedly of the splendor of the musical soirees the Maharajah of Benares used to hold at one time. Her own father, a famous sitar player, she said, was an exalted guest at such gatherings. What about Panditji? I asked, referring to her husband downstairs. She looked scornfully at me. What about him? she seemed to say. I was soon to know that this was an obsessive theme with her: how the grandeur of her family connections had been fatally undermined by her marriage to Panditji, a penniless musician who, when he first arrived at her father's mansion as a student, Mrs. Pandey would claim, owned nothing other than the clothes he had on his undernourished body.

On the evening of the party, Mrs. Pandey ate early and then disappeared into her room. Panditji was as usual oblivious to the goings-on in his house. Only Shyam showed some interest. He lived the neutered life of a feudal retainer, aware of nothing except his mistress's wishes, and he rarely spoke a word apart from a clichéd proverb in Hindi he would repeat, without regard to context, as he fanned the chulha fire: "Greed," he would mumble, "is the biggest evil. It eats away man, destroys families, sunders son from parents, husband from wife . . ." This evening, he squatted on the floor, scrubbing brass dishes with coal ash and water, his jaw jutting out as he slowly chewed on his tobacco, and stared disconcertingly at the guests as they walked up to the roof.

The musicians had been the first to arrive, wearing long embroidered kurta and shawls that had been drenched in attar. Miss West, who wore an expensive-looking chocolate-brown dress of some soft shiny material and was to receive compliments for it from everyone except myself, made the introductions. "This is Samar," she said. "He wants to read everything." That was to be my role with her: the autodidact, the fanatical reader who wanted to read everything. She seemed to take a somewhat proprietary stance toward the sitar player among the musicians, a thin young man with tense sharp features and long, flowing hair, red betel juice around the corners of his mouth. His name was Anand. "Are you treating Catherine well?" Miss West asked him, and he replied in a tone of mock complaint, and with a heavy Indian accent: "But, Miss West, she must learn to cook." And Miss West, still bantering, said, "You sexist Indian men, you never change, do you?"

Mark was the next to arrive. He was studying "alternative" medicine in Benares. Miss West had shown me an essay he had written for an American magazine on the superiority of Ayurvedic medicine; it was the kind of thing Miss West seemed to like reading, anything that proposed a radical assault on received knowledge. The essay was full of technical terms I couldn't follow. But I was struck by the biographical note, which mentioned the various careers Mark had pursued at different stages in his life: poet, dishwasher, painter, Tibetan Buddhist, carpenter, and traveler through such remote lands as Ecuador and Congo.

On that first sighting, Mark's craggy broad-shouldered handsomeness, enveloped in a long Pathan suit, seemed to match perfectly the years of hard experience his byline hinted at. He was accompanied by two women. One of them — with close-cropped hair and glasses on her round, plump-cheeked face — was called Sarah. She was German and a practicing Buddhist, Miss West had told me, and I had wondered about the word "practicing": it seemed to me superfluous for someone who had gone to the trouble of converting to Buddhism from the faith she was born in. But I didn't raise the point with Miss West. I had seen Sarah before on the ghats — Miss West had pointed her out to me — and she had appeared serious enough about her new faith. She sat on the same spot every day, a step away from the waterline, and in the same contemplative posture: cross-legged, arms held straight in front, hands resting on her knees, palms facing upward, eyes fixed on some distant invisible object out on the river. Nothing seemed to distract her: neither the banter of the boys playing badminton on a chalk-marked court down below nor the late-evening bathers and the boatloads of tourists, who would stare curiously at the woman in semi-Indian attire sitting all by herself on the ghats.

The other woman accompanying Mark was his girlfriend, a snub-nosed woman called Debbie. Short and squat, she looked a diminished figure beside the tall and sturdy Mark. She wore long silver earrings over a slightly ill-fitting white cotton sari; extravagantly curled Indian clips kept her frizzy blond hair pressed on each side of her forehead. She spoke very fast; her sentences ended with a nervous giggle and an inquisitive gaze.

I helped Miss West set out the food on brass plates: dal, tandoori chicken, matar paneer, puris, and saffron-scented basmati rice. Miss West said, "Where's Catherine? She's always late, the poor girl," as she went around pouring the bhang-laced thick creamy thandai from a brass jug into clay cups I had bought at a nearby tea stall earlier that day. Everyone except myself drank the lassi (Miss West said, "Are you sure you won't have any? You are a real Brahmin, aren't you?" and Debbie turned to look appraisingly at me). It didn't take long for the cannabis to take effect. The voices and laughter grew louder; people grew careless in their postures: Mark slumped against a bolster, his back to the river and its fickle late-evening traffic of tourist-laden boats, and Sarah was half-recumbent on the white sheet, her thandai cup precariously perched upon her stomach. Several conversations grew around me.

I overheard bits of the conversation between Debbie and Sarah. Debbie was saying:

"You know, I met this really peculiar man at the Taj yesterday. Mark knows him; he's an Indian scholar of some sort, called Prasad. . . . Anyway he started asking me all kinds of really aggressive questions about Buddhism . . . and, you know, I could tell what he was thinking inside . . . something like 'What's wrong with this woman? Why's she a Buddhist?' etc., etc. I didn't like him at all. He sounded like a real jerk with his . . . sort of British public-school accent."

"How did he know you were interested in Buddhism?" Sarah asked.

"Well, he asked me what my religion was."

"What did you say?"

"Well, just that I was raised a Christian, but I'm now thinking of converting to Buddhism."

"What else did he say?"

"Nothing much really." Debbie seemed to lose interest in the topic. "He really ignored me altogether and started talking to Mark about how people in the West had completely misconstrued Buddhism and how . . . unequipped the Western mind is to receive a philosophy of negation and how people can only be — his phrase was 'part-time Buddhists.' I thought he was being totally ridiculous. So I . . . Oh, yes! He also asked me if I had read Hermann Hesse. I said, 'Who hasn't?'

And he said, 'So did Siddhartha inspire you to come to India?' It was *really* condescending."

Anand was telling the tabla player about the concert he was giving in Paris next year. "Good money," he said, in Hindi. "When I come back I want to open up a school for sitar players, free training, free meals, everything."

Mark was discussing with Miss West his plans to go back to America and get "serious" about Debbie. "I don't want to be a rolling stone all my life," he said. "You know, one of the great things for me about coming to India has been knowing about poverty and pain and suffering and realizing that there is a whole world outside America where people don't even have the basic things in life. I mean you keep seeing all those things on television, you know, those starving kids in Africa, but somehow you never get close enough to really feel it. It doesn't register much. It's just out there on a map and you never really care as much as you should. And then you see it face-to-face and, boy, it knocks you out. I feel I have been lucky in this respect both as an artist and a human being. Not many people get the chance to experience all this. Back home we are kind of trying to forget what pain and suffering are . . . keep . . . covers . . . only . . . real life . . . winners and losers . . . this . . . machismo . . . makes . . . pathetic failures. I mean spiritually, because we don't allow ourselves to suffer, experience pain. What I want to do when I get back is find a way of sharing my experience of Benares, and find some way of integrating it into daily life."

Miss West, who had given the impression of listening carefully until now, suddenly jerked her head up. "I am frightfully sorry, but I simply must attend to the garland situation," she said and walked away briskly. Mark watched her go, and then shook the ice cubes in his glass before draining his drink.

All around me, people spoke, laughed, ate, drank; and watching them, I became increasingly aware of the strangeness the occasion held for me. Was this what always went on at parties? I wondered: the easy exchange of confidences, the casual display of personality, the quick amiability and seemingly inconsequential chatter about things that appeared important.

It all seemed to be an esoteric ritual, and I took no part in the conversation. I didn't want to say the wrong thing and had no clear idea of what the right thing was. I did once ask Debbie — safely following Mark, who had asked me the same question — what she was doing in Benares. Passing through, she said, and gave her short nervous giggle, and I was so struck by her reply that I could not add anything more to my question.

At some point in the evening, a tall striking girl wearing a blue embroidered Kashmiri caftan appeared on the roof. I knew it was Catherine. I had heard of her from Miss West, who was frank in her disclosures about people she knew in Benares, and even franker about people she considered her protégés, such as Catherine and Anand. It was hard not to be distracted by Catherine's extraordinary beauty. Miss West had said, "She's very pretty." I was struck then by this way of looking at women. "Pretty": it wasn't a word much used for women in the world I had known, where even the most beautiful women were kept unaware of their advantage. Women were obedient daughters, dutiful wives, and devoted mothers; they weren't ever considered outside these roles. Now I looked at Catherine in the light of Miss West's remark, and the word "pretty" came to be crystallized by the lovely vulnerability of her face, the clear olive skin, the large hazel eyes that looked out at the world with a mixture of uncertainty and sadness, the full lower lip, the dark wavy hair that formed a perfect inverted V over her forehead. After this, her soft French accent was all the more unexpected; it made her seem oddly childlike, more human, more manageable.

Catherine's father was a leading banker in Paris, and she had come to Benares in order to get as far away as possible from her oppressively "bourgeois" parents — this deployment of a word I had previously encountered only in Marxist texts was new to me. In Benares, she had fallen in love with Anand, whom she met at one of Miss West's musical soirees. They lived together in a nearby riverside house. At the end of the winter Catherine planned to take Anand back with her to Paris, where he would attempt to make a living out of performances and studio recordings while Catherine finished her philosophy degree.

Miss West made the introductions. Again, I was presented as the tireless autodidact. Catherine smiled and asked me the predictable question about my current reading. I told her. "Turgenev?! Oh, he's wonderful," Catherine exclaimed. "All those country-house settings and passionate people. But I haven't read that book. Will you lend it to me?" "Yes," I found myself stammering, "yes."

Miss West said, in that unnaturally loud and tense voice I had heard for the first time that evening, "Shall we have some music now?" She looked around anxiously. "Shall we? Shall we?" she repeated. People interrupted conversations to nod weakly at her, and began reluctantly to move toward settling themselves on the two large bolster-strewn mattresses that had been placed directly opposite the musicians. The sitar and the tablas were unpacked and tuned. As everyone applauded, Miss West garlanded the musicians, put vermilion dots on their foreheads, and placed several incense sticks and diyas before them.

First, one of the performers who had come with Anand — an old courtesan who had quietly spent most of the evening in one corner of the roof — sang a Thumri. It was about Radha's love for Krishna, the longing that remains forever unfulfilled, and shades into a bittersweet acceptance of life and its limits; and it was sung well, with a depth of feeling that would have been impossible to predict from the appearance of the singer, who was about seventy years old, with eyes kohl-rimmed a forbidding black. Mark, who sat in front of me, obscuring my view of Sarah, kept shaking his head and throwing up his hands in the appreciative manner he seemed to have picked up from Indian audiences. Debbie sat cross-legged and stiff in a meditative posture, her eyes closed. Miss West, her face visible to me in profile, wore that melancholy expression she often had when she sat on the roof looking out over the river.

Then it was Anand's turn, and he played Raga Yaman, one of the gravest of Indian ragas, a look of tense concentration on his face, fingers sliding up and down the strings with a vehemence that was in sharp contrast to the somber stately notes produced by his instrument. Catherine accompanied him on the tanpura. "They are very much in love," Miss West had said, and I played with the words in my head, trying to fit them to what I saw before me. But Catherine and Anand barely glanced at each other; it wasn't easy to imagine between them the continuous exchange of tenderness and passion that the words "very much in love" suggested. So dissimilar they appeared: Anand, fidgety and intense, who with his thin face and tormented looks would always be associated with the warren of dark slumbering alleys around us; and Catherine, looking in her calm self-possession, as she would always do, from another world, richer and more fulfilled than the one she lived in now.

In the months that followed this evening, I was to see her in every mood and posture, in every kind of dress and at different times of the day; such rapt gazing as mine would leave a wealth of memorable images in my mind. But it is the picture of her sitting up very

30

straight on the jute mat, abstractedly plucking at the tanpura's strings, the light from the short flickering flame of the diyas bathing her clear unblemished face in a golden glow, that has stayed most vividly with me, and is the central force that illuminates the rest of the evening in my memory.

2

It didn't take long for my days in Benares to fall into the kind of self-imposed routine I knew during my undergraduate years in Allahabad. I got up early, awakened, more often than not, by the sounds from nearby houses: radios blaring devotional music, crying babies, wet laundry being slapped against the bathroom floor, the voices of people queuing up before the municipal tap in the alley below, water cannonading into plastic buckets.

Within an hour I was ready to leave. The door to Miss West's room was still closed when I went down the stairs to have breakfast with Mrs. Pandey and Shyam. I sat on a low wooden stall in their lightless kitchen and ate warm parathas off a brass plate and drank ginger-flavored tea from a scalding-hot steel glass. Shyam squatted before the chulha fire, fanning the flames with a sooty jute fan. Mrs. Pandey sat before me, slowly slicing vegetables in a large brass plate, her broad face expressionless as always.

I walked the three miles to the library — my

meager budget couldn't accommodate rickshaw rides to and from the university every day.

A thin crimson-edged mist hung over the river when I walked out of the house. The alleys leading to the main road would be empty, the houses sunk in a blue haze, still untouched by the sun, which had already begun to tentatively probe the façades of the houses lining the river. Rubbish lay in uneven mounds, or was strewn across the cobblestone street, firmly sticking to the place where it had been deposited by an overflowing open drain. After every twenty meters or so, a fresh stench hung in the air.

The road was full of potholes, which, when filled by unseasonal downpours, reflected the tops of the overlooking houses and a slice of the sky in their dirty gray stillness. There was little traffic, except for a few newspaper boys on cycles, who would jauntily pedal past the slow-moving rickshaws bulging with noisy schoolchildren, satchels, and plastic water bottles; these cyclists were swift sprightly figures, in contrast to the rickshaw drivers, silently toiling with their heavy loads, bare feet and legs thrusting at the obdurate pedal, their shoulders pushed back and arms stretched taut over the handles.

After the constriction of Lanka — box-shaped brick houses, shuttered shops, exposed drains, pavement vegetable vendors, and tea shops spilling out over the road — there would be the ever-renewed surprise of the university's green open spaces; the broad tree-lined avenues stretching from one end of the campus to the other; the sprawling cricket and hockey grounds; the quiet cool groves of bamboo, banyan, and mango trees.

The person I knew best in this other life I came to lead on the university campus — separate from the life I led in Panditji's house, with Miss West as neighbor — was Rajesh. His name was given to me by someone I knew in Allahabad, a man called Vijay. Vijay, once a secretary of the student union, had left Allahabad University almost middle-aged, after accumulating, in the manner of student politicians, six degrees in literature, commerce, journalism, and law. He was now a "contractor" — the much-used multipurpose word that could denote anything from a supplier of building materials to an organizer of arson and even murder. Almost all of the student politicians and troublemakers called themselves "contractors"; the word was considered more weighty than "businessman." But Vijay was a Brahmin, and he felt he must affect a certain aloofness from the common run of "contractors." He had made his name after organizing a large demonstration against the then prime minister, Indira Gandhi, when she visited the university a few years before she was assassinated. The demonstration turned violent when the police attempted to break it up, and the police were especially brutal with Vijay. In hospital with fractured arms and legs, and multiple stitches on his skull, Vijay received visits from national-level politicians from parties opposed to Indira Gandhi and briefly became famous.

Too old now to play an active part in student politics, he nevertheless displayed an elder-brotherly solicitude toward the Brahmin students at the university. He lobbied hard with the administration on their behalf to postpone exams, or to reinstate an expelled student; he worked overtime on the labyrinthine university bureaucracy to get more Brahmin students admitted into university hostels. He asked for nothing in return from those he favored other than their votes for Brahmin candidates in elections to the student union. That was how he came to know me: he volunteered to help me gain a health certificate from the university infirmary, and I turned into one of the young Brahmin students under his protective umbrella. "Studious" Brahmins like myself, he would say, pronouncing the English words with relish, needed "backers" if they were to go on studying without fear of disturbance from low-caste "lumpens" and "antisocial elements."

He had probably seen himself extending his patronage to Benares when he gave me Rajesh's name and asked me to look him up at the Hindu University.

I said I would, but I had little intention of doing so. In truth, I was made uncomfortable by Vijay. I had no sympathy for sectarian, caste- or religion-based politics; I wanted to keep as far away as possible from the constant skullduggery and intrigue that went on among different political factions, and frequently resulted in violence.

But then one evening, not long after I arrived in Benares, as I was coming out of the library, I saw a boy among a group of students whip out a crude pistol from under his long, grimy kurta and fire it into the air. He couldn't have been more than seventeen years old and he was indulging only in a bit of macho posturing. The boys accompanying him slapped him on the back and burst into laughter. But he made the rest of us jump out of our skins: the birds on the massive banyan trees outside took off with a loud flapping of wings; a rickshaw coming into the library compound braked abruptly and swerved into a hedge.

The boys had laughed afterward. But for that one brief moment, I had known real fear, and now the campus had different associations for me. As I returned home at dusk it appeared an ominous place; the possibility of violence seemed to lurk amid every group of students I encountered. I didn't know anyone at the university and was conscious more than ever of my vulnerability.

The university's recent troubled past only further increased my fear. For some months, the campus had been the setting for pitched battles between the police and students. Things were quieter now. But the peace was temporary; it could be broken by one carefully lobbed stone. A few hundred meters from the main gates to the campus was the office of the vice-chancellor, a much-hated figure among the students for his iron-handed methods, which were a frequent pretext for violent agitation. Here, the droves of policemen, nervous khaki-clad rookies, lay in wait. Sunk one moment on string cots before tents of gray weather-beaten tarpaulin, playing cards, their lathis and rifles and riot shields resting on the ground, at the first sign of trouble — that carefully lobbed stone, the sound of shattering glass, the explosion of a crude hand grenade — they could turn into a rampaging horde within seconds.

Not far away on the same road lived their antagonists, the students, in a row of hostels, also built in the Indo-Saracenic style. The rage that had undermined the university had found its easiest victim here; after years of arson and vandalism these hostels wore a look of extreme decrepitude. The aggressive black graffiti on the walls were a premonition of the damaged furniture and shattered window-panes and broken balustrades inside; the lines of white underclothing hung out to dry in the arcaded two-story blocks made the hostels resemble the old havelis outside Benares that had been overrun by squatters.

But the hostels were inhabited not only by students. They were actually sought after by outsiders. To young men from the region around Benares, they represented an important stage in their attempt to lift themselves out of conditions of extreme poverty. Rents were very low and sometimes didn't have to be paid at all. You could live in these hostels for many years while waiting for that miracle government job and not spend more than a few hundred rupees. Rajesh lived in one of the more run-down hostels. Wild grass grew in the quad and ran right up to the two long wings of the hostel. Soggy cigarette packs lay over a film of scum in the open stagnant drain that ran parallel to the wings. There were large light-green scars on the walls where rain and damp had seeped through; the plaster had peeled off in many places, leaving the brickwork exposed underneath. The lower half of the pillars had on them blood-red batik-like patterns made by students spitting betel juice. Piles of legless tables and chairs lay under the dark staircase, which smelled faintly of urine. Scraps of yellowing newspaper were scattered on the steps.

Most of the rooms were closed, heavy padlocks hanging on the doors. There was hardly anyone around: along the large quad where Rajesh's room was, a bare-torsoed man emerged from his room to drape a wet towel around the balustrade and then went straight back in.

Rajesh's room was at the end of a long corridor on the first floor; the door was open when I arrived. It was close to dusk and it was dark inside, where he was lying on a cot, wearing a turtleneck sweater and cheap polyester pants of the kind sold outside the university in the rows of tiny shops. He was reading a Hindi softback edition of poems by Faiz, the Pakistani exile, the poet of heartbreak and loss. He seemed completely absorbed.

He peered at me from behind the book as I knocked on the door. I introduced myself; I told him that Vijay had asked me to see him.

He seemed to know at once why I had come. "Yes, yes," he said and got up and held out his hand to me.

He was a tall, good-looking man with a slim supple frame and a slight glint of uncertainty in his probing dark-brown eyes. There was something buttoned-up, inscrutable, in his expression, in the way his thin lips clamped shut above a strong jaw. Thick black hair fell down from one side of his head; unlike most students at the university, he did not have a mustache. He had shaved badly that morning and tiny patches of stubble lay under his throat, just above where the turtleneck touched his skin.

He spoke slowly, with a great deal of deliberation — his Hindi had a faint regional accent — and his normally vigilant eyes lost their intensity and seemed to turn inward when he did so.

"Where are you staying in Benares?" he asked. I told him. He paused for an instant, and said, "Do you know Arjun?"

I said he was the son of my landlord. If he was surprised, he did not show it. He silently mulled over that piece of information while gazing out of the room and running his hand through his hair.

And then, abruptly, he asked, "Have you read Faiz?"

I said I had.

He didn't appear to have been listening. He picked up his book from where it was lying face-down on the cot and recited a few lines from it in a low, somber voice:

Ye dagh dagh ujala. ye shab-gazida sahar
Vo intizar tha jis ka, ye vo sahar to nahin,
Ye vo sahar to nahin jis ki arzu lekar
Chale the yar ke mil-jaegi kahin na kahin
Falak ke dasht men taron ki akhiri manzil
Kahin to hoga shab-e sust mauj ka sahil
Kahin to jake rukega safina-e-gham-e-dil.

(This leprous daybreak, dawn night's
    fangs have mangled —
This is not that long-looked-for break of
    day,
Not that clear dawn in quest of which
    those comrades
Set out, believing that in heaven's wide
    void
Somewhere must be the stars' last
    halting-place
Somewhere the verge of last night's
    slow-washing tide,
Somewhere an anchorage for the ship of
    heartache.)

A strange disquietude came over his face as he recited. After he finished, he sat still for a

41

moment, eyes fixed on the open book in his hand. He then abruptly got up and offered to get me some water; his eyes when they met my face were again full of uncertainty.

The earthen pot he picked up from under his bed turned out to be empty. He said he would refill it in the communal bathroom at the end of the corridor and went out.

The room felt less small and congested without him. Besides the strong cot, there was a rough study table, a wooden chair, and a jute-and-bamboo bookstand, its thin legs askew under the weight of dust-laden old books and papers. Cobwebs clung to the high ceiling and even to the broad sooty blades of the old-style fan overhead. From a solitary nail in the dark-blue wall hung a pair of cheap denim jeans. Muddy tennis shoes lay on the stone floor. Under the cot sat a black metal trunk, a familiar object that almost invariably accompanied a student on his first journey to college, on his passage to responsible adulthood. It was a common sight in the hostels of Allahabad; I had one when I first came to the university. But it was oddly distracting to see it here, Rajesh's name painted on it in stylish white Roman letters, above the word "University" wrongly spelled "Universty."

I noticed the bag of pistols last, probably because it belonged so naturally to the room and the hostel, was so much a part of the broken furniture and the wild grass and the betel-juice stains. A couple of pistols were bulging out of a jute shoulder bag lying on the floor, next to the green plastic bucket. I had seen the type before: ugly long-barreled metallic pieces that came out of some dingy back room in the poorer parts of the city. They looked unreliable and were indeed known to explode sometimes at the slightest bit of pressure on the trigger.

Vijay had told me that Rajesh was not in politics. I was less certain about what he actually did at the university. The pistols now made me wonder; they also made me nervous. I almost wished I hadn't come.

Rajesh came back with the water and then proposed that we go out for tea. "There is no light," he said, gesturing to the naked light-bulb hanging at the end of a long electric cord attached to the ceiling. "No light all day today."

It came to me that he wanted to get away from the room for another reason. Had this something to do with the pistols? But he had made no attempt to conceal them from me.

We walked through the deserted corridors to the rusty iron-barred gate, which had come loose from its hinges and furrowed the earth whenever it was moved. I asked Rajesh about

43

the locked rooms. He said that most of the students had gone home after their "Mains" — the main examination for the Civil Service.

He was silent for a while after this. But as we went through the gate and joined the tree-lined road leading to the tea stall, he asked me, "Are you planning to take the exam?"

I said I was, but I wasn't twenty-one yet.

I needn't have told Rajesh this, but the exam had been weighing on my mind for some time. It was partly why I had been sent to Allahabad University. It was why most people — at least in North India — went to university. In the past, the Civil Service — originally set up by the British — recruited large numbers of students from the universities of Allahabad and Benares. The number had diminished steeply in the last decade. But the old reputation had endured; these universities were still seen as portals to the Civil Service. Almost every student took the year-long three-tier exams at some stage; it was the thing to do whether or not anything in your academic record justified your ambitions. Though very exacting, they still offered the quickest route to affluence and power in North India. More important, they offered a way out of the hopelessness and desperation many of the students from nearby villages and towns knew awaited them at home. These students spent the best part of their twenties in their badly lit rooms, grappling with various exam "guides," memorizing whole essays on Gandhi and Nehru, cramming their heads with arcane statistics about the Indian economy. But only a handful of them ever qualified. To the rest, the results came every year as a fresh blow. They were the ones you saw age fast, with gray hair, crow's-feet, and faltering eyesight; and every year there were at least four or five suicides.

At the tea stall — known to me from previous visits — the potbellied owner stopped pumping his kerosene stove as soon as he saw Rajesh and left his position behind the stall to come scurrying forward to greet him.

Rajesh seemed to take these attentions coolly, but I was struck by the man's obsequiousness. Only a few days ago, I had seen him take a student by the scruff of his neck, after an argument that suddenly grew abusive, and send him tumbling out into the road to crash headlong into a terrified bicyclist. Violence against students could invite immediate retaliation, but the actions of the stall owner suggested that he was indifferent to that possibility, that he was on good terms with the more aggressive elements within the student community.

With a wet rag he wiped a narrow wooden bench, placed it close to the stall crammed with kettles and glasses, and motioned to us to sit on it. It was almost night now; the birds chattered loudly in the massive mango tree above us; mosquitoes danced around the petromax lamp on the stall.

Swathed in thick shawls and blankets, a few students appeared out of the dark. They saw Rajesh and came over to where we sat waiting for the tea to arrive. There was reverence in their attitude toward him; a couple of them even made as if to touch his feet but then flicked their hands across his knees instead.

Rajesh made no attempt to introduce them, but they all shook my hand and told me their names. From their accents and names, they appeared to be Brahmins from the rural districts near Benares and were no different from the students who hung around Vijay in Allahabad — "studious" boys from impoverished families, freshly arrived and vulnerable at the university, and in urgent need of "backers."

They began talking among themselves about an incident near the women's hostel, where an outsider had been caught molesting a woman student and was badly beaten up. I was sitting there listening when Rajesh turned to me and said, "You are here to study, is that right?"

I didn't know what to say and gave a brief nod.

"Then that is what you must do," he continued. "If anyone bothers you, let me know and I'll fix the bastard."

I couldn't see his face in the dark, but he spoke in his normal voice, without emphasis. The moment quickly passed as someone turned to Rajesh to ask him his opinion of Rajiv Gandhi — the Bofors scandal had just hit the headlines then and made Gandhi, so far known as Mr. Clean, suddenly seem corrupt and devious.

He didn't say anything for a while, and when he spoke, he went on for a long time. He spoke not only of Rajiv Gandhi, who he thought was out of touch with Indian realities, but also of his mother, Indira, and then of Pandit Nehru. He was certain that the Nehru-Gandhi family had caused great damage to India. He said that Nehru wasn't tough enough on corruption. A few sentences later, he said that circumstances had forced Nehru into being excessively accommodating. The speech was full of contradictions of that sort; he didn't seem to have thought through many of his ideas. But the students listened attentively and he spoke slowly, drawing out his words with great deliberateness, eyes skimming over the faces around him. At times, he would open his palm to emphasize a point and would bring it down with a soft *slap!* on his thigh.

He stopped only when the tea came, in tiny tumblers, cardamom-scented, sweet, served by a small boy wearing a threadbare oversized jacket over a grimy vest. We drank in small sips, greedily inhaling the warm, scented fumes first.

The conversation turned to a student who, after just two years in the Civil Service, had accumulated millions of rupees in illegal commissions. Someone added, in a tone of amused awe, that he had also fetched a dowry of Rs. 12 million.

Other such civil servants and large sums were mentioned; the students grew increasingly excited discussing them. The small boy in the threadbare jacket began to spray the scraggly ground with water from a leaking plastic mug. From the big transistor radio, encased in battered leather and hung from a nail in the trunk of the mango tree, came the baritone voice of the 7:00 P.M. Hindi sports newsreader.

A few students passing by the tea stall noticed Rajesh and instinctively bowed their heads in greeting. Rajesh responded with a faint nod. I noticed all this and became even less sure of what to make of him. The admiration for Faiz, the pistols, the Godfather-like status, the monologue denouncing the Nehru-Gandhi dynasty — he had left a mixed impression on me. But it was hard to deny the sense of security his presence gave, and I felt I could disregard the rest. Sitting next to him that evening, amid the only people I knew so far on the campus, I had felt myself safe for the first time in many days. The confusing bits about Rajesh, the parts that didn't add up, didn't seem to matter much at that point.

3

I came to know Rajesh slightly better over the weeks that followed. But I felt easier in Miss West's company; the world she represented held me more than the university, whose recurring tensions I found too familiar.

There had been an awkward moment with her after the party. I had been the earliest to leave and go to bed that evening. I was always in bed by ten, although this was one of my rules I was soon to break. The party had continued — I had gone to sleep with the soothing notes of Anand's sitar in my ear.

Early next morning I was awakened by the now familiar sounds of someone using the roofless toilet at the top of the stairs. There was no flush system in the toilet; we had to splash water from a large rusty Nestlé powdered-milk tin after filling it up from a tap that seldom worked. I heard the creak of the tin door, the hollow gurgle of water rolling down into the hole in the ground, and then the futile repeated tweakings of the dry tap.

And then I heard something else: sniffling sounds, as though produced by suppressed sobs. They went on for a while. I lay there in the half-dark, listening, and then got up to investigate.

It was chilly out on the roof, where smoke from Shyam's cooking fire below was already rising through the bluish air. Miss West was still in her soft brown party dress, sitting slumped against the low parapet amid last night's mess of overturned earthen cups, mattresses, rumpled sheets, and marigold petals.

She looked completely drained of the nervous vitality of the previous evening, disheveled and strange: in her sleep her vermilion dot had spread all across her high clean forehead. She glanced at me with tear-smudged eyes as I came out of my room; her voice still seemed under the influence of last night's bhang as she said, "Oh, hello there. Did I wake you up with my blubbering?"

I said she hadn't.

But she wasn't listening to me. With her face turned away from me, she said, "It's all a waste, isn't it? Such a fucking waste."

From her, the invective was unexpected and unsettling, and I was standing there wondering what to do when she said, "Listen, will you be a dear and help me to my room?" I took her proffered hand and helped her to her feet. She put her arm around my shoulders as we walked toward her room. "You are such a dear, *such a dear*," she muttered. I felt her weight on my shoulders and smelled the rose water Anand had brought with him and sprayed on everyone, and I had a sudden oppressive sense of the density of memories, wounds, ambitions, regrets, seething inside the body leaning against mine.

Once in her room — which I was seeing for the first time — her manner abruptly changed. When I began smoothing the sheets on her bed, she said in a snappish voice, "Leave them there. I can deal with it." As I prepared to go she said, "Wait, let me get into bed first," and then half-stumbled, half-walked from one corner of the room to another, searching for what turned out to be her sleeping pills.

I stood awkwardly, gazing at the collage of photographs Miss West had stuck on one damp-scarred wall of her room. The pictures must have been of her friends and relatives; they had been taken at different times but shared remarkable similarities: there were, everywhere, the same wide, bright, laughing and smiling faces, glittering with good health and high spirits. Only the settings differed: a Sunday picnic, open hampers, paper cups, champagne bottles; a beach party; a crowded dance floor, bare shoulders and black bow ties; a Christmas dinner, animated faces around a table crammed with open tureens, plates, and wineglasses. I noticed the tiny captions beneath some pictures as Miss West, now having found her pills, poured water from her earthen pot into a glass. Here was Fiona, running away — panting, crouching, laughing — from an approaching wave; there was Juliette with her suntanned shoulders and tuxedoed companion. I lingered, in particular, on pictures of Miss West, all younger versions of herself. In one she sat in what looked like a verandah on a cliffside house, sunglassed and straw-hatted, the deep azure of the sea behind her. In another photograph, she had her arm around the waist of a tall man with the name of Christopher. His height, and the riding breeches he wore, at first conveyed an arrogance that was negated by the shy smile on his pleasant face. He was in several other pictures as well. I wondered about Miss West's connection with him. Was he her husband? If so, why was she called *Miss* West?

I left Miss West on her bed, a small, quiet bundle under the quilts, and paced the roof for a while. On a river sparkling with early-morning silvery wrinkles, the first boatloads of tourists were beginning to appear. A familiar sneezing sound was coming out of the open window in the adjacent house: it was the woman whose face I could never see, towel-drying her hair. Somewhere on the congested ghats to the north, a loudspeaker belched and burped into life and began to leak whiffs of an old Hindi melody into the still air.

I felt a little out of sorts. I had witnessed yet another side of Miss West, and I was as unsure as always what to make of it, or how to figure out the sources of her distress. I kept coming back to the pictures. I couldn't help being struck by the unique suggestions they carried. Such a full and varied life they spoke of, such pleasures of untroubled prosperity! It occurred to me that much care and energy had gone into assembling and mounting these pictures, and my view of Miss West shifted yet again. I now began to see how closely she was still connected to her past, and this awareness suddenly made me melancholy.

It was an odd moment; but when years later I returned to it in memory, I was to discover in it the necessary prelude to my time in Benares, to the many tumultous events of that winter.

Miss West knocked on my door a day after the morning I had seen her crying on the roof. I was getting ready to go to the library; it was where I had taken to spending my days.

"Just checking to see whether you are dead or alive," she said as I opened the door. She looked jaunty in her oversized straw hat and pleated khakis, and she was full of news. She was going out to the market, and she had overheard the newest row between Mrs. Pandey and her errant tabla-playing son, Arjun.

One of Mrs. Pandey's obsessive topics concerned Arjun, who she said was plotting to throw her out and take over her house. She claimed he was encouraged in these nefarious plans by his wife, Sitadevi, who she thought was the most corrupting influence over her son's mind and soul. "She says she comes from a Brahmin family, the witch," Mrs. Pandey would say, "but she's really the lowest-born among the low"; and Shyam, who never said anything else, would intone: "Greed is the biggest evil. It eats away man, destroys families, sunders husband from wife, son from parents . . ."

I had occasionally run into Arjun and Sitadevi on the stairs. Sitadevi, a tall, thin woman in her mid-twenties, would raise her angular face from under her *pallu* to throw me a sharp searching glance and then would wordlessly pass on, her high-heeled shoes tick-tocking against the stone floor.

Arjun barely registered my presence. He was a short, bearded man with thinning hair and thick lips; his slow, sly manner made him seem capable of the brutality his mother feared.

I stood with Miss West on the roof and talked for a while about Arjun and Sita. It was only when she turned to go that she said, averting her eyes from my face, "I'm sorry I was such a bore the other morning. I hope you won't mind too much."

I had been thinking more about that time. But I was not closer to knowing what had made her so unhappy, and her quick recovery suddenly made my questions seem irrelevant.

Before I could even think of saying something, she had proposed a boat ride in the evening. "I haven't done it for ages," she said. "Will you come? You should do it at least once to get a feel of the city."

I said yes. I never went out on such excursions on my own; the city was still an unexplored place for me.

Miss West had her own favorite boatman: his name was Ramchand and he came running up the steps as soon as she and I appeared on the ghats that evening.

He was a strikingly handsome man with beautifully sculpted muscles on his lean chocolate-brown body, most of which was bare, his only item of clothing being a dhoti, which he wore like a G-string, tightly wound around his hips and buttocks. He held his palms together before Miss West; he bowed his head; he looked eager to serve. Miss West, speaking to him in broken Hindi, inquired after his health and family; she asked about the house he was building for himself as he led us to his boat, a ramshackle affair of nailed-together planks lying still on the black, scummy water.

She brought an un-Indian naturalness to her exchange with the boatman, and watching her, I felt a trifle awkward. Although I spoke the same language as Ramchand and lived in the same country, the scope for conversation between us was limited. Countless inhibitions of caste and class stood in our way; the only common vocabulary between us was of the service he offered.

"He's quite dishy, isn't he?" said Miss West as we got into the boat, and Ramchand began to disentangle the ropes that tied it to the iron picquet on the muddy bank.

I was too embarrassed and flustered to respond; the word "dishy" was new to me, but it wasn't hard to guess at its meaning.

"Back in England, he'd be a film star, or at least a model," Miss West said. And then after a short pause she added, "But you don't go for men. I know that. I noticed you gawking at Catherine that evening. Tell me," she asked in that sharp demanding tone of hers, "do you like her?"

This embarrassed me further. There was so much here that was weird and unfamiliar to me: women commenting on the physical allure of men, particularly men socially inferior to them; the notion that I could "like" men in that way. What seemed worse (for it was partly true) was that I would be so taken by Catherine in that brief meeting that other people would notice the change in my demeanor.

I mumbled something about Catherine being "nice" and was relieved when Miss West didn't ask me any more uncomfortable questions about her.

Instead, she said, "Poor girl. How badly she needs to be loved. She's obsessed with Anand. She thinks of him as the next Ravi Shankar. But I wonder how long that will last. I don't think he can give her the stability she needs. He's too dependent on her."

I thought: But hadn't she herself said that they were very much in love? These second thoughts of Miss West's perplexed me at first. But they also sounded truer; and I acknowledged these new facts of Catherine's relationship with Anand with the sudden thrill that accompanies the truths that in some unconscious way matter deeply to us.

Soon we had moved away from the ghats, Ramchand pulling at the oars in a slow graceful motion, the varied sounds of the city becoming a steady background hum to the soft *plop-plop* of the oars against the water.

We passed a few fishing boats anchoring themselves for the night, their tattered sails fluttering against the soft breeze blowing in from the other bank. On Harishchandra Ghat, amid piles of wooden logs and mounds of swept-up ashes, there was a lone burning pyre, and the grieving friends and relatives of the deceased stood motionless around it. At Kedar Ghat, the piercing oboe-like sounds of shehnai from a wedding procession traveled over the water in brief gusts. Up ahead in the far distance, a train rattled across the Dufferin Bridge, its windows flashing the last of the day's sunlight.

My mind was still a mess of confused thoughts about Catherine and Anand when Miss West said, "There, that's Mark's house, just above the Shiva" — she pronounced it Sh-ee-va — "temple, with the iron-barred windows. Do you see it?"

I looked in the direction she had pointed, but it was too dark to distinguish the house from the mass of gray masonry in which it was embedded.

Miss West said, "Such a nice chap, but so American. So excessively sincere about everything he does. He's taken up with that perfectly ordinary girl, Debbie, and thinks the world of her."

"What he wants to do is get home," Miss West went on. The light was almost gone and I couldn't see her face. But the voice still traveled through the darkness in sharp, clear bursts. "He's sick of gadding about the world. And so he's gone and fallen for the commonest American he could find here. A perfect example of *poshlust* — do you know the word? It's Russian, absolutely brilliant, it stands for commonness, banality, smugness, all together. She gets her parents to send her videos of *David Letterman*, she misses her dog, all she wants to do in Benares is sunbathe and get a great tan, and then she says she wants to convert to Buddhism. It doesn't make sense."

She was silent for a while and I tried to guess who or what *David Letterman* was. Miss West turned to talk to Ramchand; she asked him to take us to Narad Ghat. The evening sounds of the city — conch shells, temple bells — began to reach us as we rowed toward the bank. The water shimmered with the broken reflection of the huge sodium lamps looming out from behind the ramparts.

Miss West tipped Ramchand generously. He bowed his head low in appreciation; that eager expression came back to his face. As he walked away from us, through a row of flower and coconut sellers, he fell in with a friend he had greeted while coming up the steps from the river with us. His manner changed immediately. His shoulders lost their supplicant's stoop. I saw him point his thumb in our direction, and laugh, his teeth white against the dark-brown skin of his face.

Later, walking through the dark alleys, a party of jovial pilgrims from Tamil Nadu ahead of us, I asked, "Where's Debbie from?" It was the question I was accustomed to ask people in India. The answers usually helped put their backgrounds in sharper focus.

"Debbie?" Miss West echoed. "She's from Providence, Rhode Island. A perfectly vile place."

I tried to find Rhode Island on a mental map of America. I had heard about the provinciality and backwardness of Oklahoma and South Carolina. But Rhode Island? The name brought up no associations in my mind. I tried to visualize Providence to myself, and speculated about the reasons for it being so, in Miss West's word, vile.

Miss West couldn't have guessed at the degree of uncertainty her remarks induced in me. They made me overturn all the notions I had formed so far. "He's so American. So oversincere," she had said. Were Americans oversincere as a rule? Such generalizations lay beyond my limited knowledge of the world; they made me feel ignorant. And they made Miss West herself seem a repository of bits and pieces of odd wisdom.

I had no means of assessing on my own the character and background of people I had met at Miss West's party. Mark had appeared solid to me; the eventfulness of his life, the various careers — it all suggested a substantial endeavor to me. Miss West's remarks made him seem different, someone much less certain of himself, and drifting from place to place, from one secondhand idea to another. It was the same with Debbie. The bits of dialogue with Sarah I had overheard at the party, her interest in converting to Buddhism, had intrigued me. The idea of conversion lay so far from anything in my experience; such an effort of the will and intelligence it seemed to imply, such a depth of dissatisfaction with the conventions of one's society. But when I now thought of Debbie, I remembered best her quick nervous giggle and ill-fitting sari, and I tried to see in them the sign of the commonness Miss West had spoken of.

4

I hadn't forgotten Miss West's remarks about Catherine and Anand when I ran into them a few days later, walking back from the library at BHU.

I saw Catherine first; she stood out in the crowd at Lanka Crossing in her pale-yellow sari, her hair loose and luxuriant over her shoulders. Anand followed a little behind her, stylish, as he had been that evening, in a long white kurta and churidar. Together, they attracted, I noticed, the lecherous malevolence of the student idlers who usually hung out at the adjacent tea shacks, gossiping about, and verbally goosing, every passing girl.

It was Catherine who saw me and waved. They walked across to my side of the road. I felt the students watching me and grew very self-conscious. I was relieved when the conversation ended quickly, before the students could get up to anything more than gesturing at us and laughing.

Catherine was now working part-time at the French Tourist Information Center. A steady traffic of French tourists passed through

Benares, and they often ended up losing their passports or becoming seriously ill or getting robbed, or worse: it was her job to help them out.

"We get some real cases sometimes," Catherine said. "Otherwise the job is easy."

They had recently moved into a new house not far from Assi Ghat. Catherine said I should visit them there. They had no phone, but I could simply drop in any time in the afternoon. Anand seconded her. I promised to do so, and then we parted.

A few days passed before I went one afternoon to their house. I would have gone immediately, but was held back by my very eagerness to see Catherine again: I sensed something coarse in it, and unhealthy. That scruple faded in time, but was never to disappear altogether.

The spools of memory have suddenly begun to roll faster. Jolty progress on a rickshaw through brick-paved narrow alleys splattered with lumps of fresh cow dung. Overhead, torn paper kites lie trapped in the dense tangle of electric wires, over which sit, in neat rows, gray pigeons. On both sides, claustrophobically small houses pushing against each other, jostling for space; balconies with arabesque fretwork streaming with saris hung out to dry; a tea shop with sooty interiors, the corpulent halwai ensconced before his enormous cauldron, poking with a long-handled skimmer at the lone samosa sizzling in the black oil. An ocher-robed sadhu with mattlocks sits on the raised porch of a bangles shop and eats roasted chana from a paper cone. I walk up a narrow and steep staircase, the sides of which are covered with a mural depicting Ram and Sita on the throne of Ayodhya, and onto a tiny landing. A door on the left leads to two box-shaped rooms on the roof, where a sagging string cot lies in one corner.

It was Catherine who opened the door, her face breaking into a wide welcoming smile as she saw me. She was wearing a starched white kurta over blue jeans; her hair was wet and glossy from a recent washing and had created a damp patch on her back. Seeing her, I was once again aware of a peculiar inner slackening. The self I knew and displayed to other people sank into a strange torpor; something weak and pliable took its place.

Catherine showed me around the house. It wasn't very big: two squarish rooms on the first floor, a bathroom and a kitchen, approached through a landing they shared with their landlord. The windows, overhung with pots of bougainvillea, looked out on the congested houses across the street — small dark rooms choked with furniture and bawling babies. The walls, painted a light yellow, were bare; on the floor there were mattresses and bolsters covered with hand-printed Kalamkari sheets; two handsome gleaming sitars stood in one room, and the only item of furniture was a cane bookcase, crammed with Gallimard paperbacks.

Catherine said, "We decided not to have too much." She laughed, as if she had just remembered something, and added: "My friend Louise was saying the other day, it's too bourgeois to have too many things cluttering up your house. It reminds you of Paris."

My mind was full as always of something I had just read, and I quoted Flaubert, from some probably inaccurate translation, about how one should live like a bourgeois but think like a bohemian.

Catherine laughed — a full, throaty, generous laugh — and said, "That's good. That's *very* good."

And then, suddenly growing serious, she said: "Really, I would like to live as simply as possible in India. We can sleep on the floor, we can do without a fridge, washing machine . . ."

Anand, who was wearing a flimsy lungi and T-shirt and lying against the bolsters on the floor, peeling a banana, interrupted at this point, saying, "But we need an air conditioner, no?"

Catherine sought to humor him: "Do you really want an air conditioner? I can buy you one anytime."

Anand's expression suddenly drooped; he grew very quiet. Catherine's answer had put into unwelcome focus what I knew about from Miss West: his almost complete financial dependence upon her. It wasn't something he could refer to without embarrassment. There were a few moments of awkwardness before Catherine turned to describing their landlord, Major Aggarwal. He had retired some time back and constantly worried about finding adequate dowry for his four young daughters. Catherine suspected him of being better off than he let on. The sources of his income were unknown, but they were various enough in the past to enable him to buy prime property all across Benares. Major Aggarwal's wife was a mousy woman; the daughters were no less subdued. Catherine said that Major Aggarwal's military discipline had stunted their characters.

Catherine's mother had just gone back to France after a month's stay in Benares. Her time in India was still a new topic between Catherine and Anand; we went back to it often during this first evening at their house.

The three of them — Anand, Catherine, and her mother — had recently traveled together to Rajasthan. It hadn't been easy for Catherine's mother, who was used to another order of comfort altogether from the one she found in India. She had had to suffer the indignity of traveling back from Jaipur in the crowded cockpit of a truck, crushed with beedi-smoking villagers who hawked and spat out of the window every two minutes; she had not spoken to Catherine or Anand for many hours after the trip. Then she hadn't ceased complaining about the cheap, unheated hotels Catherine had booked them into in every town.

Catherine said, "We would go to a restaurant for lunch and she would not stop complaining about the dirty cloth the waiter was using to wipe the plates dry."

Anand spoke for the first time since the remark about the air conditioner. He said, "She was so unhappy with the way Catherine was living in India. She said she would not come back again."

Catherine said, "I told her this is the way people live in India and you have to do the same when you are here."

It seemed a bit excessive and unnecessary to me, imposing "Indian" ways upon a first-time visitor. But I said nothing, only kept listening: nothing more was required of me. Presently, Catherine disappeared into the kitchen to make some coffee, and Anand told me more about the visit.

He had been with Catherine's mother when Catherine was interviewed for her job at the French embassy in New Delhi. With them in the waiting room was the director of the French Tourist Information Center, a somewhat arrogant and pompous man from Anand's description. He was talking to Catherine's mother in English instead of French, and if that wasn't odd enough, he was talking — in Anand's presence! — about the need for Catherine to steer clear of devious Indian men. The director knew of many instances where French women had fallen for them, only to find themselves used as passports to Europe; it was imperative, he said, that Catherine stay away from such sordid liaisons.

That the director's words were intended more for Anand's ears than Catherine's mother's was obvious. What wasn't apparent to me was Anand's motive in telling this story to me. Was he telling me this to show he was different from the "devious Indian men" the director had spoken of? Was he making a political statement about the director? Or was he complaining about Catherine's mother's passive complicity?

Catherine appeared with the coffee, which was aromatic and French: a gift, Catherine said, from her mother. She talked about Miss West's party, how much she had enjoyed it. But the conversation came back, in stages, to her mother. It was a topic that seemed to absorb both Catherine and Anand endlessly; its special intimacies could shut out the visitor completely.

Catherine said that Miss West (she called her Diana) had helped offset some of her mother's shock on arriving in Benares. Miss West had even tried to reconcile her mother to Anand.

Anand said: "She told Miss West that she didn't know about what you wanted to do. If you want to live in India, she could buy you a house in Benares."

Catherine poured scorn on the idea. Anand silently watched her, his face a blank. I could not be free of the suspicion that, however briefly, he had been held by Catherine's mother's suggestion, if only for the wealth and privilege it suggested: that someone, or more specifically his girlfriend's mother, could so easily talk of buying a whole house in Benares, something for which people he knew saved and scrounged all their lives.

I remember coming away that evening with a sense of wrongness. I couldn't put it in words then: all I knew was that something wasn't right. There was the incongruity of Catherine's presence in that small house, the French coffee and Gallimard paperbacks surrounded by the teeming obtrusive life of old Benares; there was the incongruity of her relationship with Anand.

And yet I was tempted into going back to her house again and again. That first visit, as I remember it now, was to set the pattern for all other visits over the next few weeks. I remained shy and awkward before Catherine. She was the first woman I had known outside my family; the frank directness of her gaze and the assurance of her speech were new wonders for me. They inhibited me, and I felt at ease only when talking about literature; even then her obviously greater knowledge, acquired and systematized at a famous university, awed me — I, who gobbled down books without any sense of the larger civilization that lay behind them, the hectic world of big cities and writers and publishers, of urgent social concerns and existential anxieties.

The allusions she made to her life in Paris were very faint clues to that great mystery of her background I was always trying to figure out. The even greater mystery was the peculiar chemistry between her and Anand. With Anand she did most of the talking, Anand just about managing to keep up with his broken English. They frequently quarreled or withdrew into sullen silences. These frictions embarrassed me, but they were too self-absorbed to notice. They were like people trying out their new roles, charging into, or abruptly retreating from, freshly opened areas of perception and feeling; and watching them together, the quarrels, the silences, their small gestures toward each other — she absentmindedly caressing his hair, he interrupting his sitar practice to make her tea — I would often wonder if this was "love."

5

When I next saw Catherine, she was about to leave for Anand's village in Bihar. Anand had written to his parents about Catherine; they had wanted to see her in person.

Miss West, who accompanied me to Catherine's house that evening, told me this. She knew of Anand's father: he was a farmer and headman of an upper-caste village, a conservative man from all accounts. But she didn't remark on the potential awkwardness of Catherine's visit, or on how Anand had explained Catherine to his parents. Patron, girlfriend, fiancée: they all would have been alien and difficult concepts for them.

Miss West said, in that slightly bored, offhand voice I was beginning to recognize, "He's so full of enthusiasm, that boy. Wants to win the world, and more. Makes the rest of us seem so dry and sterile."

We were in a rickshaw, bumping along over cobblestone lanes, and Miss West's voice came out in short hiccupy bursts. Despite the continuous jolting, she sat very erect on the narrow seat. She always traveled with the hood down, wearing her oversized straw hat. People turned to look at her; they often shot a brief slightly mocking glance at me. Miss West didn't seem to notice them, but I invariably grew self-conscious in her company.

Catherine was alone at home, writing official letters to the French embassy: a French tourist, she said, had been found in the city's red-light district, unconscious, with no money or identification. "Probably a drug overdose. The doctors are looking into it," Catherine said. "These wretched day-trippers," Miss West remarked as she took off her hat and shook her tousled hair, "why can't they go to Costa del Sol or wherever. Why do they have to come all this way to mess themselves up?"

In her reading glasses, and with her hair tied in an Indian-style ponytail, which made her forehead look wider and cleaner, Catherine appeared slightly different from the last time I had seen her. She always dressed elegantly, wearing bright Indian colors in many different combinations. These fresh sightings of her made her strangeness, her unknown past, even more intriguing, and I had to remind myself not to stare too long at her in Miss West's presence.

Despite the complications with the unconscious tourist, she was in a buoyant mood, humming to herself as she made coffee in the kitchen.

As usual, I said little to her. I asked her only if she was looking forward to her visit to Anand's village. She replied, "Yes, of course. I am very excited."

Then, turning to Miss West, she added, "It was really long overdue. The more time we waited, the more awkward it would become."

It was also to Miss West that she confided her nervousness about the visit. Anand's parents had never met, or even seen, a white person in their entire lives: it would all be a bit bewildering for them. She wasn't expecting to be received warmly. Anand himself had warned her about that. They were likely to be wary of her, and they were likely to resent her for her influence over their son.

When she came out of the kitchen, she began to speak of Anand's difficult childhood in her soft French accent, frequently mixing up the English tenses. Miss West and I settled ourselves on her bed, leaning against the bolsters, and drinking coffee. Catherine hadn't put on the lights yet and the room was full of the smoky blue light of the evening. Street sounds drifted in through the tiny window: the squeaks of Bajaj scooter horns, the jangle of rickshaw bells. In one of the rooms in the congested house across the street a fluorescent tube kept flickering in and out of life; and the pigeons, so neatly arrayed one moment on the electric wires, kept exploding into the air with a loud flapping of wings.

Anand's parents had two daughters to marry but no money for the dowry, the current rate for which was very high within families of their caste. They had looked to Anand for help; they expected him to do well in his studies and find a salaried government job somewhere. They had actively discouraged Anand from developing his musical talent, and they had almost disowned him when he dropped out of school and declared his intention of going to Benares to find a music guru. There had been vicious rows at home. Anand was often beaten up by his father.

"Now," Miss West interrupted, "I didn't know *that*. How absolutely *awful*."

Catherine said that it had indeed happened — not once or twice but several times. "And," she added, with a sudden sharp edge of passion in her voice, "this was when he was already eighteen years old."

Catherine mentioned similar cruelties, the passion in her voice unmistakable now. It was odd to hear her talk about Anand in his absence: he suddenly appeared a man of deeper personality and experience than his own quiet, slightly bland presence made him out to be.

Presently, Catherine got up to turn on the lights and came back with a few photos of Anand's village. Shoddy printing and tiny white disfiguring spots made it impossible to isolate any detail on them. But the overall picture they added up to was clear: the jumble of low mud huts and naked brick houses with cowsheds in the front yard or narrow lanes rutted by bullock-cart wheels, beyond which lie the whitewashed shrines, the buffaloes floating on algae-covered ponds, the sea of yellow mustard fields, and the emptiness of dusty country roads.

How hard it was to imagine Catherine in this setting! Or to visualize the journey to the village, to see Catherine amid the overflowing crowds on Bihar trains, packed tight together on hard wooden bunks and the floor and spilling out on the roof; to see her among the even more ragged passengers on the ramshackle country bus of dented abraded steel, its tires worn smooth by the broken roads, the windshield cracked and grimy. Such aggressive curiosity she would arouse! How exposed she would be to the blank insistent stares, the intrusive questions in pidgin English, the lewd speculation about her connection with Anand.

As it turned out, I didn't see her for many

days after she returned. The first time I asked Miss West about the visit, her sole remark was: "It didn't work out." Judging by her tone she didn't want to invite more questions on this matter, but later, in an absentminded moment as we stood on the roof one evening, she came back to it without any prompting from me.

"Did I tell you about Catherine's visit to Bihar?" she said. "They were hard on her, scowling and suspicious: they didn't say anything to her — they hardly speak a word of English — Anand got all the flak. Poor girl, she was in tears. But that's something she'll have to live with. You can't expect people like Anand's parents to change: they'll always disapprove of her, and in some sense that disapproval is important to them; it's part of their identity; they can't let go of it."

Catherine herself had moved on to other preoccupations when I next saw her. The biggest source of anxiety now was her own parents. She had discussed with them the possibility of arranging some concerts in Paris so that Anand could pay, with the advance money, for his air ticket to France. They had replied that he ought to earn the necessary amount in India before he even started for France.

This greatly exasperated Catherine. How

on earth was he going to do that? she exclaimed. Didn't they know the difference in scale between the two economies? That kind of money doesn't come easily in India. Her mother had been here after all; she must have taken with her at least some idea of Indian conditions; she was expected to be more understanding than her husband.

We were at Mark's house. Miss West had taken me there, on one of her rounds of late-afternoon visits after the mornings spent reading and listening to music, and we had found Catherine, along with Sarah, the German Buddhist. Miss West often asked me if I wanted to accompany her on her trips. The visit to Mark's house, as with the previous visit to Catherine's, was her attempt to create a social life for me. Lately, she had also undertaken to introduce me to Western classical music; she played me CDs of Schubert's String Quintet in C Minor and the String Sextet No. 2 by Brahms, and directed my attention to specific bits. I didn't always like the music or understand what she said, but I was glamoured by this contact with names that I had encountered only in print.

I had seen Mark's house several times from the river ever since Miss West pointed it out to me. This was the first time I had been inside it. It had three rooms huddled around a courtyard that offered a wide, unrestricted view of the river. The rooms were filled with a medley of self-consciously ethnic knickknacks — Azamgarh dhurries, Himachali wall hangings, Gujarati lampshades, Tibetan tankas, and various kinds of pots and pans.

As we walked into the half-enclosed courtyard, where they all sat, catching the last bit of warmth before the sun disappeared behind the houses to the west, Mark was reclining regally on a jute mat, facing the glinting river. Sarah and Catherine were leaning against the wall a few inches away, but it was Debbie who caught my eye. She was lying on a saggy string-cot, stripped down to her bra and panties, her skin already a leathery-brown, her legs drawn up and parted in a rather graceless manner.

Miss West had told me that a widow from Bengal lived in one of the rooms in Mark's house; she had long stopped paying the rent but the landlord had been unable to evict her. It was her white saris that hung on a clothesline in the courtyard. Mark, Miss West said, got along well with her.

But what about Debbie? I wanted to ask Miss West, who had remarked once before on her sunbathing: one of the signs, I remembered, of her "commonness." No one seemed to see anything amiss in her present appearance; Debbie herself seemed profoundly un-concerned about it. But it was shocking to me, and I knew it was very far from anything a widow from Bengal, living out her last years in prayer and near-destitution, could have coun-tenanced. All through the visit I kept worrying about the possibility of her making an unex-pected appearance upon the scene.

We had arrived in the middle of several bustling conversations. Mark smiled at us and gestured toward the vacant space in front of him. Sarah paused for the briefest while in her conversation with Debbie, acknowledging our presence with a smile that momentarily animated all the wrinkles on her face. Debbie abruptly sat up, revealing the freckled top of her breasts, and waved.

Catherine was in the midst of a serious-seeming conversation with Mark. On the last occasion we were together at her house, I had heard her say to Miss West, "I don't like Americans very much, but Mark is different. He is deep, deep." I couldn't see Miss West's face; she had her own opinions of Mark, opin-ions she had expressed to me. But she said nothing to Catherine, and it pleased me to think that there were things she would con-fide only in me.

Catherine had gone on to describe a con-versation with Mark. He had told her about his life, his various careers, how they brought him little satisfaction in the end. Catherine said, "He has suffered a lot of pain." It was Benares, she said, that had healed him.

Later, while Miss West chatted with Mark and Sarah, I listened to Catherine talk to Debbie, who was saying, "No, I didn't want to come to India as much as I wanted to go to Latin America."

"Why Latin America?" Catherine wanted to know.

Debbie screwed up her face and adjusted the bra straps aslant on her shoulders — the skin of her shaved armpit, when she lifted her arms, was rutted and bristly. "I don't know," she said, "but I had this really deep urge to go there after reading Márquez. You know, *Love in the Time of Cholera.* It's my all-time favorite novel. . . . It's just *so* romantic. . . . I just *love* the way he writes. I mean, the people in his books, they are so *emotional,* so free with their feelings, their bodies, everything. I don't know, I'm not much of a literary critic, but I can't think of a writer who can hold a candle to Márquez when it comes to . . . when it comes to . . . I don't know."

"I don't think it is a good idea to rank writers like that," Catherine said, a slight touch of reproof in her voice. "There are so many we don't get to read." She paused and then added: "Personally, I like Kundera. He says serious things about contemporary life . . ."

I could also hear Miss West talking to Sarah and Mark about a new guru who had appeared in Lucknow and acquired a large following among European and American tourists — "seekers," as Miss West usually called them, with a derisiveness she was now underplaying in deference, I surmised, to Sarah, who was a "seeker" in her own way.

With these conversations humming in the background, my mind wandered to Rajesh, whom I had seen at the library earlier in the day. Surrounded by his hangers-on, he had talked about the possibility of student violence in the coming days. He had got the students worried; they had started to talk among themselves of leaving the university before they were caught up in the police crackdown that followed such student-inspired disturbances. I remembered briefly what they had said, and as I did so I remarked to myself at the same time about the great chasm between where I was — sitting here in Mark's house, an expatriate corner of Benares, among foreigners who fascinated me endlessly — and the life I led at the university, whose problems from this remote distance appeared uninteresting and petty.

Catherine and Debbie were still talking

about Kundera. Debbie was saying, with a combative tone in her voice, "The great thing about these European novels and films is that they have no inhibitions about sex and nudity. . . . It's all presented so naturally, not like America, where you have these disgusting middle-class moralists like Jesse Helms . . . and you end up distorting everything."

"But that's not Kundera's point," Catherine protested. She was suddenly aware that I was listening, and flashed a brief smile at me. "In fact, nudity for Kundera is partly this state of unbearable lightness. And actually the movie has been made by an *American*. It's *not* a European film."

"I am not saying that *that* was the film's point," Debbie retorted. "I mean it in the way the characters behave toward each other, toward their own bodies, being so unashamed about their desires . . . I don't know . . ."

The conversation went on for some time, until Debbie said, "Oh, God, it's getting cold," and went, much to my relief, to change into warmer clothes. Catherine glanced at me once or twice while talking, as if inviting me to say something. But I kept quiet. I hadn't read the books or seen the films that were mentioned, and even if I had, the terms in which they were discussed were so unfamiliar to me that I wouldn't have been able to say much with any degree of confidence.

Catherine seemed restless and troubled when I saw her together with Miss West toward the end of the visit. In that mood she was unexpectedly frank. Talking about the trouble with her parents, she digressed into a description of their marriage, which, from her account, wasn't a particularly happy one. Catherine blamed her father for this. He was, she said, vain, arrogant, short-tempered. She herself had never got along well with him. She had rebelled early, and from that point she never sought his permission for anything. When she was sixteen, she one day declared her intention of going off to Germany for a few weeks. He said no. She ignored him altogether. He raged for days after she left. The same had happened when she came to India. He had now given up trying to control her life.

But she feared his reaction to Anand. Her mother, with whom she got along better, had barely accepted him; her father's rejection was almost certain. He was a conservative man, a Catholic; he could still disapprove, in this day and age, of premarital sex. He could never approve of her relationship with a poor Indian.

And his approval was important. In a few weeks they were to go and live in France, where her life would have to be partly subsidized by him until Anand's situation changed. And that's why it was important that the concerts be arranged, that he have some kind of performance record and income.

But Anand, she said, had created more problems. He had lied to his parents about the sources of his livelihood in Benares. He had unwisely invented a fabulously well-paid sitar-playing career for himself. His parents had naturally demanded to know why hadn't he, if he was so flush with money, sent some their way; why hadn't he wanted to improve his sisters' chances of early marriage. So now, in order to maintain this deception, Catherine had to send part of her own salary to Anand's parents. She didn't mind the money bit at all, she said with a dismissive shrug; it wasn't much anyway. It was the lies she couldn't deal with.

Miss West said, "I am so sorry to hear this, I really am. It shouldn't happen this way. But this is not an ideal situation. These things are inevitable, given the disparities, I mean the differences in terms of money and background, things like that. But I wouldn't worry too much if I were you. I am sure it'll work out in the end, one way or another."

I listened, feeling embarrassed by Catherine's disclosures, and said nothing.

I was walking home alone — Miss West having gone off to Godhulia on her own for some shopping — when it occurred to me that in some unconscious way Catherine might have been speaking for my benefit. It was a flattering supposition, and I almost dismissed it at first for that reason. But it seemed more plausible when I thought of my last visit to Catherine's house. After all, Miss West already knew of the events of Anand's past that Catherine spoke of so passionately; they were what she had had in common with Catherine since the time she had introduced her to Anand at one of her musical soirees. Catherine's words were perhaps meant for me more than either of us realized, and I now felt I should have said something to her — even if it was little more than the slightly banal generalities Miss West uttered on such occasions.

I couldn't see it then, but for Miss West, Anand's welfare was a small private concern, which coexisted with the doubts about his artistic potential she had recently admitted to me. For Catherine, lonely and insecure in Benares, it was nothing less than a cause, and she seemed to want it to be shared, or at least known, by more people.

It was clear to me even on that evening in her house — listening to her quietly emotional voice in that darkening room, the fluorescent tube outside flickering away — that the stories about Anand's childhood had affected her deeply. What wasn't apparent to me then was that in telling them, she wanted to have their injustice acknowledged by others. She also wanted to protect Anand and keep him from further hurt.

This was her primary motivation, and now after the new complications created by her own and Anand's parents, with these growing troubles, she needed to have it attested by others; she needed to know if she was doing the right thing.

Anand, when I next met him, was already looking forward to going to Paris; he spoke of this with the curious serenity that I had seen come over him, the serenity that came from his belief that with Catherine by his side things could not but turn out well for him. Paris had become for him a locus of several desires. He spoke solemnly about the visit as expanding the narrow vision he had inherited from his rustic background; he spoke with childlike enthusiasm about the sold-out concerts he would give, the best-selling recordings he would make. I had already heard him speak at Miss West's party of the school he wished to set up for talented and needy sitar players; he expanded on the subject now, speaking as though the school were already a reality.

It was peculiarly disquieting to hear all this. I had no awareness of how the music industry worked but felt that the success Anand projected in his immediate future couldn't be so easily achieved. I thought he had very little sense of the world he was about to enter, and watching the hopeful unclouded expression in his eyes, I couldn't help feeling — as on that first visit to Catherine's house — a sense of wrongness and incongruity.

But it was too late to withdraw. Without quite realizing it, I had become addicted to their company; it was the regular fix I needed in addition to my daily visits to the library. I went often to Catherine's house, and stayed for long periods. The sadhu with mattlocks in the alley outside her house and the halwai with the enormous paunch in his sooty sweetshop became familiar, reassuring figures. But these visits weren't without their secret torments: I saw in Anand's serenity the serenity of a sexually satisfied man, and I was often pursued, after leaving their house, by dark imaginings of that unknown part of his relationship with Catherine, its physical side. These imaginings were limited and made yet more intense by my own lack of experience. But they gave an edge to my impressions of

Catherine, to her soft voice, and to her face that seemed to change its appearance every time I saw her; and another layer of awkwardness was created between us.

In any case, I didn't speak much. I would tell Catherine about my recent discoveries at the library — and that was all I had to offer by way of conversation. I mostly listened to their plans and anxieties about the present and the future, their disagreements, their playful bantering.

I can see now that for Catherine and Anand I had my role cut out. They were so self-contained and content when in each other's company, but like all couples, they needed witnesses from the external world, and in this most tradition-minded of Indian cities, the presence of people like Miss West and myself was to them an important fact; it was a positive endorsement of their new fragile status as an unmarried couple. Catherine knew barely anyone in Benares, apart from Miss West, Mark, and a few French semipermanent residents I would see occasionally, middle-aged, harassed-looking men wearing ponytails and earrings. Anand, too, had few friends in Benares: timid, depressed-looking sitar or tabla players who would sometimes be at Catherine's house, hunched over in one corner, not saying much, unsure of what to make of Catherine, or indeed Anand. I now see how his relationship with Catherine, a rich European woman, must have put a strain on these older relationships in Benares; it would have set him apart from the people he knew among the musical fraternity, most of whom lived improvised lives in the poorer quarters of the city.

But there were my own needs. I had no friends: growing up alone, I had developed no skills for intimacy, or even ordinary camaraderie; friendships seemed to require from me a degree of self-abnegation I could not achieve. However, a large part of the loneliness I had increasingly come to feel had been offset by my obsessive reading, the regard I had for the life of the mind. With each book, I entered into what I felt to be an exalted bond with its writer, to whom I gave all the care and attentiveness I could not bring to human relationships.

But as I grew older the substitution of books for friendship had seemed to work less and less. In truth, I had been lonely for a very long time. In Benares, the unexpected company first of Miss West and then of Catherine had only made the fact more apparent to me — a fact that never struck me with greater poignancy than when I knocked on Catherine's door, and the sound of the heavy iron bolt struck against the old bleached wood traveling up the empty stairs seemed to carry some of my loneliness. It explained the speed with which I grew to cherish the long evenings in Catherine's house, in the room filled with smoky blue light, the fluorescent tube outside flickering away as usual, and the pigeons periodically responding to unseen provocations by exploding into the dusk.

So it was that I began to dislike leaving her house late in the evening and walking up three flights of stairs to find my tiny room in darkness and, when I switched on the weak bulb, all my things in it exactly as I had left them: the books slumped on the table, with the markers jutting out, and crammed into the octagonal niches, the pajamas spread-eagled on the bed where I had thrown them, the Hawaiian slippers flung beneath the chair where I had changed into shoes, the postcard picture of Proust on the windowsill where I had put it up several weeks ago. It was as though I expected them to have changed position during my absence; that they hadn't was proof of the loneliness and boredom I increasingly felt when in that room.

6

In the years since then, I have often thought about the evening of Miss West's party. I have wondered about the strange emotion I felt the morning after, standing alone on the roof, Miss West having drugged herself into sleep after an anguished night. It has taken me time to see that the loneliness I was to know later, when I returned to my room from Catherine's house, was only another aspect of that earlier emotion.

So little did I know any of the people present at the party that in the brief time I had seen them they became even more mysterious to me. I was tormented by my ignorance. I wanted to know more; I wanted to know everything about them. The knowledge was one way of dealing with the troubled, if undefined, sense I had after the party, a sense of the largeness and diversity of the world, and a simultaneous awareness of how little of it was accessible to me, how someone like me — someone with no money or clear prospects — was placed at its remotest fringes.

The reality of my position was made more

apparent by Debbie's reply when I asked her what she was doing in Benares. "Passing through," she had said, and the words had stayed with me. They had suggested a kind of perpetual journeying through the world, a savoring of life in a way I had no means of knowing, the life itself seeming — as it did in the pictures in Miss West's room — unimaginably adventurous.

And the more I knew of it, the more inadequate I felt. I knew nothing of Miss West, but had presumed to see sadness and disappointment in her past: this was the romantic idea that had been spawned by the idle solitude of those fog-bound first days in Benares. That morning after the party, gazing at the pictures in Miss West's room — the pictures that spoke to me of the pleasures of untroubled prosperity — I was given a truer idea of Miss West, and it had brought with it only more pangs of loneliness and self-pity.

So many tangled roots our personalities have: the social and emotional circumstances of our early years, of our parents' lives, and, if you go back even further, of our ancestors'. In some sense, the emotion I felt that morning after Miss West's party, although never fully defined, had always been with me. It had cast its shadow upon my childhood, and it came to me then as a fear of being abandoned and un-protected. In later life, the fear lost its raw-ness; it became part of the larger preoccu-pations of a solitary adolescence. I had never analyzed this fear; there had been no occasion to do so. It is only now as I write, and attempt to link disparate events and emotions, that I see the larger context to which it belongs, the long way it goes back, to a past that has grown dim in all except its broadest details.

My ancestors were Brahmins, originally from Kanauj, the capital of the great seventh-century Indian empire founded by Harsha-vardhana. There were no dates for their exo-dus from Kanauj. We vaguely knew, by way of family lore, that the sixteenth-century Mogul emperor Akbar had created a native aristocracy by awarding large grants of land to the Brahmins of the region, and that our own ancestors had been among those so favored. No one, however, had any details. It wasn't the kind of thing anyone cared to document, or even remember; the past was too much a part of the present to be categorized in a strict historical sense.

For centuries after Akbar, my ancestors had remained wealthy landowners in the flatlands enclosed by the foothills of the western Hima-layas. During all that time, the turbulent his-tory of medieval India touched them little.

My own knowledge of that past went only as far back as my great-great-grandfather in the last century, but I can't imagine his own ancestors deviated much from the well-worn Hindu grooves in which he and his son and grandson spent their own lives: studentship in Benares, adulthood and marriage, late-middle-age detachment, and then the final renunciation followed by a retreat to the Himalayas.

With India's independence in 1947, this regulated life was unraveled with bewildering speed. My grandfather and his sons found themselves thrown into the new ruthless go-getting world of independent India with none of their old certainties intact. Successive land reform legislation undermined the family's assets to the point where ancestral jewelry had to be sold off to pay for the education of my father and his brothers. There was a time when neither studentship nor marriage seemed a possibility.

My father grew up knowing both a kind of feudal grandeur and shameful penury. From a life of secluded leisure, he was catapulted into the ranks of desperate millions seeking jobs under the new regime. I did not know until after my mother's death how deeply marked he was by that period of difficult transition.

In time, the years of struggle were left behind. He joined the Public Works Department (PWD); he worked his way to a kind of middle-class security and equilibrium. But he never spoke about his early years. Once, in an uncharacteristic burst of nostalgia, he mentioned the caparisoned elephants he rode to his grandmother's village. On another occasion, he spoke of the time Pandit Nehru had come to the family house to borrow a horse from the stables. These memories alone came to represent for me the life he had known as a child.

For me, born in 1969, and growing up with cricket, the books of Enid Blyton, and Tintin comics, there could be no such memories. That past of my father — and also my mother, whose family had suffered a similar upheaval — was very far away from the series of PWD bungalows and mediocre Christian-run schools in which I had spent my childhood. The serenity of the old Brahmin world in which his family had lived for centuries was even more remote from me. I had an intimation of it on Sunday mornings, when my father, freshly bathed and bare-torsoed, would sit on a tiger-skin rug before a fragrant fire of sandalwood and recite Vedic hymns in an approximation of a much grander ritual his ancestors had performed for millennia. I felt great reverence and awe for these ancient practices. But at the same time I could feel my own life had drifted apart from them; it had attached itself to another constellation of desires and reverences.

I had the sharpest sense of this at the time of my mother's death. My mother had chosen to live in an ashram in Benares when she knew that she didn't have much longer to live. Her decision was in line with an immemorial Hindu belief that to die in Benares was to be released from the cycle of rebirths; it couldn't be argued with.

Before I could arrive in Benares, she died and had to be cremated quickly. I was secretly relieved to be spared of my duties in this regard. I couldn't have coped with the physical facts of a Hindu cremation — the cold flesh, the open-mouthed grimace, the bridal gaudiness inflicted on the helpless female corpse, the breaking of the skull with a bamboo pole. It would have intruded too much into the memories I had of my mother, this neglected figure of my childhood, her happy flushed face and eager embrace as I arrived home for the school holidays, the sad fragrance and reticulated feel of her forehead as I kissed her goodbye a few weeks later, both of us restraining our tears under the disapproving gaze of my father.

I was alone in my grief now; whatever emotion my father felt, he was unlikely to share it with me. I went by myself to the room in the ashram where my mother had spent her last years, slowly subsiding into a mist of religious piety and illness. It was where I had once seen her tiny figure huddled on the bed, quietly crying to herself. That was also the time when she first told me — out of what depths of desolation, I now wonder — that she did not wish to live any longer; and I, though taken aback, had taken after her husband, who thought her incapable of independent thought, and had not really believed she knew what she was saying. In that room, devoid of furniture and resonantly silent, there was now an altar of sorts. Bouquets of fresh flowers and incense sticks — a special tribute to my mother from the ashram's inmates — stood on a table before a newly framed picture of her. As long as I could remember, she had refused to have her picture taken; my father had chosen for this commemorative moment a very old photograph of hers, one that I had never seen. It showed her in her graduation robes and cap, cradling her rolled-up degree, her face — as was the preferred pose in the 1950s — in half profile, with the beginnings of an uncertain smile, the smile of the marriageable girl student who has already had an intimation of the savorless life in store for her.

Standing in that room, I thought of my

mother's various kindnesses to me, the jars of homemade snacks and sweets she would bring to my school, the rupee notes she would push into my pocket, when my father wasn't looking; I remembered the letters she would write in her large-eyed script, overflowing with maternal anxiety. It was only after these memories exhausted themselves that my attention turned to other things, and I began to notice her various personal effects that had been transferred to this room, everyday items that death had raised to the status of memorabilia: the clothbound volumes of the *Ramayana* and *Mahabharata* and the collected works of Sarat and Tagore, her diary with its accounts and laundry lists, old issues of the religious magazine *Kalyan*, rosary beads in a frayed velvet pouch, small idols of Krishna and Rama.

These things had accompanied her all her life; they had made up her world; but it was not until I came across the heavily annotated Hindu calendar she kept hung in her room all her life that I realized how inviolably whole that world had been to her. It had been a realm of existence over and above her sorrows and disappointments on the material plane, a world with its own rhythms and seasons, virtues and habits. Magh, Aashaad, Phagun, Sankrant, Amavasya, Nau Ratra: the sonorous poetry of these Sanskrit names, the musical chiming of these months, festivals, and fasting days — they had brought a subliminal order to her time on earth; they had measured out, and made bearable, her life.

But how alien those names sounded to me! How hard it was in that room, facing that calendar, my mother's possessions all around me, the soft chanting of the ashram's inmates wafting in through the open windows, to deny the knowledge that the past that had given shape and coherence to my parents' lives was no longer available to me.

I was very much on my own: this was what my father sought to convey to me in the days that followed my mother's death. Until then, I had never exchanged more than a few words at a time with my father. He had been the same with my mother. Practical matters were briefly discussed before both withdrew into their respective private worlds. He had been a less distant figure when I was still a child; I remember him reading me stories from the *Mahabharata*, and explaining to my young, uncomprehending mind the complex dialogue between the sage, Yagnavalkya, and his wife, Maitreyi, in the *Brihadaranyaka Upanishad* about the illusoriness of love and attachment. But he was by nature a reticent man, and his reticence grew with time.

I remember one dappled afternoon — the last of its kind before summer — when I was sitting out in the courtyard of the ashram my father and I were staying at in Benares. I was trying to read when I looked up to see my father walking toward me. How infirm he looks, I suddenly thought with a twinge of pity, how old he was, half-leaning on his stick, his hair and mustache a uniform gray, the sun highlighting his deeply lined face.

I stood up as he approached. He came closer, and then stopped and tilted his head sideways to peer at my book. I immediately held it out to him, but he waved it away and, looking me straight in the eye, asked me if I would go with him on a walk through the ghats.

There, amid the crowd of late-evening bathers, my father explained to me his plans for the future. He had decided to wind down his present life. He wanted to retire and move to the Aurobindo Ashram in Pondicherry. It was where he had long wanted to go; if he didn't go now, he would never be able to leave. As for me, he would make all possible arrangements. He had built no house to pass on to me, and there wasn't much money. But he could set aside a small allowance that would see me through college. After that, it was up to me to make what I could of my life.

He then concluded these abrupt announcements with an even more uncharacteristic personal-philosophical statement. He said he had never wanted to get married; his marriage was a mistake from the very beginning, and both he and my mother had suffered for it. Another mistake lay in joining the PWD. But there was no choice for him. It wasn't anything he ever wanted to do, and he had ended up spending the best years of his life in joyless drudgery. But then, he didn't have too many regrets about all that anymore. Experience had taught him that of such mistakes were most lives compounded.

What he had always desired was freedom: freedom from all bonds that tie one down to the vanities of the world, freedom from all duties and responsibilities to other people. It had come to him at last in old age, with the death of his wife, when he could not take full advantage of it. He was going to make the most of it in the time left to him.

It took him a few more months to wind up his affairs. I was still in Allahabad and didn't see him leave for Pondicherry. He wouldn't have liked that anyway: the sentimentality of goodbyes. He did ask me to visit him during my holidays. But I never went. I sensed the awkwardness of such a visit for both of us. I went instead to Kerala, Kashmir, Darjeeling, and Simla; I stayed in cheap hotels and traveled on buses. I wrote to him about my journeys. He seemed to approve of them in his replies. I wrote to him from Allahabad; my letters grew more brisk and confident.

It was in Allahabad that, amid all the disorder of the university, I was able to carve out my own life. It was a life I wished to continue in Benares when my three years in Allahabad came to an end. Benares was a choice by default. In Allahabad, I had developed no clear ideas of what to do or where to go next. I rarely attended classes, and spent the long, empty days in the cool arbors of Azad Park, where I would read and read for hours. Away from the chaos of the university there existed a different city of broad sleepy avenues and old colonial mansions peacefully crumbling behind overgrown hedges, and it was there I sought those peculiar delights of the solitary and the eccentric, and even managed to know happiness of a sort.

In my mind's eye, I see Allahabad now as I often saw it from the top balcony of a high tower in the middle of the university campus, the crinkled green silk of its many trees held down here and there by domes and spires. The epicenter in this toy town of the imagination is the ramrod-straight street down Civil Lines, on which were located in close proximity Wheeler's bookstore and Palace Cinema. Wheeler's, as it was called, was bigger and better stocked than the bookstores you would find in a small town. The books were well organized and arranged on long, dusty shelves, and the store was — unheard-of luxury! — air-conditioned. Palace Cinema offered another, more readily accessible kind of haven for the imagination. It was there that I once watched James Bond cheerfully outwit a global cast of villains in Cuba, Berlin, and Rajasthan. From this dizzying world tour I remember emerging through dark staircases not into drab reality but into an enchanting night, transformed by an inaudible shower into a soft-focus, blurry glimmer, bright lights trembling behind the thin mist rising from puddle-smeared pavements, a lone bicycle rider imprinting a trail of treadmarks on the gleaming wet road.

7

In Allahabad I had been on my own. I found my own byways and cloisters in the city. But in Benares, to which I came seeking little more than an extension of the idle, bookish life I had in Allahabad, I had found myself in a different world. I knew more people, and their presence in my life filled me with new emotions and alerted me to old inadequacies.

Restless and lonely in my room, I began to spend more and more time outside it. I spent the longest time at the university library. Many memories of my days inside its dark, cavernous echoing rooms have survived. The random browsing through the long row of shelves in the badly lit stacks, where students smoked foul-smelling beedis; the fly-infested rough wooden tea stall just outside the main gate, where I would eat, standing up, a hasty lunch of omelette and sticky-sweet tea; the view from my windowside desk of the patch of sunlight carpeting a lawn, the dewy grass ablaze but the neem trees bordering it luxuriantly dark and still — the images speak of a time of serenity and quiet fulfillment, and insofar as they do so, they are not false.

But they edit out a small but significant part of my experience. They do not quite convey the fact that this serenity was precarious, always under threat from the chaos that was the rule in the university in those days, the chaos that I frequently witnessed from close quarters but took for granted.

The university campus had been patterned on some design of the cosmos found in the Vedas; its sylvan seclusion owed much to the Hindu equation between students and hermits. The various departments lay on the diameter of the semicircular plan; behind them were the hostels and playgrounds.

Set in the middle of large lawns and gardens, the buildings looked like products of an extravagant imagination, the predominant style being Indo-Saracenic: a mishmash of neo-Victorian and Hindu-Islamic styles, cupolas, arcades, colonnaded balconies, castellated towers, classical porticoes, domes, minarets, all jumbled up together in stone.

Indo-Saracenic: I knew the name but I didn't then have much of an idea about architecture. In Allahabad, I had lived among the very first buildings of the Indo-Saracenic style; but the fact had escaped me altogether. The buildings were much like the crumbling colonial mansions elsewhere in the city, sites of decay and ruin. India was full of such buildings. I saw them everywhere; they were too familiar; I asked no questions about them.

This wasn't complacency, or lack of curiosity. I saw what I saw, but there was nothing to compare it with. Decay and ruin were so much a part of one's environment that one took no notice of them. It was the visitor, the traveler from other lands, looking to figure out a new place and its people, who brought an inquisitive and trained eye to things one took for granted — as did Catherine, who once asked me about the Hindu University.

She often spoke of her tramps through Benares in a way that attached significance to the smallest things. Coming into the house from somewhere, she would remark on the quality of the light over the river; she would speak of the dappled effect of the water on the rooms of the riverside houses, or mention the fretwork on a particular balcony of a house on Narad Ghat. I was always struck by her great alertness to the world around her, which made her discover style and beauty in the most unexpected places. It made me want to see the city through her eyes, and always pretending to more knowledge than I possessed, I often adopted her opinions about something I knew nothing of.

She had been to the university museum a

few times, and had wandered about the campus: it was, she said, unlike anything she had seen in India or elsewhere.

I promptly read up on the university's history the next time I was at the library. The university, built in the early years of the twentieth century, was the work of the pre-Gandhi generation of Indian nationalists, such leading figures as Madan Mohan Malviya. You could see the statues erected to commemorate them at important traffic intersections in Benares — statues that were now forlorn, neglected, discolored.

The larger aim these nationalists had, apart from independence, was the regeneration of India through direct and vigorous contact with the best of what was being thought and said in the Western world. The aspiration was shared not only among Indian nationalists, but many British men and women subscribed to it too. Among the inspirational figures behind the Benares Hindu University was Annie Besant, the English theosophist and Fabian socialist and friend of George Bernard Shaw. I remember reading this one afternoon in the library, sitting among the criminalish young men playing cards, the bored young women with long, painted fingernails, tracing their initials on the wooden desktop, and for a moment the internationally famous names seemed to make the university appear a more important place: a place designed for a noble cause, to which great men and women had devoted their time and energy.

But the moment didn't last long, as the more I read, the more I felt that I was reading about another university in another world.

In this, the university resembled the one in Allahabad I had gone to for my undergraduate degree. The break with the past, whenever it had occurred, had been clean; the early years of idealism belonged to an unremembered time. You could get the details in books. As for the present, you had to figure it out for yourself. You had to know where you stood and you had to be careful.

One morning, shortly after meeting Rajesh, I was walking to the library when my attention was diverted to a large and noisy crowd assembled outside the university museum. It was a building in the same Indo-Saracenic style, secluded from the road by a tall hedge and trees. Inside it, as a reminder of the university's better days, were miniature paintings and sculpture of much distinction.

The crowd was growing every moment, students on foot and bicycles, and even a couple of motorcycle riders, joining it from all directions. It had spilled out onto the road by the time I reached it. I heard the slogans as I came closer: *VICE-CHANCELLOR HAI HAI!! VICE-CHANCELLOR MURDABAD!! DOWN WITH THE VICE-CHANCELLOR!!*

I knew about the students' hostility toward the vice-chancellor. I remembered, too, Rajesh's recent warning about the possibility of student violence. I now wondered what fresh provocation had caused the large frenzied gathering.

When I asked a bystander standing alongside me, he barely looked at me as he replied, "The vice-chancellor is inside the museum."

It seemed odd: What was the vice-chancellor doing inside the museum? And why were the students here?

I stood there for a while, wondering if I should move on, when in a sea of unfamiliar faces shining with excitement I suddenly spotted someone I knew.

It was Pratap, one of the young students I had met with Rajesh at the tea stall.

He, I remembered, had been particularly excited during the talk about the civil servant and his millions, such talk among poor students being part of a consoling fantasy about the future. His hair was cropped close to his skull — it was the kind of haircut many students had, from the roadside barber outside the campus gates, the bearded hunchbacked Muslim with the rusty hand mirror and rickety wooden chair. His shoulders lay bunched under the thin shawl draped around them; his trousers, tied at the ankles, were of a shiny synthetic material.

He saw me looking at him and his large impassive face broke into a smile. He pushed his way through the crowd, provoking mild protests; then he was standing next to me and shaking my hand with great vigor — a gesture of friendliness that I felt owed much to my connection with Rajesh.

He explained that the vice-chancellor had come to garland a statue inside the museum, and some students had got wind of his presence there. They had surrounded the museum, refusing to let him leave until he revoked expulsion orders he had issued for three students. He had been trapped there now for almost an hour. In the meantime, the students had locked up his personal staff in the adjacent canteen and damaged his official car. Pratap pointed to the white Ambassador car that stood marooned amid swirling groups of students. The front windshield had been knocked out, giving it the appearance of an eyeless skull; the headlights had been smashed, the shattered glass on the ground glinting like tiny diamonds; wires stuck out forlornly from the hole on the roof where there had been a revolving blue light.

Pratap said, "Look over there: it's Mohan!"

I looked and saw a student in a white khadi kurta and vest, his thick-rimmed glasses jutting out from his face. He was being held aloft by outstretched arms and then placed on someone's shoulders. I didn't know who he was, and when I asked Pratap, he was surprised that I didn't know. Mohan was an old student, a member of the Communist student wing, and famous across the campus for his revolutionary poetry.

A loud voice appealed for quiet, and when the students had quieted down a bit, someone else announced in a dramatic tone that Mohan was to recite his poems.

All eyes were now on the poet, who started fumbling through the sheets of paper in his hand; someone guffawed, and a few protesting voices immediately rose up. A relative quiet briefly ensued as Mohan kept searching. He finally found the page he wanted and began.

The poem, recited in grave, admonitory tones, was about the need for a new freedom struggle and independence for India; the freedom that came in 1947 had turned out to be a fraud; it had merely replaced foreign oppressors with homegrown ones.

As Mohan went on, the crowd's attention began to wander. He started on another poem. It was a poem about the Nazi siege of Leningrad. The crowd remained as distracted as before. Someone broke into a fit of giggles; a few other people followed.

The student who had giggled first now screamed: *DOWN WITH LENINGRAD!!* A ripple of frank laughter ran across the large crowd. Pratap whispered to me: "These are mostly men from the Hindu Pride party. They don't like this Russia-China, Chou-Mao stuff."

Mohan seemed totally unperturbed as he began his next poem. This was a Hindi translation of Pablo Neruda's poem on the fall of Allende in Chile.

It went on for some time: the tenacious poet, a derisive audience. I was about to leave when a tremor of apprehension originating from the western end of the crowd reached me. An instant later, I heard the familiar siren; the students became very quiet and tense. A few of them even started to extricate themselves from the crowd. Mohan stopped midway through his poem; then, as if recalling his courage, began to recite again, his voice very clear in the sudden hushed silence.

Presently a white Ambassador with a blue siren light came into view. It was followed by two jeeps, both crammed full of policemen with lathis and wire-mesh shields.

Heads turned toward the gate, where the car and jeeps stopped. Someone now took Mohan's place and began in a loud voice to beseech the students not to leave the area. "It is our rightful struggle," he said, in broken English, even as the crowd parted to make way for the policemen striding up to the museum where the vice-chancellor was held captive.

I knew the car with the blue siren belonged to the local superintendent of police. I even knew his name — I had seen it mentioned once or twice in the local newspapers. He was known as a dedicated campaigner against local mafias. I craned my neck to get a better glimpse of him as he passed us, surrounded by a posse of constables. He was a short, corpulent man, and the expression on his face was nervous and fidgety. His cap sat askew on his head and he walked with the gait of a man with some muscular trouble in the groin.

The man who had replaced Mohan was still haranguing the students to stand firm and refuse to bow to police pressure.

Later everyone, even the local papers, would offer different versions. No one apparently was close enough to see what actually happened. Too many people pressed onto the SP and his men making their way through the crowd. But people did recall seeing the SP's head suddenly capless; they would remember seeing him turn around angrily and slap the boy hard standing nearest to him; they would remember the boy throwing himself upon the SP with a mighty roar; they would remember the wrestling bodies sprawling into the crowd, which quickly receded and let them fall to the ground.

After that there was chaos.

The policemen left standing beside the jeeps and the white Ambassador panicked, and in their hurry to get to the commotion invisibly developing inside the crowd, they frantically swung their lathis to clear the congestion. In the restricted space allowed them, they couldn't swing lathis much. One student got hold of the other end of one of the lathis and snatched it away from the terrified policeman.

This encouraged the students. Angry voices rose in unison. The policemen were easily outnumbered. A few more lathis were snatched away, and even used, and the air was filled with the sickening thwack of wood crashing down on human bones, yelps of pain rising from the crowd.

And then I heard a big boom: it was the kind of noise a big Diwali firecracker makes, except that the sound came through slightly muffled. I turned toward the direction the noise had come from and saw a policeman — not more than twenty, tall and lean, with the beginnings of a faint mustache around his lips — totter forward, his face distorted with agony. He had been hit by something from the back, and as the crowd instinctively cleared behind him, I saw his attacker. It was a young student; his big-collared white shirt stuck to his emaciated torso like a second skin. I noticed his polyester bell-bottoms — seventies-style clothes passed down to him from someone much older in the family. His long, thin arms hanging at his sides, his feet well apart, he watched the policeman fall to the ground with a mixture of fascination and horror on his face.

As the policeman staggered and fell, almost as though in slow motion, watched by colleagues momentarily stunned into stillness, his back came into view: a mess of furrowed skin and blood. His khaki shirt had been torn to shreds, which stuck to red raw chunks of flesh that had been loosened from beneath the skin.

He had been hit by a hand grenade. I had seen the kind before: filled with small rusty nails, it was small enough to be concealed inside a fist, and it exploded on impact.

Two things happened simultaneously. The bystanders threw themselves to the ground —

it was a reflex inspired by action films. And as we did so, there came to us the sound of a large motor vehicle. We looked up to see a large khaki-painted truck coming to a stop behind the parked jeeps. It was part of the original team of policemen and had somehow arrived late.

The tables turned in an instant. The newly arrived policemen jumped down from the truck and charged into the crowd to rescue their beleaguered compatriots. It was the students' turn to panic, and most of them simply abandoned the lathis and took to their heels. In seconds, the dense crowd dissolved into many rapidly lengthening streams, the air suddenly full of the fast patter of leather shoes hitting the asphalt road.

I was one of the students running fast away from the museum, full of fear that my sandals would break and leave me barefoot and stranded. I ran wildly like everyone else. Not knowing where I was going and concerned only to get as far away as I could from the museum, I ran deeper into the campus. It was after I was some distance away, the sickening sight of the wounded policeman finally out of my eyes, that I took stock of my situation. The police were certain to go after the students now. They would cordon off the area and raid every building in the vicinity of the museum, every building that seemed to harbor students. I wasn't a student, but I looked like one, and the policemen were indiscriminate in their vindictive fury.

I looked around me. I had run a fair distance from the museum; I had crossed the large cricket and football grounds — a handful of students were crossing them now, running toward where I stood. I realized I was very close to Rajesh's hostel. From where I was I could see the tea stall he had taken me to, and the cupolas on the roof of the hostel. Things looked quieter around here: deserted roads, deserted hostel. It seemed unlikely that the police would come so far as this. It was to Rajesh's hostel that I went.

He was in his room, but preparing to go out, to the Hanuman temple in the old city, he said, tightening the laces on his tennis sneakers — sneakers no longer muddy, but freshly washed and sparkling white. It was Tuesday, a day of fasting and prayers for him. I told him he couldn't go, and when he looked at me quizzically I told him my news, panting a bit with excitement and breathlessness.

He listened to me attentively, without a shift in his expression at all. But when I stopped and he looked away, that uncertain look came back to his eyes.

He said nothing for a while. When he spoke

it was with his face still averted. He said, "I had told you this would happen. Why didn't you listen? You shouldn't involve yourself with such people. You are a Brahmin, you are here to study, and that's what you should do."

That's what he had said to me the first time I met him. It irritated me a bit now. I hadn't involved myself with anyone or anything. I had simply been, like many other bystanders, caught up in the events of the morning. It was true that he had warned me. But I couldn't have known how or when exactly the students would initiate the disturbances.

And the Brahmin bit didn't make sense. It smacked of melodrama; it harked back to an India that had long ceased to exist, the India of classical times, where learning and the arts were the almost exclusive province of Brahmins.

But I couldn't say that to him. Our relationship, so new and unsettled, couldn't have permitted such frankness. I was still made nervous by him. They weren't there now, but I hadn't forgotten the pistols in his room. I didn't know him at all well and felt that he could easily have been the student who attacked the policeman. I wondered if the grenade that was used came from sources known to Rajesh, whose foreknowledge of the events of the morning was one sign of his proximity to the rioters.

But instead of expressing any of these doubts and hunches, I said, "There were Communist students in the crowd; also, Hindu nationalists."

He was unexpectedly quick in his response. "No," he began, his eyes fixed on me now. "No, these were just students. You can't call them Communists or Hindu nationalists or Congresswallahs."

He paused. "Never make that mistake, never." There was a new vehemence in his voice. "These were just students with nothing to do, nowhere to go, with no future, no prospects, nothing, nothing at all."

He went silent again and sat there, his face turned away from me, his shoelaces pulled but still untied.

He got up and paced the room, the laces trailing on the floor. He stopped before the table and stared at the pile of books on it. His voice softened when he spoke again. "Have you read Iqbal?" he asked.

I said no, a bit surprised. He had previously asked me about Faiz. His interest in Iqbal, the poet-advocate of Islamic Pakistan, was even odder.

He extracted a slim book from the pile on the table and leafed through its Bible-paper-thin pages.

I was exhausted from all the running, and

the memory of the policeman's awful bloody wound was still fresh; at the back of my mind was the fear that the policemen would decide to raid all hostels in the campus. I was eager to get out of the campus as fast as I could. And so I barely listened to what Rajesh recited. But stray words from the poem stayed in memory, along with their gloomy sentimentality, and I recently found an English translation of the poem.

"Love fled, Mind stung him like a snake";
he could not
Force it to vision's will;
He sought the orbits of the stars, yet could
not
Travel his own thoughts' world;
Entangled in the labyrinth of his learning,
Lost count of good and ill;
Enchained the sunbeams, yet his hand no
dawn
On life's dark night unfurled.

8

It was around this time that Catherine's friends from France began to appear at her house. They would come in groups of two and three, leave after a few days, and then come back again after a week or so. The chaste spaces of Catherine's rooms, still without furniture, came to be littered with grubby backpacks, empty Perrier bottles, bundles of laundry, old copies of *Le Figaro*, and *L'Express* and *Newsweek* in Air France folders.

She had known these friends as fellow students during her undergraduate years at the Sorbonne. Nearly all of them had been active in left-wing student movements, with a special interest in Third World causes. It was Catherine who told me this. I think she was eager to establish the credentials of her friends. So that when I saw them first, they were inseparable in my eyes from those massive French demonstrations led by Danielle Mitterrand that made it occasionally to the front pages of Indian newspapers.

After just a few years out of college, they

had taken good jobs in various fields. When Catherine said this to me soon after the first of them arrived at her house, I had to ask her what she meant, and I noticed a tinge of envy in her voice and manner as she listed their flourishing careers in advertising, journalism, design, and so forth. I now see that she must have felt left behind in Benares, that meeting old friends with new and varied accomplishments in their recent past would have aroused an old student competitiveness within her.

In their company, Catherine became a vivacious yet somewhat remote person. She and her friends spoke among themselves in English out of consideration for Anand and me. But she would frequently lapse into rapid-fire French in the middle of a conversation. The effect was disconcerting, and not the least because I already felt disconnected from the conversation, from the names of unseen cities and cafés and films tripping off their tongues.

Faced with such mature experience of the world, such casual yet intimate knowingness, I felt the fragility of my own personality, my lack of opinions and taste.

Catherine did make several attempts to bring me closer to her friends. With Anand her friends' attitude could only be that of an interested and kindly patron. He had nothing to say to them. They were bored by Indian classical music and sat through the couple of private performances Catherine persuaded Anand to give only because it would have been rude to leave. She felt that I was the Indian friend she had in Benares whom they could profitably converse with. She enthusiastically introduced them to me, describing me as an "intellectual" — a word so quintessentially of Paris that it embarrassed me. But in using it Catherine was probably hoping only to set off some sort of frank exchange.

However, things didn't turn out that way. I knew so little about her friends and I had no means of finding out more. Catherine had made me think of them as people concerned about the Third World. The simpler truth was that they had moved on from their student days to professional careers; their visits to India, on Catherine's repeated invitation, were in the nature of safe adventures, forays from secure positions into the unknown world for which they had once possessed an abstract political passion.

But I didn't know this then. Whatever else I knew of their social and intellectual background came to me from books, from the nineteenth- and early-twentieth-century utopian philosophers I had been directed to by Edmund Wilson, the American critic, whose books I was then reading at the library. The dated and mostly irrelevant knowledge I possessed only confused me further; it made me look for meaning and nuance where none existed.

Almost the same kind of book-created confusion existed on their side. I recall one episode with particular clarity. Seconds after we were introduced, one of Catherine's friends — Jacques, a tall shambling man with a permanently aggrieved expression on his face — had set about interrogating me about Gandhi. It took me some time to figure out what he meant by his questions, and by then it was too late to go back to basic history.

In the vision that had come to him from books and films, every Indian was axiomatically a Gandhian, and the country on the whole an Edenic setting of self-sufficient villages and their cotton-spinning nonviolent inhabitants. His great desire was to explore the "real" India — the Gandhian India, as opposed to the "fake" India he said lazy tourists saw.

I had lived in India all my life, but I couldn't divide it up between the tourists and the Gandhians. Jacques's way of looking at India intrigued me. I felt, as I often did with Catherine, that he was bringing a larger vision to something that had grown overfamiliar. I wished to enter that vision, to see things the way he would see them, and I felt oddly protective about him when I heard — from Anand — that he had had a hard time on his travels. He had left Benares with the intention of finding this Gandhian India and was ready to sacrifice all comfort and luxury to this end. He had returned a fortnight later, sick and feeble with food poisoning and dysentery. The horrors of semiurban and urban India, Anand said, had repelled him so profoundly that within the very first week he had shed his ascetic resolves and sought refuge in those very same sanctuaries of five-star hotels he had earlier derided.

My encounters with Catherine's other friends were equally unsuccessful. Once past the barrier of language (they spoke English with considerable difficulty and with a heavy, almost incomprehensible accent), our conversations floundered in prejudice and artifice. Most of them couldn't think of India as anything other than an exotic hotbed of illiteracy, poverty, and religion: they would come back from their travels around Benares, speaking excitedly of sadhus who had been standing on one leg for ten years, of beggar children without limbs, and of the huge rats scurrying about in the alleys.

In trying to correct their notions of India, I

became false to myself and others. I turned into a performer, one eye and ear always open for Catherine. I became eager to flaunt my book-learning, and I dropped names right and left: Nietzsche, Mann, Proust, James, Kierkegaard, Pascal. I was keen to demonstrate I had read them all and, what's more, remembered everything I had read.

I couldn't tell how far I succeeded in impressing them. Perhaps very little. For their attitude remained one of gentle condescension, some of which I sensed, and thus became even more aggressively knowledgeable about everything. I remember, in this regard, a brief argument with one of Catherine's closest friends, Claire, a thin, bony woman with close-cropped hair. She claimed to be in love with England and Englishness; and she had found them best represented, she told me, in Evelyn Waugh's *Brideshead Revisited*. I had read the novel, and found only the first part somewhat accessible. The later descent into Catholic theology had left me perplexed; people and motivations had grown suddenly obscure, even preposterous. Then, recently, browsing through the dusty stacks at the BHU library, I had come across Edmund Wilson's famous attack on the novel, and much of it had struck me as true and just. I repeated before Claire some of Wilson's arguments only to elicit from her this retort: "Who is this Edmund Wilson?" I said he was an American critic, to which she said, "You know you must never trust an American on these matters. What do they know about European literature? Nothing. Why are you Indians reading these Americans?"

It was unsettling to see Catherine so quickly assume her place in this private circle of friends from her past — people whom I, despite her best attempts, couldn't get to like. I was struck most by the casual intimacy with which she and her friends spoke of their own and other friends' private affairs. I had never known anything like this kind of intimacy, which, I now recognize, must have developed during their university days, during night-long coffee-and-cigarette-aided confabulations in student digs. It explains the ease with which they disclosed their anxieties about their post-university future, the joviality and light melancholy with which they discussed their current and past romantic relationships.

With these friends around, I felt Catherine recede, grow less familiar. The house itself seemed to change; it created within me a different, more melancholy mood, with the intimations it now held of a richer, fuller life elsewhere — the glossy French magazines with their housemaking advertisements and holiday offers, the wine bottles from the Dordogne, the catalogues of new exhibitions at the Louvre — the world she had known all her life, and to which, after this brief interlude in Benares, she would soon return.

The thought, every time it occurred, came to me with new force, and it brought with it little twinges of anguish. On evenings when I came back from Catherine's house, my disheveled room seemed a meaner and shabbier place in the low-voltage light from the exposed lightbulb.

Outwardly, nothing changed. My life remained fixed in routine. The day at the library passed off calmly, and anxiety and restlessness built up only toward the end of the day, when routine faltered.

I went to the library every day and stayed there until it closed at six. I often saw Rajesh there. I hadn't thought of him as a frequenter of libraries. But he came quite regularly, apparently with no specific purpose in mind, and every time he came he would seek me out. He behaved with less formality toward me; the stiffness and awkwardness of our earlier meetings were gone. He would still look away in the middle of a conversation, his eyes suddenly clouded with uncertainty, his face unreadable, and I would wonder again about the other life he led, the life in which I suspected he was in league with the student rioters.

But he was now less difficult to be with. He knew where I sat and would come and stand behind me, peering over my shoulder at my book.

"Edmund Wilson!" he would begin, always reminding me when he did so of Catherine's friend Claire. "Why are you always reading the same man? What's so special about him?"

I felt I couldn't explain to him the circumstances in which Wilson had become an attractive and important figure for me: my semicolonial education, which had led me to spend more time than was necessary on minor Victorian and Edwardian writers; my own confused self-education, which had seen me randomly read books without grasping the concrete social and historical backgrounds they had emerged from.

It was in my usual random manner that I had once chanced upon Wilson. I had read his book on the American Depression. In Benares, I found that the library had other books of his. I read them as well. They directed me to other books and sent me back to those I had already read. That winter Wilson became an indispensable literary and intellectual guide. He seemed sensitive to the artistry of great books. He could also place them in history and link them up with larger movements of men and ideas.

There was also the image of Wilson suggested by his various diverse endeavors: it was the image of a man wholly dedicated to the life of the mind, immersed in intellectual pursuits of the noblest kind; a man with a clear vision of the world, which new discoveries continually expanded — in short, the man I secretly longed to be.

I wasn't completely unaware of the disparity between this ambition and the circumstances of my life. My anxieties about the future, kept at bay until I reached the eligible age for the Civil Service exam, were of a different order altogether. The future itself seemed so circumscribed — as much for me as for countless others at the university — no matter what we strove for in the present. A part of me knew I was aiming too high with the ambition to emulate Wilson. I was never far away from feeling absurd and embarrassed — which is what made me feel more abashed before Catherine's friends.

But none of this, I felt, would make any sense to Rajesh. So, in response to his inquisitiveness, I would make a few general statements about the importance of Wilson. He wasn't satisfied, however. Once he saw me reading *To the Finland Station* — Wilson's book on the pre-Marxist and post-Marxist tradition of historical analysis — and demanded a summary of Trotsky's ideas.

These demands could exhaust me and I would wonder, in a fit of irritation, why Rajesh, who seemed to read nothing apart from the local Hindi paper and Faiz and Iqbal, should be so interested in Trotsky or Wilson, people so far away from us, from Benares.

As if sensing this, he once brought to the library a notebook of thin, damp, double-lined pages, with a red-lipped Murphy Radio Baby on the cover. Inside, he had copied some of Wordsworth's and Shelley's poems. He had studied them as part of his undergraduate course: "The Solitary Reaper" was his favorite among them. But, unlike the works of Faiz and Iqbal, Romantic poetry was something he only read, never recited. He said he had trouble pronouncing certain English words — he was working on it, however, he said. One couldn't get anywhere in India without a good knowledge of the language, and the poems helped him, he said. But when I asked him exactly what it was that he liked about the poems, he wouldn't say anything. They seemed to exist in his head alone, as a kind of private music.

He would often join me at the fly-infested tea stall outside the library where I had lunch. Invariably, the students who hung around it at all times of the day recognized him, and within minutes a small crowd would gather around him to discuss the latest gossip, corruption, and sleaze scandals: the size of a politician's wealth, the imaginative ways in which the World Bank or some other rich development agency had been conned, the bridges that existed only on paper, the dual-carriage highways that had never been built.

When asked to respond to something, Rajesh would retreat into one of his long monologues. Some of his themes soon became familiar to me. Gandhi, he claimed, would have set a proper course for the country had he not been murdered so soon after independence. Though a good, well-intentioned man, Nehru had little understanding of India. He believed too much in imported formulas: industrialization for an agricultural country, state secularism for a religious people.

This was one theme. Another related to politicians and businessmen (he would refer to them as *dukandaar,* shopkeepers) who, together, had betrayed the country. The only hope, he would say, lay with honest civil servants.

And so it would go on until I slipped out of

his small eager audience and made my way back to my windowside desk at the library.

I occasionally speculated about his other friends. Who were they? What did they do? Once I saw him step out of a dark-green Ambassador with tinted-glass windows — a sure sign of dubious character. With him in the car were two paan-chewing thickly mustachioed men dressed in the garb of local politicians: white khadi kurta and tight churidars. I wondered if he was planning to go into politics, if the students he patronized were part of a larger strategy to build up his electoral base in the university. But I couldn't be sure of any of this — even after the riots in which I thought he had played a role. It did occur to me to ask him, but he never talked about anyone he knew at the university or outside it. I was sure that he would take the question badly, and the thought of how he might respond made me nervous.

He did once mention Arjun, Mrs. Pandey's errant son. He already knew I lived in his mother's house. He said, "That Arjun. Do you know what he tried to do?"

Puzzled, I said, "No."

He continued, "He tried to mortgage the house you live in — a house which doesn't belong to him."

How and where had he acquired this piece

of information? I didn't say anything then but rather thought I should speak to Mrs. Pandey, who was forthright on the subject of her son's misdemeanors and would have liked to know about any fresh instances.

But it slipped my mind each time I saw them. On those evenings when I did not visit Catherine's house, I ate with Mrs. Pandey and Shyam in their dark, windowless kitchen. Dinner was a quiet affair. Shyam kept dropping perfectly shaped chapatis into my brass thali, his face almost demonically intense in the glow from the chulha fire. Mrs. Pandey watched, wordlessly, without a flicker of expression on her broad, large-featured face. Long shadows leapt over each other on the soot-encrusted walls, and bells and conch shells rang out from the adjacent temple courtyard, where a small group of devotees performed the evening aarti. From downstairs would come the faint twanging of sitars and the hollow beat of tablas — Panditji winding up the last of his evening lessons for the American and European students, who often came up to the roof afterward to smoke opium, much to Miss West's annoyance. "Wretched addicts!" she would exclaim. "I must have a word with Mrs. Pandey about them."

In fact, she had already complained to Mrs.

Pandey, but since she had only an elementary grasp of Hindi, she hadn't understood when Mrs. Pandey expressed her helplessness in the matter. The students were acquaintances of her son, Arjun, and they brought in much of Panditji's income — his occasional singing at the temple brought a pittance; they couldn't be antagonized.

Of Arjun I saw little. But I remember one incident well. One evening as I came up the stairs, I saw someone slumped on a string cot just outside the kitchen threshold where Mrs. Pandey and Shyam were sitting. The figure stirred slightly and then raised himself up on his elbow, the cot creaking, and looked at me out of a black-eyed, swollen face. It was Arjun, almost unrecognizable at first, his thick lips chapped and bruised, his beard and balding head covered with bandages and bits of sticking plaster.

He squinted at me, figured out who I was, and then slowly sank back onto the cot.

I walked up the stairs. Later that evening, sitting before Mrs. Pandey in the kitchen, Arjun still slumped on the string cot outside, I asked her, "What happened to Arjun?"

"Someone hit him," she said. Her tone was neutral. She might have been speaking of someone else's son.

"Who?" I asked.

She nodded her head as if to say she didn't know. Then, after a pause, she added, "It's his own fault. He gets involved with unsavory people; he gambles; he takes loans he can't pay back . . ."

She went on to enumerate more faults. Shyam kept nodding and saying, "Greed is the biggest evil. It eats away man, destroys families, sunders son from parents, husband from wife . . ."

As he mumbled on, Rajesh's words abruptly came back to me: "He was trying to mortgage a house that doesn't belong to him."

I thought I should tell Mrs. Pandey. There might have been a connection between what Rajesh had told me and Arjun's present state. But the moment — Mrs. Pandey denouncing her son as he lay outside groaning softly with pain — didn't seem right then.

And when the moment passed it never came back. The story sunk into memory, where it remained until many years later.

PART II

1

February had just turned into March, the afternoons steadily growing warmer, when abruptly one day Miss West announced her decision to go to Mussoorie for a few days ("to the hills," she said, in her old-fashioned way).

She told me that she had already discussed her plans with Catherine, who was to go with her.

"Her interesting friends have gone traveling in different parts of the country," she said. "The poor girl wants to get out of Benares and do some traveling herself before she goes back to Paris."

Miss West knew friends in Delhi — actually a former maharajah — who owned a house in a less crowded and touristy part of Mussoorie. She asked me if I wanted to come along. "There'll still be snow on the ground," she said, her face shining with childlike excitement. "You would like that, wouldn't you? And the views of the Doon valley from the house are absolutely gorgeous."

My first thought was: Can I afford it? I had

to count the money I kept in an imitation-leather pouch in my room before I could say yes.

It was impressive, after that, to watch the speed with which a journey could be arranged, tickets bought, clothes packed — my parents used to plan for months before stepping out of the house for a short train journey.

But when we were almost ready to go, Miss West's plan developed complications — and, as it turned out, was never to recover from them. She had to stop over in Delhi to complete certain very important formalities at the Foreigners Registration Bureau. She gave me all the details of the Mussoorie house and then left for Delhi by an earlier train, promising to join us in Mussoorie after a day's delay.

So it was that Catherine and I came to travel together to Mussoorie.

Throughout the days leading up to our departure, I felt an odd growing excitement: it was the first time I would be traveling alone with a woman, and then there was the always-redeemable promise of the Himalayas. Anand, on the other hand, looked morose, even depressed. I knew from Miss West that Catherine had asked her not to invite him to Mussoorie. Catherine had wanted to do this trip without him; it was meant to be a change from her usual life in Benares, a life recently grown more tense with the growing anxieties about their future in Paris.

Anand was parting from her for the first time since he came to know her. With me he had always been polite. In the past, he hadn't seemed to mind being left out of the few conversations about books I had with Catherine. Practicing his sitar in the next room while I talked to Catherine, he had appeared confident of his own special claim on Catherine's time and attention. But he didn't like being excluded from the trip to Mussoorie, and there was now a new, appraising wariness and even a touch of antagonism in his attitude toward me.

He came to the railway station to see us off, looking slightly haggard with his unshaven face and crumpled kurta. He helped us store our bags on the overhead bunk and then we all stood outside the coach. Around us seethed the usual mass of people and things: toy stalls blared Hindi film music; the waterless urinals gave off a strong stench of ammonia; pornographic magazines covered with crinkled yellow plastic lay in a prominent heap on the magazine stall; half-naked child beggars with stringy rust-brown hair tugged at people's clothes; and there were several men who kept running from one end of the platform to another for no apparent reason, their faces distorted with acute anxiety and weariness.

With a palpable air of disinterest, Anand went over his plans for the coming week with Catherine. He was to visit his parents in Bihar — they needed him for a family wedding. But before he left he was to try again to arrange a studio recording with All India Radio, research cheap air tickets to France, chase up his passport application. He impatiently nodded when Catherine, who was in a contrastingly cheerful mood, reminded him of some further tasks he hadn't mentioned.

The train stayed on beyond its scheduled time for departure, well after the goodbyes had been said, and in the strange limbo that developed, communication first dwindled and then ceased altogether.

Anand looked increasingly glum, and when the train finally jerked into movement and began to slide down the platform, it was with a great effort that he held up his hand, as if drawing on his last reserves of energy — but did not wave.

The train picked up speed; dust blew in through the windows. Benares — this part of it newly developed and ugly — soon petered out in ponds of stagnant water and rows of corrugated-iron sheds and yards filled with rusty junked cars and trucks. The five burkadraped women with us in the compartment began to whisper among themselves. I heard the word "Angrez" — the all-inclusive term for foreigners. They were speculating about Catherine, who was sitting by the iron-barred window, gazing out at the darkening flat fields and ditches.

Night swiftly descended. A weak yellow light came on in the compartment. We clattered past a series of dark, deserted stations. Little points of light punctuated the blackness outside. Catherine didn't shift from her position by the window. The Muslim women played cards, pale white arms and long, pink-painted fingernails darting in and out of their burkas.

It was still dark when we reached Dehradun and transferred to the small, crowded bus that was to take us to Mussoorie. I sat next to a bleary-eyed Catherine, our bodies separated by a couple of inches, and touching when the bus driver took a sharp turn on the deserted sodium-lamp-lit road — a new, awkward intimacy ensued, reinforced by the curious backward glances of the army cadets in the row before us.

I must have dozed off soon afterward, for when I woke up, the bus was speeding along a brightly lit stretch of roadside petrol pumps and Catherine was asleep on my shoulder, the garish lights outside flickering across her face, her reposeful eyes and slightly open mouth. Careful not to disrupt her sleep, I sat stiffly on my seat, flinching each time the tires hit a pothole, and watched the orange glow of dawn fringe the towering snow-capped green hills of Mussoorie. Most of Doon valley still lay under deep-blue shadows. But on Rajpur Road, the dew-drenched lawns of retired civil servants and army generals were beginning to glitter, and rolled-up newspapers on wide graveled driveways patiently awaited their first readers.

Catherine blinked into wakefulness just as the bus began its groaning spiraling ascent to Mussoorie. We hadn't spoken at all on the train. In any case, the loud clatter of the train's wheels would have made it difficult to talk. We had retired to our bunks early. She now apologized for having gone to sleep on my shoulder. "I hope I didn't stop you from sleeping," she said. I said she hadn't. She smiled and then in a sudden access of energy began gently to massage my slightly numb upper left arm. "Did you sleep well then?" she pressed and asked. I lied again.

The air in Mussoorie, when we left the diesel-smelling warmth of the bus, felt chilly Snow lay in grimy mounds at the side of the road: coolies from Kashmir squatted around little charcoal braziers; thin columns of smoke rose into the crisp air from the tin-and-timber shacks huddled down in the valley. Outside shuttered shops stood men wearing thick mufflers and pajamas, and brushing their teeth at municipal taps.

The house arranged by Miss West was on the large hill in Landour Cantonment. It was a substantial cottage with a white roof and green trim around the door and windows: In its size, scale, and setting, it wasn't like anything I could have imagined. Set in a large clearing of level, grassy lawn, and secluded by a thick screen of oak and pine trees, the cottage was the biggest on the hillside. From within, the large glass wall of the living room provided a panoramic view of Dehradun quietly smoldering in the wide and deep Shivalik valley — the valley itself was brilliantly visible, with enough dry riverbeds and green clumps of forests and hollow depressions to resemble a gigantic topographical map. Closer, down the hill, irregularly patched with snow, lay the dollhouse-shaped Wynberg Allen School, and even lower, the cluttered slopes of downtown Mussoorie, the jumble of new hotels and restaurants. On the far left of the valley I could see the Ganges, hurtling past Hardwar on its furious descent from the Himalayas, but reduced, from such distance, to a curled silver ribbon on a map.

And after all this, there was the house itself, the maharajah's possession, with its rich oak paneling and gleaming kitchen and springy sofas and soft carpets and expensive stereo systems and televisions and large porcelain bathtubs.

Catherine seemed delighted by the house and the surroundings. "Miss West has some rich friends," she said as she dragged an armchair out to the lawn and settled herself in it.

I said nothing but felt vaguely oppressed by the opulence of the house and unable to put any words to what I felt. Odd, meaningless thoughts floated in my mind as we sat there in perfect seclusion and quiet for some time. Dry leaves softly rustled as someone came down the path that ran behind the house. Once or twice, the sound of a bus or truck horn came piercing through the clean air. Overhead, in the blue, birdless sky, the white clouds were like wisps of shaving foam.

The sense of oppression grew when we went for lunch. Before that, the caretaker of the house had come around while Catherine was taking a shower. I heard footsteps behind me and turned around to see a short old man in faded khaki shirt and pants limping across the lawn. I stiffened in my chair, suddenly vulnerable, suddenly feeling myself more and more of a usurper in this setting. The man frowned at me as he came nearer; his small scaly face held a question mark. When I told him that we were guests of Miss West, he smiled: a wide obsequious smile that added more folds to his reptilian face.

We were to eat at a nearby hotel. Miss West hadn't wanted to bother with cooking during her time in Mussoorie. The hotel was owned by the same maharajah who owned the house we were in. It was his mansion — built in Swiss chalet style, with gables and fretwork — that he had converted into a hotel after the government of India stopped paying privy purses to the former maharajahs. That's what Miss West had told me, the maharajah and the mansion seeming very much a part of the glamour of India for her.

I expected her to have informed the maharajah of our arrival. But he knew only of Catherine — he bowed and flashed a wide smile at her and asked her if everything was all right at the house. His response to my presence took me completely by surprise.

"So you are a tour guide with Miss Catherine? From Delhi?" he asked, in gruff Hindi, of the kind I later heard him use with the menial staff. His eyes were large below bushy eyebrows. His thick mustache was unwaxed and drooping and flecked with gray.

Tour guide? I recovered to say, "No, why do you think that?"

But he only nodded; he wasn't listening; and his staff took their cue from him. The manager, a tall, ramrod-stiff military type, insisted that I put down my name in capital letters in the hotel register. "What is this handwriting, please? I am not being able to read anything. Please write clearly. We need the name for police record."

Turbaned bellboys wore smiles of mockery as I complied. They were still smiling when a cavalcade of dusty Dodge Caravans and Land Rovers with blue diplomatic license plates came crunching up the gravel driveway. They shuddered over the cattle guard and then slid to a halt under the gabled portico. Children in rumpled clothes poured out, followed by weary-looking adults. Twangy American accents filled the small forecourt. The maharajah, pouting over the newspaper, snapped to attention; so did his staff. The manager abandoned his peremptory military manner behind the desk. He roared at the bellboys; he rushed to the cars to supervise the unloading of the luggage.

In the midst of this, Catherine was busy chatting with a couple of French tourists she had spotted in the lobby, backpackers wearing identical crimson anoraks. She seemed so distant and unfamiliar in her black overcoat and a stylish blue beret I had not seen her in previously.

I suddenly wished she was with me, and overcoming the pathos of my own vulnerability, I went and stood next to her.

She turned away from the tourists to look at me and smiled — a brief quizzical smile — and then turned back to them again.

My uneasiness deepened as we went in for lunch. The soft-hued interiors, the quiet conversations and subdued laughter at surrounding tables, the clink and clatter of spoons and forks, all intimidated me into a restive silence, and once again I sought strength from Catherine's unfazed demeanor.

Among the strange faces at our table was that of one of the newly arrived Americans, a tall, balding middle-aged man, a visiting scholar of Indian history. His wife was a stout and somewhat fidgety woman who kept going off in the midst of lunch to apply fresh coats of powder and lipstick to her face and came back each time seized by a fresh anxiety.

"Andrew, Andrew," she would start, "I just wanted to say that the bathroom hasn't been sterilized this morning." Or it would be: "Andrew, Andrew, I just wanted to say that Prakash hasn't returned from the bazaar yet."

Interrupted in the midst of a long story he had been telling the French tourists with great detail all through lunch — about the Maharajah of Jodhpur, whom he referred to as His Majesty — her husband would grunt and then ignore her altogether.

At one point, he turned to Catherine and asked her what she was doing in India and how much longer she planned to stay. Catherine told him. She also told him about Anand, describing him as "my Indian boyfriend." He asked her more questions, and Catherine now went into a long litany of her anxieties regarding her return to France.

There were no good jobs to be had for people like her, who had waited too long after finishing their first university degrees. The universities were reducing their staff. There was little scope in publishing firms. It was why a lot of young people were going off to London or America to look for work. She blamed Mitterrand; she blamed socialism for the failing economy.

As she went on, sounding, I felt, quite overwrought, the French tourists kept shaking their heads in agreement. Once or twice, Catherine's eyes met mine — the profound worry in them was unmistakable. The tourists said a few words in confirmation. Once, Andrew's wife came down from her room to suggest a person in Paris who might help Catherine find a job. The conversation moved to Gorbachev and *perestroika*. The French tourists turned out to have strong views on this subject: they argued furiously with Andrew when he said that Yeltsin was the only hope for the Soviet Union.

Catherine said when we reached the house that she was tired and wanted a nap. She threw herself on the living-room sofa, and she lay all afternoon, curled up sullenly on her side on the chocolate-brown silk cover, her hair falling in a thick mass almost to the carpet, exposing the delicate down on the nape of her neck.

I sat out on the sunny lawn. The deep midday stillness was disturbed only by strangled shouts from a basketball court and echoes of a recorded muezzin on a loudspeaker in the town below. I read *The Leopard* and ambled through Sicilian landscapes in melancholy reverie all afternoon.

Catherine emerged from her sleep several hours later to propose a walk. Bleary-eyed, she stood at the door to the living room, smoothing her hair and saying, "We have to go out anyway. We must call Miss West in Delhi and find out her plans."

We did so. Miss West sounded cheerfully

resigned on the phone, and inquired about her friend the maharajah, but also told us that she had been detained for a few more days and would not be able to reach Mussoorie until after we were gone.

Later, after the phone call to Delhi, we sat in a glass-roofed restaurant full of Punjabi vacationers from Delhi — the men in three-piece navy-blue suits, the women in glossy salwar-kameezes, the squabbling children in fluorescent Disney colors — and wondered how best to spend our time in Mussoorie. I was keen to go somewhere else and get away from the overappointed house and the hotel, the maharajah and the American visitors, and so when Catherine suggested making an excursion to Kalpi, a riverside village she had heard of from one of her friends, I immediately agreed. We made inquiries at the local tourist information center and were told there was a bus for Kalpi early next morning. We decided to take it.

Walking back from the mall, past the busy restaurants and the electronic beeps and peeps of video-game parlors, to the forested hill, Catherine abruptly began to speak of Anand.

He was impractical, she said, and had no idea of what was in store for him in Paris. He thought it would be very easy to perform, to make albums, to be recognized, not realizing that people in Europe hang around on the fringes of the music world for years before they are noticed.

And so she went on in her soft strained voice until she suddenly stopped and said, "What do you think you would have done in my situation?"

It was the very first time she had asked me such a direct question, and it put me in a quandary. Until now, I had been merely a listener. Like Miss West, I had been a witness to her dissatisfactions; I had never actually wondered what I would do in her situation simply because I couldn't imagine it ever developing in my own life. Then, it wasn't my place to offer advice. I didn't know Anand well, and of Catherine I had only a broad fuzzy image in my mind. With her knowledge of literature, her instinct for style and elegance, she was the cultured European woman who for some half-understood reasons had chosen to live in Benares, and had, for even less understood reasons, fallen in love with an Indian man from a very different background and outlook.

Yet I felt I was called upon to say something — and I felt that this time, unlike on other such occasions in the past, I couldn't get away so easily. I thought hard of something appropriate, Catherine quietly expectant beside me. But I could only remember my father's homilies about the importance of detachment, homilies drawn from classical Hindu scriptures, and they were what I was just beginning to repeat before her, a little embarrassedly, when she impatiently interrupted me.

"Are you saying I should be more detached from Anand?" she asked.

She didn't wait for my reluctant nod. "Yes," she said, with a new tone of zestful certainty in her voice. "That's exactly what I have been thinking about recently. I have invested too much in Anand and I need more detachment. Yes, detachment is right, absolutely right."

She fell silent as we trudged back to Landour on the leaf-strewn and flinty paths through the forest, our backs turned to the glorious chaos of colors on the western horizon, where the sun was slowly disappearing behind starkly outlined hills.

The light had turned an aquamarine blue when we reached the top of the Landour hill and strolled through the language school, where a couple of American students stood shining a torch over a spectacularly abscessed dog, on the way that went past the disused British cemetery. Snow lay thick on the paths in this densely forested part of the hill, where tall pines and oaks brood over the sad human waste of empire, the graves of very young women and children. Behind the trees glimmered the villages of the valley behind Mussoorie, the low tin-roofed wanly lit huts, which on moonless nights were like sallow gems scattered all across the dark folds of the hills. A somber silence hung in the air, the silence of aging trees and the dead, and the snow in the dark seemed to glow with a soft inner light.

Catherine was silent all the way back to the house. Her earlier voluble mood had gone. Shrouded in a thick white blanket, the chokidar was waiting for us outside the living-room door. He had seen us at the hotel in the afternoon; now that he knew that we were guests of both Miss West and the maharajah, he was eager to please. He addressed Catherine as Memsahib, his teeth, when he smiled, gleaming in the darkness. He brought out chairs for us to sit on and then paced the lawn behind us in short assertive steps, sporadically slamming his lathi into the ground in the overassertive manner of chokidars.

Down in the valley, the scattered points of light seemed to mingle with the stars in the vast arching sky overhead. A lone owl somewhere on the trees around the house hooted repeatedly at short intervals. The undergrowth was full of brief rustling anxious noises. A childhood memory stirred within me, of sleeping in the open on clear spring nights, curled up on cold velvety sheets under the mysteriously luminous sky.

Catherine said she was sad Miss West wasn't with us to enjoy the view. It was the first time she had spoken since the cemetery; I was getting used to her long silences. "Poor woman," she said, "there are so many troubles she has to deal with."

I wondered about this. Which troubles? But I did not get a chance to ask, as Catherine quickly spoke again to ask me about the university. Did I enjoy my time there? I told her about the riot I had witnessed, the agitated students, the badly wounded policeman. She seemed shocked: it was far beyond anything, she said, she ever suspected on her trips there. She asked me about the kind of life students at the university led. She had asked me that question before in Benares. I remembered because I had had problems with it. The life of the students at the university was the only one I knew, and I would have had to know other kinds of student lives to be able to define our lives properly.

This time, I told her about Rajesh, without naming him. I described his room at the hostel; I mentioned the friends he hung out with.

I told her about the Civil Service exam, and felt at that moment at least — sitting out under the night sky in the hills, so far away from Allahabad and Benares — immune to all the anxieties normally associated with it.

It was later — after some talk of the day ahead, the chokidar now silently sitting behind us, the blackness and stillness of the night present almost like a solid substance around us — that she came back to Miss West. She said she had been reading a book about women who love too much. She said it reminded her of Miss West.

She said, "Diana has been involved with this man for a long time, almost twenty years: a married man, a man with school-going children. The man's wife knows about the affair, but not his children. She pretends it doesn't exist. It's hardest for Diana, because she wanted to marry this man, have children, settle down. But he won't leave his wife, and Diana can't bring herself to leave him. It's a hopeless situation for her. Of course, when she was young and beautiful she had many admirers; even now it wouldn't be hard for her to find a good man to marry. But she won't do it; she is completely in love with Christopher. They never see each other in England; they meet in Europe or India, spend a few days together. Christopher's father was in the Indian Civil Service and stayed on for a while after independence; he's been to India so many times and it seemed natural for them to meet here. He doesn't even come to Benares; he wants to keep it entirely secret. Diana goes along with him on this. It's for his sake — he's a senior corporate executive and may go into politics, he's a public figure and I think wants to avoid a scandal — so it's really for his sake that she lives in India for most of the year, and she lives from meeting to meeting . . ."

Christopher: the name struck a note in memory, and even as I sat there absorbing Catherine's words I remembered the captions to the photographs in Miss West's room. The smiling man who featured in so many of the pictures.

Catherine went on and I sat there listening with a growing sense of unreality. So hard it was to connect her words to the person I had spoken to just this morning, to connect the image Catherine's description gave me, the image of a life and personality so compromised by passion, to the confident, humorous voice on the phone: the voice that had always struck me as that of someone who knew what she wanted from life and the world and was capable of getting it. So enviable had Miss

West seemed to me, her background, the apparently untroubled self-knowledge, her quick ironical assessments of people and situations, which put her on equal terms with the maharajahs of the world.

I had admired and envied these gifts — the gifts that I thought were of an easeful life, a life made comfortable by money and travel, the many-dimensional life I had glimpsed in the photographs on the wall of her room. The discovery that complete fulfillment still lay far beyond Miss West's grasp confused the image I had had of her. I was troubled, because Miss West's disappointments seemed to point at an even harsher fact: the cruel-seeming asymmetry between desire and satisfaction that could exist in the most privileged of lives.

Catherine had been speaking in a low soft voice so as not to let the chokidar hear anything. But it wasn't hard to discern the restless mood she was in. The private disturbance that had earlier made her speak so obsessively of Anand had now made her disclose confidences Miss West had probably entrusted to her at an equally unguarded moment.

The mood explained the impulsive gesture that left me flustered as we went indoors, to the quiet, warmly humming house. Just as we were going to our separate bedrooms, Catherine paused in midstep. I reflexively stopped, too. "Goodnight," she said, and smiled. "Thank you for all your help," she added, and gave a tiny wave and then suddenly reached forward and gave me a quick, light embrace. A rustling of clothes, the pressure of her arms and shoulders, a whiff of shampooed hair, and then she had withdrawn, and with a brief backward smile slipped away into her bedroom.

I slept badly that night. I missed the certainties of my life in Benares, the measured day, the focused mind. The long journey from Benares, the strangeness of my new surroundings, the hotel, the house, the maharajah, the manager, the Americans, the French tourists, the new complicated knowledge about Miss West's past, Catherine's unsettled and unsettling presence, her many alien, inscrutable emotions and preoccupations — I felt them beginning to work on me. Thoughts combined, interlocked, ramified. I felt tense, oddly exposed.

2

We woke up late the next morning and had to sprint down the hillside to the bus station. But the bus to Kalpi was already packed full by the time we reached it, with not an inch of sitting or standing space anywhere. The only vacancies were on top, and as other passengers — mostly peasants with sackloads of vegetables — gawked, Catherine and I clambered up to the tin-plated roof with our bags.

The bus started late and when it did I immediately felt the cold; the dry and bracing wind cut right through to the skin. I gradually took out all the woolen clothes I had brought with me. But I still shivered every time a fresh gust of wind blew across the roof.

As the bus groaned out of the ungainly clutter of downtown Mussoorie, wide unobstructed vistas opened up all around us: lushly forested foothills wreathed in early-morning blue mists; sharp-edged stripes of sunlight angled against the soft mulchy ground of pine groves; thin columns of smoke rising from the tiny houses with thatch or tin roofs scattered all across the hillsides and deep in the valley

— the sallow gems of last night, now dwarfed by the huge immensities of space daylight had revealed, the vast landscape over which the snow-covered mountains to the north, resting on plinths of deep blue air, serenely presided, giant white mountains that often appeared in altered perspective and sometimes were obscured as the bus twisted and turned in tortuous loops, but were always solidly, immutably present.

All morning, we circled down into a flat-bottomed valley, into the gigantic needlework of rice fields, where tiny bent human figures appeared as minute colored stitches; then, as we descended farther, the bright red kerchiefs of the women and the water-soaked fields with their jagged reflections of the sky grew clearer. Another season, another kind of climate existed here; the air became less chilly. The bus stopped to let off passengers at little thatch-roofed tea shacks, where a smell of cooking oil and tobacco hung in the crisp air and ancient gray-bearded men in thick woolen vests sat coughing over hookahs, a pinecone fire crackling away on the ground. Coming around a bend, the bus would occasionally startle a party of hook-nosed Gujjars on their way to the high passes after the winter down in the foothills; with flailing arms and a stick they would herd their flocks, all curved horns and glittering eyes, to the side of the road and then with wary red eyes watch the bus sidle past.

At a raffish highway town, where we stopped to switch buses, Catherine was accosted by a young entrepreneur from Delhi. Thick-lipped, leonine-browed, with the beginnings of a paunch visible even under his bulbous warm jacket, he wore cowboy boots and Levi's jeans and was standing at the paan shop combing his hair with rapid stylish flourishes. Hands dug deep in his jacket pockets, he sauntered over to where we stood waiting for the bus. He ignored me altogether as he spoke to Catherine. "You must be going to Kalpi," he said, "but it's very inconvenient by bus. You can come in my car. It's very comfortable, air-conditioned and all that." He gestured to the steel-gray Maruti parked before a paan shop.

Slightly taken aback, Catherine turned to me and rolled her eyes comically. She asked him, "Are you going to Kalpi, then?"

"No," he said, "I am going back to Mussoorie. You see, I have big business there, hotel-restaurant, whatnot. I have many big business in this area," he added, taking one hand out of the jacket pocket and waving it around. "But I can drop you at Kalpi. No problem. Honestly, no problem."

Catherine said, "Thank you, but I'd prefer to go by bus."

He looked crushed. He stared wordlessly at her for an instant, his face drained of all its assurance.

Then as he turned to go back to his car, he asked, "Which country are you from?"

Catherine, toying with him now, replied, "India."

"*India?*" Suspicion darkened his countenance; his thick brows twitched. "Which state?" he asked.

"Rajasthan," Catherine replied, still straight-faced, and then added, "District Ajmer, have you been there?"

His confusion was complete. "No," he weakly replied. There was a brief moment before the truth of his situation dawned on him, when he uncertainly stared at Catherine. Then, face reddening fast, he turned and lumbered back to his car.

We turned out to be the only occupants of the bus to Kalpi, apart from a few gray sacks of mail tossed in behind the driver's seat where leaking diesel-oil had blended with dust to produce a black paste of sorts. The road began to curl up steeply minutes after we left the bus station. Soon, the snowy peaks, temporarily occluded by mist and clouds, came back into sight, grave and majestic against the deep blue sky; the frothy river we crossed on a jittery, jangling bridge turned into a winding silvery trail; the fields we had raced through knitted themselves back into elegant patchwork quilts.

There were more flocks of yaks on the winding road here, each flock carrying its own little cloud of dust as it scampered to the side of the road. Tiny monkeys with red, hirsute faces crouched and gawked at the passing traffic. The sacks of mail were heaved out and thrown onto the ground before tiny red-painted post offices. Little hamlets lined the road, houses with slate roofs and neat dung-paved courtyards with rose bushes and tulsi plants. School-going children stood at ramshackle bus shelters painted with signs for Four Square cigarettes, their white shirts and blue shorts and skirts unexpectedly formal in this setting. When they saw us, wide smiles would break out across their ruddy cheeks and they would start waving at us with hectic energy. I once turned to see Catherine waving back delightedly, her hair blown back by the wind, the tip of her nose red, her eyes streaming, a smile of pure happiness on her face.

She saw me looking at her and shouted: "Wouldn't it be nice to live here?"

"Yes," I shouted back. "Yes."

The same thought had come to me, had, in fact, been with me from the time the bus left Mussoorie. It came out of the happiness I always felt amid the Himalayas, a kind of private exhilaration that made the tensions of the previous days dissipate fast, made them seem part of another, not quite real or significant, life. It wasn't just the beauty of these snow-carpeted mountains and broad green valleys and surging rivers — the beauty that could move even those with no aesthetic feeling. It was because so much of this landscape was marked for me; the peaks and valleys and rivers held so many associations. It was the first landscape I had known in my imagination, in the stories from the *Mahabharata* where it was the setting for exile and renunciation. The Pandav brothers had walked on this ground, their presence commemorated by innumerable small temples across the ranges; great Hindu sages had made their homes on the banks of its famous rivers. It was always oddly exalting to think that these secluded mountains and valleys were where in unknown times my own ancestors had wandered after long, fulfilled lives on the plains. They were linked to my vague but cherished sense of the past, my memories of Sunday mornings, rooms filled with the fragrant smoke of a sandalwood fire, my father meditating on his tiger-skin rug, before a miniature temple, whose ascending spires, I knew even then, approximated the soaring peaks of the Himalayas.

Presently, the school appeared, to which all the children had been heading. It was perched between shimmering rice fields, a single small building on a flawlessly clean lawn, with a red corrugated-iron roof on which the school's name had been painted in wavering white letters. A deep gorge appeared on our left, the river in it seeming to sneak shyly past all obstructions. The illusion was broken when, after we had been traveling for an hour down into the gorge, the river appeared roughly parallel to the road, and all the bus's relentless grumbling and rasping and clanking could not muffle the thunderous boom of thick white jets of water pummeling the huge white rocks squatting in its way. Away from the angrily frothing river, the thinner, humbler streams flowed into small quivering pools on whose banks grew delicate irises.

Slim, tall waterfalls draped the hillside in many places; old grimy snow lay in shaded gullies from under which water leaked out in muddy trails. Overhead, the hills were all sheer rock, with young shepherds perched on the serrated slopes, sheep grazing on grassy narrow cornices. The gorge widened into a valley with dry riverbeds, white smooth boulders piled up on the side of the road. The bus rambled through forests of pine and oak, the river lost from sight, the sky reduced to a patch of blue pawed at by the tops of pine trees. More snowy peaks came into sight; the valley narrowed and the road rejoined the river and almost immediately deteriorated. Fine chalk-white dust rose into the air as the bus lurched across the rock-strewn flinty surface. Finally, at the end of the dusty track was Kalpi, a scattering of slate-roofed huts on a green meadow, deserted on this drowsy late afternoon, with long, cold shadows creeping down from the snow-clad peaks towering above the raging river on both sides.

There wasn't a single person in sight. With stiff legs and humming head, I followed Catherine over a rope bridge across the river and up to the only solid-seeming building in the vicinity. It was a forest bungalow, with wooden lattices in the verandah and a small patch of lawn, now covered with snow. The chokidar was asleep in one of the outbuildings, in a squalor of firewood logs, old smelly clothes, and charcoal braziers. His eyes were red; his speech was slurred; he smelled of cheap rum. He said we were the first visitors of the year, and the bungalow wasn't ready to be lived in yet, except for one room. The room that he unlocked for us contained the sullen chilly dampness of many airless months. The damp seemed to come off the walls and penetrate the several layers of woolen clothes we wore. There was no power. The mattress on the sole bed was bare; the coir rug on the floor gave off a sour smell of old dust. Stiff, tiny morsels of rice from the last dinner lay on the oilcloth top of the dining table. In the bathroom, with a skylight that framed the white peaks, the taps rattled and shook at first and then, after some noisy expostulations, settled down to produce a steady stream of muddy, hand-numbingly cold water.

Gradually, with many incomprehensible mutterings, the chokidar brought in fresh sheets and quilts smelling of mothballs, and candles, and logs of firewood. Catherine knelt before the stone fireplace for a long time, striking matches one after another, before giving up. The wood was too damp. We'll have to do without the fire, she said, smiling, and gave a mock shiver.

The long drive had filled her with high spirits; she was amused by the chokidar — his slow mincing gait, his slurred speech — and attempted to mimic him when he was out of sight.

I was tired and when Catherine went to the bathroom for a bucket bath I lay down on the narrow double bed and soon dozed off.

I woke up to find the room in pitch-darkness — Catherine had blown out the candle — and Catherine next to me, her face buried deep into the pillow, the back of her neck with its delicate down gently rising and falling.

I lay there stiffly for a while, not daring to shift position lest I wake her up. The exhilaration of the ride hadn't done away with the peculiar tension I had known in Mussoorie the day before, and I now felt even more keenly, lying next to Catherine, the somewhat comic strangeness of my situation: a Brahmin student from Allahabad all alone with a French woman in a room at the edge of the known world.

This wasn't how I had imagined ourselves when we first set out from Benares. In the days past, when such vague and exuberant hopes accompanied me repeatedly to Catherine's house, I hadn't gone on to visualize such perfect proximity to her. Something had held me back: a puritanical fear, perhaps.

But it was a situation that seemed to have its own odd logic and momentum. I felt I had already surrendered to it, was no longer in control. My nervousness had been replaced by a quiet excitement.

★ ★ ★

I must have drifted back into sleep at some point. I opened my eyes to find Catherine moving around the room, searching for something, her shadow dark and looming in the light from the candle.

"Would you like to go out?" she said. "It's wonderful outside."

It *was* wonderful outside, the day dying in a sea of indigo ink; the snowy summits in front wreathed in cotton-wool clouds that caught the last light of the day and held a pinkish tinge; the tall hills behind us silently silhouetted against the darkening sky, where a star or two had begun to glimmer.

We walked up to the temple we had seen on the way to the rest house. It was very small, shaded by an old oak tree, with elaborate and elegant wood carvings on the eaves. There was no one around, but the gate to the sanctum was open and the sequined idol inside was of Krishna, purplish instead of the normal dark blue. A smell of freshly burnt incense hung in the thin air. Moths whirled around the lantern that stood on the brick-paved porch. On the left of the temple was a storeroom of sorts, on stilts; behind it was a wooden lion's head from which water, fed by a stream, gurgled out into a narrow drain.

Someone finally emerged out of the darkness. It was the priest: a young sadhu, an unexpectedly handsome man. His well-muscled torso was uncovered — astonishingly so, for the cold was intense. He wore a white dhoti over bare feet. There were marks of sandalwood paste on his broad forehead. His long, black hair hung down over his shoulders. He saw us; his eyes lingered slightly longer on Catherine but not a flicker of surprise crossed his fine sharp-featured face. We had come late for the evening puja, he said; it had just finished.

He spoke Hindi with a strong Sanskritic emphasis. There was a grave courtesy in his manner. He invited us to sit on the porch and share his evening meal. Catherine hesitated, but he assured us there was enough food for all. In a few brisk precise movements, he brought out brass thalis from the storeroom and ladled out dal and rice from large steel containers and filled chipped enamel cups with water from the gargoyle. We ate with our fingers. He apologized for not being able to offer us spoons or forks; he said the water came from a nearby spring and was safe to drink. He said little more of his own accord; he asked us no questions — no questions about where we came from, and what we were doing in Kalpi.

I asked him how long he had been at the temple.

For five years, he said, his head bowed over the thali, fingers nimbly mixing dal with rice.

And where had he grown up?

"Lucknow," he said, his mouth full. He then paused in his chewing and looked up at me with his clear confident eyes and added: "But that was another life, less meaningful, less substantial."

He bowed his head; he went on eating. So beautifully he spoke, with such resonant Sanskrit phrases: they weren't something he could have picked up in Lucknow; they spoke of a different kind of training. Intrigued, I asked him more questions. Slowly, the details came out, sketchy but significant; and it was with some difficulty that I translated them into English for Catherine's sake.

He came from a middle-class shopkeeping family and had been conventionally educated at a local school and university. His parents had arranged a marriage for him when he reached twenty-one. He hadn't wanted to get married, but his parents had been attracted by the large dowry that came with the bride. His wife died soon after the marriage — he barely knew her, but it was a devastating event for him; it had set him thinking about his life and made him question everything he

175

had held to be true. With that growing estrangement from the world he had grown up in, he had begun frequenting temples and ashrams; he had started to read religious texts. Then one day he had left home and traveled with some sadhus to Gangotri, the source of the Ganges. He had wandered around for some months, staying at various ashrams, and then had come to Kalpi. Here, he had lived with the man who was previously the priest at the temple. The man was old and ailing. He had looked after him, and when he died, he had decided to stay on in the village.

Catherine, who hadn't spoken at all until now, and had been struggling to eat with her fingers, asked me to translate a question for her. She asked: "Do you keep in touch with your parents and brothers?"

"No," he said, his handsome face impassive in the light from the lantern. "When I left, I left those relationships behind me. I didn't bring them here. They belong to the past."

It was dark when we returned from the temple, moving slowly, with the aid of Catherine's torch, down the steep, muddy slope, past sweet whiffs of Rajnigandha. The sky overhead was luminous with stars; the black hillsides, their outlines blended with the sky, were punctuated by the tiny, wan lights of kerosene lanterns; a dog somewhere nearby kept barking; the rope bridge was dark and still against the white glowing water.

Catherine said she wanted to sit by the river for a while. We took the narrow dirt path that led to the water, past scattered boulders and twists of pony excrement, and found a suitable place on one of the huge rocks just above the water. The river was calmer here. I sat next to Catherine, legs dangling over the rock, feeling a fine cold spray on my face.

We sat there for a while, without exchanging a word. I thought of what the sadhu had said about his rejection of the past. It had briefly reawakened a feeling that had come to me earlier in the day, the old, almost religious sense of the Himalayas as a refuge from the futility of life elsewhere. I thought of his earlier life, his grief on his young wife's death, his wanderings in the mountains.

I could sense Catherine's thoughts weren't far away from the sadhu. After sitting silently for some time, I asked her, "What did you make of him?"

It seemed as if she had been thinking of him; she instantly replied, without turning her face, "He is a weird man."

"Why weird?"

She thought for a while and then said, Well, maybe 'weird' is not the right word. I don't know. Not normal, perhaps . . ."

She stopped. A few moments later she said, "But I liked the serious way you spoke to him and took an interest in his life."

I said, "But it's an interesting life."

She immediately spoke up: "Not for me, not for me. I find it empty, hollow. There is no love in it. It's a life without love. What's interesting about it? Nothing."

The sudden passion in her voice startled me. I turned to look at her. She was wearing her blue beret, which accentuated the paleness of the skin on her face and sharpened her profile against the night sky as she looked out over the river. Out of nowhere, as though from a forgotten life and world, and so foreign in this setting, the words of Miss West came back to me — "How badly she wants to be loved" — and I felt a strange sad feeling come over me.

I wasn't prepared when she abruptly asked me, giving a bizarre turn to the conversation, "But have you been in love? Do you know what I mean?"

The question held an implicit challenge. It flustered and abashed me. What could I tell her? I had no ready-made answers; the truth was too complicated and I was shy about revealing it to anyone. I had lived so far away from human contact of the sort Catherine im plied. I hadn't known any women apart from those in my family. Of love and romance, the less regulated but natural order of things, I knew only from books, and I followed other people of my background in suspecting it of being not natural. In the world I had known, romantic love was looked down upon as a kind of sensual derangement that briefly affected insufficiently acculturated or Brahminized youth and then left them broken and disillusioned soon afterward. In this world, men and women were ushered into marriage after their elders had matched horoscopes and convinced each other about their respective social and financial status. Love was supposed to follow marriage, not the other way around; and it mattered little if it didn't.

Catherine said, "You are not saying anything, which means you haven't." She suddenly laughed; it was her full-throated generous laugh. "Maybe you want to be like that sadhu back there, no? Is that your real ambition? To be a lifelong celibate? Admit it, come on, come on," she said, gently pummeling my back with tiny fists, her beaming face turned toward me.

Her new bantering manner defused the tense awkwardness I was beginning to feel. She mentioned one of her friends, a gay man, who had become a monk and then fallen in love with a fellow monk. She told more stories of his later defrocking; she became more and more voluble.

Later, once back in the room — she said she was too cold and wanted to be under a quilt — later, we lay propped on pillows, unopened books on our chests, looking up at the wooden beams on the ceiling, and aimlessly talked late into the night.

It was she who did most of the talking. I listened and occasionally asked questions. She spoke of her life at the university; she spoke of her school friends; she spoke of a great attachment she had formed as an adolescent to a middle-aged man who never became aware of her feelings toward him; she spoke of other unfulfilled loves.

She recalled these with unsettling frankness — unsettling, because I hadn't ever heard anyone speak of the past in so direct a manner. She spoke of these relationships as something in which she had invested much of herself. In them had existed all the possibilities she thought had been denied by an indifferent, over-intellectualized atmosphere at home. Different men at different times had seemed to offer an escape from the emotional sterility she thought she had grown up with, and time and again she had succumbed, only to find that she had made a mistake. She spoke of men courting her for her beauty alone; she spoke of being constantly misunderstood.

I listened, suddenly entranced, but also sad. I had known next to nothing about Catherine's past. The officious father, the disapproving mother, that was all I knew. These stories now began to fill in her background, but I wasn't so held by the plain knowledge they offered about it. The fascination lay elsewhere: it lay in the enormous longing for love Catherine seemed to have, the promise of a lasting fulfillment that shaped her life. That the longing seemed to cause a kind of perpetual discontent only added to its appeal. It made for empathy; it made me see how much Catherine's struggles resembled my own.

Most of Catherine's stories, even the happier ones about her university days, looked back to wasted endeavors, to a time irretrievably lost and rendered futile by later events. They suggested a larger continuing failure and drift. But it was something I knew, to a lesser extent, in my own life, existing as I did so very far from the richness of the world as I imagined it, with no means of getting closer. The sense of a life somehow not working out, a life whose true flowering had yet to come, was familiar to me, and it was by this feeling, suddenly renewed, that I felt myself deeply moved — as I had earlier in the evening beside the river, remembering Miss West's words.

As she went on, Catherine's tone grew more and more melancholy; her voice grew softer. She often fell silent and then for long stretches stared at the tall flickering shadows on the ceiling.

It was during those spells of silence that I felt her turn away from the ceiling and look at me with her sad and tentative hazel eyes, her soft curly hair falling over her face and spread across the pillow, gently ticklish where it touched the side of my neck.

It wasn't a moment I had, or could have, anticipated; but suddenly now, in that cold damp room with the dingy rug and sour smells, the giant shadow of the candle's flame restlessly licking the walls of the room, the world outside shut doors and windows reduced to a dim murmur of falling water, I wanted that moment of intimacy to stay.

3

Later that night, during one of her spells of melancholy silence, Catherine reached out and kissed me. I responded, fumblingly, but with an avidity that filled Catherine with mirth and left me feeling embarrassed.

It is hard for me to describe the physical aspect of what happened next. It was made memorable only by my incompetence in everything that followed upon Catherine's first disencumbering kiss: the first nervous explorations, the fumbling with buttons and hooks, the awkward impasses and shameful lonely climaxes.

Even if I could describe it without being meretricious, I would still be false to my memory of the event, which matched at only a very crude level the usual adolescent fantasies I'd had about the savoring of unknown pleasures.

The revelation was of a different order, and in it lay all the sweetness of that moment — the moment I wanted to prolong indefinitely, for it had awakened a part of me I had never known. It came to me later, in a calm moment after the disorder of the physical act, as I lay next to Catherine, listening to her endearments, her declarations of love — the declarations she said she had long wanted to make to me, and which I reciprocated clumsily, making her laugh — watching her face, so tender and beautiful, in the candlelight, the vision reminding me of the first time I saw her, playing the tanpura, sitting very straight on the mat, her face bathed by the golden light from the flickering diyas.

I couldn't get over the affinity that had so abruptly and spontaneously sprung up between us, this intimate proximity with someone who was until a few minutes ago a remote and unsettling stranger. Our nakedness; Catherine's glowing face, which had never failed to hold me and which was now so close to mine that its features took on an unfamiliar cast; the infantile nature of our conversation; our quick easy laughter over silly things — it all appeared miraculous.

Was this love? Was this love? I kept asking myself, more insistently than in the recent past, when I witnessed it only from a distance, and the part of me that was made uneasy by the unreal quality of it all — listening to Catherine's words of love for me, which referred to someone other than the person she saw before her — was soon overwhelmed by the part that embraced eagerly the possibility that Catherine had seen things in me I hadn't, the part that wished to surrender to the mood of the moment, to the new intense emotion it released within me — the emotion which was also a suddenly acute awareness of the great yearning that had lain suppressed within me for a long time.

I wanted the moment to go on forever; I wished never to let go of its intensity, and the morning, when it came, felt like an unwelcome intrusion.

I had stayed awake for a while after Catherine drifted into sleep, her head resting on my shoulder, the shadows from the candle still swaying across the walls and ceiling of the room. I felt restless and exuberant; strange wild thoughts crisscrossed my mind and then faded out of sight. At some point after the candle burned itself out and the room plunged into darkness, I, too, fell asleep.

I woke up, and in the first wakeful moment was suffused with the thrilling memory of the previous night's events, before being almost immediately assailed by panic.

Catherine was gone. A mess of bedclothes and wrinkled sheets was piled where she had lain the previous night.

Where was she?

I then heard the noise of the tap and the din of water falling into a steel bucket. She was in the bathroom, and between registering this rather too plain fact and the panic of finding her absent from my side, I felt the memories of the night recede.

The room itself looked ordinary, stripped of drama, in the bright glare filtered through the dirty green curtains. Random sunbeams fell on discarded backpacks, untidy bundles of clothes and shoes; there was something monotonous about the even noise of the riverfall.

The tap in the bathroom was turned off. I heard the quick, squelchy sounds made by her flip-flops and then after a short mysterious spell of silence the flush toilet with the rusty chain roared and gurgled.

The door opened, and Catherine appeared, wrapped in a black towel, her hair wet and glossy, tiny beads of water on bare shoulders, which were bunched up against the cold. She didn't turn to look at where I lay, half-propped on my elbow. With short mincing steps, she went up to where her backpack rested against the wall, rummaged for a brief moment through it, brought out, first, a white T-shirt, then her underclothes, and holding them in a bundle she turned, as I knew she would, toward the bed, where her jeans lay on the floor.

She noticed my gaze. She walked toward me, a small reluctant smile on her face. I smelled the sandalwood soap she had used as she leaned down to plant a quick kiss on my forehead. She withdrew abruptly and untied the towel around her.

Naked, her breasts shaking slightly, she dressed herself, and I, still supine on the bed, couldn't help but watch: first the under-clothes, and then the T-shirt and jeans and the woolen pullover. All this — elastic straps slapped into place, hooks and buttons fastened, zippers zipped — was accomplished with a practiced ease and a matter-of-factness that left me oddly flustered, and the exchange of tenderness that I half-hoped for as she came into the room began to feel inappropriate.

She bent her torso to one side and began to dry her thick mop of hair.

She said, between the sneezing sounds the towel made, "I see . . . Indian women . . . doing this . . . in Benares. . . . They do . . . it really . . . well."

So composed and remote she already seemed, so different from the tender and high-spirited person I had held in my arms. It was painful to hear her mention Benares — the larger world that the last few hours of our intimacy had managed to keep at bay and to which we were now going back.

Every time Catherine hit her hair with the towel a fine spray of water rose out of her hair and briefly passed through the golden sunbeams crossing the room.

I suddenly remembered something. "There is a woman who lives right next to my house in Assi," I said. "I can never see her face but I hear her drying her hair every morning."

She didn't respond. When she stopped and straightened up, her expression was solemn. She was panting slightly; loose strands of hair fell over her eyes.

She said, her voice neutral and low, "We must not let Anand know what happened last night. He would not be able to deal with it. It would crush him, and I can't let that happen. I feel responsible for him. I love him, too, you know."

My thoughts had been far away from Anand; this emphatic reminder of her connection with Anand — after that already painful reference to Benares — couldn't have come at a more vulnerable moment. She saw the puzzled hurt on my face. She leaned down to embrace me. I smelled the sandalwood soap; the wet cold hair against my skin made me shiver.

Then, as it was too uncomfortable to hold me while standing, she slipped into bed next to me and held me tight against her.

She repeated her endearments of last night, her conviction of a lifelong friendship. Soon, we were babbling in the childlike way we had discovered, without, it seemed, any effort on our part. Then, a few fervent kisses later, we were reenacting the rituals I had learned the previous night.

It was done with only a bit more competence on my part. Catherine joked about it and then, seeing me slightly put out, burst into laughter.

"You men are all the same," she said, laughing, her teeth large and white, dimples on her cheeks. "You all worry about these things."

The thought came to me, with a pang of jealousy, of the men she had spoken of last night, the men who had not worked out for her.

But the moment passed; I was eager to fall in with her cheerful mood.

Catherine mimicked the chokidar's gait as we packed up our things; she spoke excitedly of the journey back through the mountains. As we walked away from the rest house, weighed down by our backpacks, Catherine stopped abruptly and turned back.

"One last look," she said in a cheerful voice.

The sentimental gesture surprised me at first; but it was gratifying to notice her somber face and sad eyes when she turned toward me.

Later, while waiting for the bus to Hardwar, we sat out on the rock by the river, eyes half-shut against the blinding reflection from the water. So new the world seemed, and everything of value in it present in this moment, when neither the discontentments of the past nor the desires for the future existed, everything touched by the pure happiness I felt — the snowy peaks, glorious in the sun, the rushing river, the rope bridge, the grassy hillsides spangled with dew, the whitewashed temple, and the ocher pennant fluttering from the very top of the oak tree.

The sadhu from last night performed his morning rituals a few meters away, a picture of grace as he stood facing the sun, pouring water from a glittering brass jar, his long hair wet, his muscular torso gleaming with oil.

How remote and neutral he appeared to me now, so easily blended into the brilliant morning scene, all the complex melancholy feelings he had brought on last night defused and almost unremembered now.

He nodded at us as he left. I suddenly noticed Catherine watching him unseeingly, her face a mass of quick conflicting emotions, and she broke down as soon as he had disappeared from sight.

She felt oppressed by the confusion of her life, she said between sobs that shook her entire body, the confusion and the uncertainty. And it was getting worse. There was her attachment to Anand, with all its attendant responsibilities, and now there was a new one, to me, and it had come with its own complications. Instead of becoming detached, she was getting more and more involved with other people.

Even in the midst of her tears, it was heartening to me to be spoken of as an encumbering attachment. I tried to console her, and after some time, she stopped crying. I brought her water in a plastic cup from the river; she washed her tearstained face and wiped it with my handkerchief. She gave me a quick surreptitious kiss, complimented me on my gallantry. Some of her gloom appeared to recede.

But the pattern was set. Her moods kept changing; and by following them as anxiously as I did, I became a prisoner of them. My eyes didn't stray far from her face. The few moments of pleasure on finding her calm would be immediately canceled out when she collapsed into a fresh fit of remorse and self-pity. There were more tears from Catherine on the bus — tears hastily concealed when inquisitive peasant eyes turned in our direction. The landscape so closely observed on the way to Kalpi — the villages teetering from high cliffs, the neat little flowerbeds in dung-paved courtyards of houses along the road, the ancient men with wizened faces smoking hookah in chai shacks, the primly dressed school-children, the hook-nosed shepherds with white dust on their beards, the clean blue sky overhead and the white mountaintops — all of this now slid past unseen in a blur.

At Hardwar — where we went intending to take a direct train to Benares — a tout at the bus station led us to a dungeonlike guest house in a lane crowded with garishly decorated sweetshops and vegetable stalls. We remained there all day, too exhausted from the bus journey to do much, and drifted in and out of sleep. People came and knocked randomly on the door and then went away. Tinny devotional music blared through the windows and a voice on a nearby loudspeaker kept announcing the numbers of lucky-dip winners.

Between spells of sleep, Catherine broke into fits of weeping. Once again I tried to console her but was helpless. Her tears seemed to come from a source unknown to me and often moved me to tears myself; but they were also puzzling and filled me with every kind of fear and insecurity. They created a new physical awkwardness between us: lying close together on a narrow hard cot, under a ceiling fan with broad rusty blades, we didn't kiss even once.

Hunger finally forced us out of the room, where mosquitoes had begun to collect in busy swarms. We went to a roadside dhaba. Catherine didn't eat much; calmer now, she talked about her travels in South India, and drank glass after glass of mineral water, fetched by an agile waiter-boy, who sat at the next table when he wasn't serving us and stared unblinkingly at us.

Afterward, we walked through the brightly lit alleys and their crowd of pilgrims and cows to the ghat at Har-Ki-Pauri — Hardwar appearing a miniature version of Benares — and sat there watching the evening aarti.

Gray-haired pandits with wrinkled paunches stood before the idols dressed in shiny doll's clothes and waved large brass lamps, tracing large golden haloes in the fog of incense smoke. Tonsured young initiates blew hard into conch shells. Down below where we sat, the lights of the ghat glimmered in the blackish river, which, so gracefully serene in Benares, heedlessly rushed on here, cruelly overturning and extinguishing the diyas which devotees had so gingerly set afloat upon it.

Catherine asked me about my father: How did he live by himself in Pondicherry? What did he do all day? She said she was intrigued by the idea of retreat and renunciation. She said she wanted to visit him; she said that parents were often the key to understanding people you cared for.

"But I am happy," she added, with a sudden giggle, "that you are not following in your father's footsteps anymore, you are not a celibate Babaji anymore."

I smiled weakly, to fall in with her mood, but could not but feel the flippant remark as inappropriate, especially the casual reference to my father.

After the aarti ended, little boys with vermilion marks on their foreheads went around with collection thalis; they sprinkled holy water on devotees, who warmed their palms and face on the camphor flame and dropped a coin into the thali. A couple of them came toward us. Catherine dropped several coins in the thali, and then caressed my face with her warm palms.

Disappointment awaited us at the railway station. There were no sleeper berths available on the train to Benares. My somewhat abject entreaties to a thick-jowled ticket conductor managed to obtain a single berth directly opposite the toilets. But the door to the toilets didn't close and a stench of urine and excrement kept wafting out all through the long insomniac night. The train languished interminably at morguelike platforms strewn with slumbering white-shrouded bodies and then lurched off again, creaking and groaning, into the night. Far-off lights beckoned in the dark, and came nearer and nearer, only to swerve away at the last instant; the train would mourn each such abandonment with a heartrending wail.

We took turns lying down on the narrow berth. Still sleepless, we sat side by side in the end, wordlessly watching the fleeing night through the open windows. Between spells of normalcy, Catherine cried quietly, and long after the journey I would remember how the dust blowing in through the window marked her wet pale cheeks with dark trails.

Morning brought Benares, huddled under a dark canopy of rain clouds; shuttered shops and broken roads and slime-covered drains and defecating men passed our weary eyes. At the railway station truculent coolies bargained with passengers driven to near-hysteria by the simple act of offloading family and luggage, ragged urchins screeched *"Chai, chai"* while cracked loudspeakers above droned out details of delayed arrivals and departures. Outside, rickshaw drivers with thin unshaven mustachioed faces and blood-red eyes jostled, harangued, and taunted arriving visitors.

The world, held at bay for so long, was beginning to filter in, but my own gloom was yet to come.

It had drizzled for a brief while earlier that morning and the sky was still overcast. Muddy water ran down the broken pavements in narrow self-made channels. The streets were littered with tiny soaked slips of paper and rotting vegetables and cow dung, the profound silence cleft only by the slow grind of rickshaw wheels. The houses on both sides looked wretched and dark. Here and there on rickshaw seats lay slumbering bodies in cramped postures.

"At least," Catherine said, as if reading my thoughts, "at least we have got another day together."

She was referring to the fact that Anand was still in Bihar, visiting his parents.

It pleased me to hear that. I was beginning to long for some reassurance of her affection for me. I wanted to be alone with her again, and it was with a thumping heart that I ascended the staircase with the familiar mural of Ram and Sita.

Catherine leaned forward and lightly kissed me as she turned the key to her door. I followed her into the room to encounter, first, a chaos of sitars and tablas and discarded clothes and overflowing ashtrays, and then, Anand spread-eagled lifelessly on the floor — not dead, as I thought in one instant of great alarm, but sleeping.

All through the long journey from Kalpi, I had been more conscious of the little time I had alone with Catherine. I had known again and again the sharp, wounding realization that the hours we had between ourselves before we reached Benares were few and dwindling fast. To see Anand now was to be jolted into an awareness of the problems that lay ahead.

I felt a new kind of unease: it was the beginnings of the guilt I had not known until this moment. Watching him as he lay there, appearing so vulnerable and exposed in his deep slumber, I had a dark, heavy sense of the relationship that now bound me to him.

Even as I stood there, the first moment of shock wearing off, I was surprised to see how adroitly Catherine handled the situation. Such great reserves of calm she drew upon as she woke Anand up and, as he opened his eyes sulkily and squinted at us, began to ask him why he was still in Benares. Had he gone to Bihar at all, or had he returned early?

She went on with her questions. Anand, still lying on the floor, kept wearily staring out of sleep-blurred eyes at her. I began to notice that he looked distinctly unwell: his hair was rumpled, he hadn't shaved for some time, there were dark shadows under his eyes, and his mouth had a pinched look.

Catherine finally ended the questioning, but with a request: "It's wonderful to see you," she said, smiling, and then added, a contrived note of weariness in her voice, "but could you make us some tea now? We are both exhausted, totally, completely exhausted."

Anand seemed to have been waiting for that cue; he got up in an access of fresh energy, kissed Catherine on the cheek and started making tea, apologizing all the time for his inaction of previous days.

Later, the tea made and served, he brought out photographs of Catherine's friends from their time in Benares. Most of them were fairly innocuous: smiling faces backgrounded by temples, ghats, and restaurants. It was the photographs taken at Ramnagar, on the sandy beach across the river, that held my attention. In one of them, Anand appeared in a skimpy bathing suit, his thin hairy body exposed, splashing water over the broad sunburned back of an oblivious Jacques. He seemed so different in these pictures, so free and relaxed; Catherine and her friends seemed to have brought out in him such a childlike enthusiasm for life.

I watched the pictures with growing discomfiture. They made me feel guiltier about Anand. I saw Catherine, her face freshly washed and glowing, exclaim and smile over the photos, and felt even worse.

Within minutes she had slipped into her old role with Anand: here, she was strong-willed and purposeful, hard to recognize as the fragile person I had known in the last few hours.

The small room suddenly felt oppressive. I left soon after finishing my tea. Catherine and Anand came to the top of the stairs to see me off. I had noticed Anand scrutinizing my face, frank curiosity in his eyes; he now looked especially closely at me as I said something to Catherine about meeting soon.

Outside, boredom hung heavy over familiar alleys and shops. The day, only just begun, already seemed stale, the white light dull, the river, glimpsed sporadically from the alleys, torpid.

The mattlocked sadhu did not look up as I passed him. Behind him, a boy attempting to ride a bicycle much bigger than he was tipped over and fell; a veiled woman watching him from the roof suddenly broke into laughter. The vegetable vendor kept on monotonously reciting the price of tomatoes and cabbage.

Back at the house, Mrs. Pandey and Shyam looked up from platters of sliced onion, tomatos, and garlic as I came up the stairs and then hung their heads again. A shiny new padlock glistened on the door to Miss West's room. The open-air bathroom was without water, and there was no power in my room. Street sounds — snatches of excited talk, the jangle of rickshaw bells — rushed in through the window I opened; dust swirled in the rays of sunshine that struck the floor; dust rested in a thin film over the books on the table; a new cobweb hung from one of the ceiling beams.

On the floor lay a letter from my father, postmarked Pondicherry; Shyam would have slipped it under the door. The letter had come registered. Why the importance and urgency? I wondered as I opened the envelope.

Inside, there was a brief precise note in unfamiliar handwriting that said that my father wasn't well, the old heart problem, and hoped I would come to Pondicherry soon to see him.

I untied my shoes and lay on the bed and imagined my father in Pondicherry, in a whitewashed house along the coast. I thought of leaving Benares and there came to me immediately the painful thought of being separated from Catherine.

4

So began my last days in Benares — days of gnawing restlessness and gloom.

The weather, so beautifully benign, clashed with my mood. Winter was slowly receding, and though the mornings were still misty and chilly, the afternoons were one long stretch of breezeless sunshine. Scarcely a cloud lingered overhead, and the smell of roasted peanuts hung all over Assi and Lanka. The evenings steadily lengthened.

The violence I had witnessed at the university had had ramifications. The student agitators had eventually organized themselves and declared a general strike. More violence had followed while I was away. Police excesses had become the new rallying point for the strike leaders, whose list of demands grew to include the withdrawal of all policemen from the university. A big crackdown by the authorities was now expected; the talk at chai shops was of more instability and violence, and for a few days after I returned to Benares I kept away from the university.

I stayed in my room all day — it was too hot

to sit out in the sun for long stretches — and randomly browsed through books that seemed either to match my mood, or to offer a palliative to it.

The thought of my ailing father came occasionally to me and brought with it fresh pangs of guilt and self-reproach. I hadn't dared read the note again. It lay next to my bed and every time I saw it I wondered if I should go to him immediately. But the idea wasn't allowed to linger long, crowded out, as it was, by thoughts of Catherine.

I had stopped going to Catherine's house. It was her own wish. She said she felt uncomfortable and nervous being with Anand and me under the same roof. She wished to see me separately. I didn't complain. It was difficult for me as well to see her with Anand. I never had much to say to him, and in the couple of times I met him after my return from Kalpi, that inability had turned into self-reproach. I wasn't able to face him with an unclouded mind; guilt and unease hung over even the most commonplace of conversations between us.

I would see Catherine in one of those modernized sweetshops-cum-cafés that were just beginning to replace the old sooty halwai stalls in Benares. It was she who suggested it. She seemed to imply that there was no question of our meeting in any place more private.

There at the sweetshop we talked for a half hour or less over cups of milky tea. Catherine was always full of fresh news regarding her plans for France — plans steadily progressing now. Her parents had agreed to help her find a flat; she was to leave soon, in a few weeks if Anand's passport came through. Each one of these developments infused her with new energy; a seeming nod from her father about anything could make her day.

She would come into the café, beads of perspiration on her forehead, an embroidered bag hanging from her shoulder, and give me a quick furtive kiss on the cheek as the owner, sitting under a profusely garlanded framed photo of his father or grandfather, absent-mindedly swatted the flies whining around the gleaming glass cases, and the under-worked waiters, grime-stained hand-towels draped over their shoulders, looked out blankly at the empty bright street outside.

These meetings left me weary with unexpressed emotion. I wished nothing less while they lasted than to recapture the intimacy we had known, however briefly, in Kalpi. This desire — which arose fresh and was thwarted every time we met — was only partly physical. Its most compelling aspect was that mysterious affinity I had never known before, except as a witness, when I saw, with wonder and curiosity, Catherine and Anand together. In my memory, it had become part of the wonderful strangeness of the time — the bizarre concatenation of events and desires and emotions that, among other things, had made two full-grown adults revert to the long-forgotten language of childhood.

A part of me also wished, in some vague yet optimistic way, to talk about the future, about where we saw ourselves in the next few years. I could not bring it up myself. I feared being presumptuous, and I feared, too, the harsh truths such a line of thought might expose me to.

Catherine made scarcely any reference to what had happened between us; the terrible thought often came to me that the time in Kalpi, unforgettable for me, had already been forgotten by her. I wondered then if it had become for her yet another one of the inconsequential experiences she had disclosed to me, a minor distraction that would soon be swallowed up by other memories from her long, eventful past.

Often, listening to her speak about Anand and her anxieties, I felt full of resentment. I felt with greater intensity what I had dimly recognized the first time I saw her with her friends: that her life previous to Benares had a greater claim on her, and the person with very ordinary concerns was more authentic and tangible than the person who had bestowed her gift of tenderness and happiness on me.

But then she would, in the midst of speaking of other matters, offer one of her endearments — French, but rendered quaint in English — her eyes suddenly full of concern for me, and our "beautiful friendship," as she called it, and my discontent would subside for some time.

But not for long. I imagined her going back to her house, through the crowded alleys, past the mattlocked sadhu and the halwai, up the stairs with the mural, to the room where Anand lay half-propped on bolsters, and the thought of this other life of hers, with its greater, more significant intimacies, would once again plunge me into gloom.

I would make my own way back to Assi. I went through the ghats; I avoided the alleys, whose bright liveliness in the evening — the men playing cards or chess, the groups of loudly bantering men at tea shops, the snatches of sitar or sarod music floating out of open windows — depressed me. In my mind, I would keep thinking of things Catherine had said to me, turning them over, searching for signs of affection, and feeling more disappointed and saddened than before.

The hole in my stomach growing large, I loitered on the ghats until it was dark, amid a mixed company of touts and drug pushers; washermen gathering clothes that had rested on the stone steps all afternoon, white and sparkling in the sun; groups of children playing hopscotch on the chalk-marked stone floor; a few late bathers, dressing and undressing under tattered beach umbrellas; and the groups of old men, silently gazing at the darkening river.

As I came back to the house, walking down the dark alley that led to it, I would be suffused by a strange sense of anticipation; the sense that there might be something, someone — a letter, a person, a telegram — waiting inside, who or which at one stroke would change my life forever and, leaping across all the intermediate steps, transport me instantly into a world cleansed free of such exacting cares and anxieties.

Each time I would meet with a keener sense of disappointment as, after washing my hands downstairs in a tiny dark washroom, where the floor was slippery with slime and often caused Panditji's students to fall, I would go up to the second floor, where Mrs. Pandey and Shyam sat waiting, and settle down on the floor to eat the unvarying meal of dal, chapati, and sabzi.

Wearily each evening I watched Shyam garnish the dal in his slow methodical way. He warmed the ghee in a small steel bowl, added some sliced onion and garlic and cumin and coriander seeds; he tilted back a bit, his eyes half-shut, his lips curled, as sparks of ghee and blackened cumin seeds flew out of the bowl with a loud fizz and crackle; then, after the fumes from the bowl began to grow steadily thicker and rise — filling the room with an aroma that was to be forever associated in my mind with the restlessness of those days — after the onion and garlic turned a deep golden-brown, he would tremulously lift the bowl with a steel pincer and gently pour it into the brass tureen, where, after a brief noisy protest, the ghee would tamely spread across the watery surfaces of the dal.

I now heard a special reproach in Shyam's voice when he said, "Greed is the biggest evil, it destroys families, sunders son from parents, husband from wife . . ."

Something of a cautionary message also came to me from a book I was reading at the time. There are certain books we read which, no matter how celebrated or acclaimed, make little or no impression on us. It is because, intellectually and emotionally, we aren't ready for them; our experience and understanding of ourselves and the world isn't rich and deep enough to match that of the writer.

I had first read *Sentimental Education*, a novel by Gustave Flaubert, a couple of years earlier. I had bought a secondhand 1950s edition of it for twenty rupees from a pavement seller in Allahabad. The name of the first owner and the red rubber stamp of the bookseller, Wheeler's, were still legible on the flyleaf, and from the pages, when I opened them, fluttered out pressed rose petals. I had been attracted by the prestige of the writer's name as well as of the publishing imprint, Penguin Classics. But the novel had passed me by, like many other books at the time: it had struck me as flat and overly long. I did persevere to the very end, but it was with the bloody-mindedness with which a man might finish a marathon long after he has run out of energy. After that the book had moldered on my shelf with some other conscientiously read but unabsorbed books.

Then, just before leaving for Mussoorie, I had come across an essay by Edmund Wilson on Flaubert's politics. It talked about *Sentimental Education* in so lively a fashion as to make me think I had missed almost everything that was of value in the novel. I picked it up again. Unlike other books, which at this time I started and almost immediately dropped, this one I read straight through, in a few sittings. And, amazingly, I now found this account of an ambitious provincial's tryst with metropolitan glamour and disillusion full of subtle satisfactions. There were things in it I was particularly receptive to at this time. The protagonist, Frédéric Moreau, seemed to mirror my own self-image with his large, passionate, but imprecise longings, his indecisiveness, his aimlessness, his self-contempt. Also, the book — through its long, detailed descriptions, spread over many years, of love affairs that go nowhere, of artistic and literary ambitions that dwindle and then fade altogether, of lives that have to reconcile themselves to a slow, steady shrinking of horizons — held out a philosophical vision I couldn't fail to recognize. Something of Hindu fatalism seemed to come off its pages, a sense of life as drift and futility and illusion, and to see it dramatized so compellingly through a wide range of human experience was to have, even at twenty, with so little experience of anything, a chilling intimation of the life ahead.

But the moment passed, as all such moments inevitably do; and my thoughts kept coming back, through familiar routes, to Catherine.

The situation at the university improved

the student leaders were arrested; the strike fizzled out. I started going to the library again, and tried hard to rediscover all my old satisfactions of habit, the kind of undistracted, single-minded pursuit of knowledge in which I had spent so many hours at the library.

There were moments of panic now when I felt that my life had changed in some irrevocable manner, and that its old certainties had disappeared, with no purpose to replace them.

At other times, these uneasy reflections would be replaced by memories of Kalpi, from which I could still derive a heartening sense of well-being.

These inner dramas dissolved my concentration, and the time when I could sit for long, still afternoons on a straight-backed wooden chair, the lawn outside my window slowly passing into shadow, when an extra minute spent outside with Rajesh and his friends would lead to pangs of guilt, that time became frustratingly hard to retrieve.

Rajesh often showed up at the library, and once when I saw him, he asked me about the trip to Mussoorie. I told him whatever I could. He listened intently. He asked me more questions about the Himalayas, for which he seemed to have a feeling not unlike mine, although, like everything else, he did

211

not express it very clearly. I also told him about Miss West and Catherine, and he was an even more attentive listener. From that point on, he often asked me about them. I felt that he had always been curious about my life outside the university, and the nature of my connection to Miss West and Catherine genuinely intrigued him for being so far from his own experience — the experience of someone who had never met a white person, had never traveled outside the region.

Beyond the library gates where I would have lunch, there were his usual hangers-on, with their talk of politics and large bribes and dowries. Rajesh hadn't been at the university for the past many days and didn't know much about the latest spell of student unrest. But the other students had all the details. It was now known that the student who threw the hand grenade at the policeman had been tortured by the same policeman in custody some time back. The attack had been a planned act of revenge.

I still wondered if Rajesh had had something to do with all that. But the students said nothing that could have hinted at his involvement. He himself gave little cause for suspicion. The next time I visited his room — it was to pick up a xeroxed article I had lost and one of his hangers-on had found at the library

— the bag with the pistols was gone. I suspected he had hidden it somewhere, and looked in his almirah when he was briefly out of the room, but there were only some clothes, a jar of coconut hair oil, and a framed and garlanded picture of Hanuman on the bare shelves.

He was more relaxed with me, often asking me about Arjun. His disconcerting habit of creeping up behind me as I sat and read was intact. After surprising me, he would peer at my book, and once again, he would say, "Edmund Wilson?! Why are you reading the same man all the time?"

Slightly fed up with this line, I one day showed him Wilson's essay on Flaubert's politics. I said he should read it to find out why I read Wilson. I asked him to get the essay xeroxed at the library's photocopying room, and he in turn asked one of his hangers-on to do so. As an afterthought, after covering the frail paperback with brown paper, I gave him *Sentimental Education* to read. I told him he'd have a better sense of the essay after reading the novel.

I said so, but I really didn't expect him to read all, or even any, of the material I gave him. He hardly read anything apart from Faiz and Iqbal and the Hindi newspapers scattered around the university's tea stalls. I didn't think Flaubert and Wilson were writers he would like or understand.

Miss West finally returned to Benares. New, unfamiliar music floated out of her room. I was particularly struck by one haunting melody she played over and over again. Prokofiev's Fifth Symphony, it was one of the new CDs she had come back with, she said, and I wondered whether the CDs had been sent to her by Christopher, whose picture I now looked at more closely whenever I was in her room.

I now saw her in the light of Catherine's revelations. I thought I could see dissatisfactions in her bright eyes and offhand manner, neurotic irritations appearing in her brusque speech. I saw the troubled past I had suspected when I first came to Benares appear again as she sat out on the roof late in the evening, looking over the moonlit river.

But I no longer felt the confusion Catherine's revelations had induced in Mussoorie, as I sat out under the luminous sky at night. It no longer struck me as strange that a life could be so exclusively dictated by a single passion. That past of Miss West's I had wondered about, the past that had seemed to me like a prison, now seemed an essential part of her life, her personality, her sense of humor and malice, and even her love for music, which I now understood better, along with the music itself, when I listened to some of her favorite composers: Brahms, Schubert, and Schumann.

She told me about her new connection with Benares. She had earlier mentioned to me a great-aunt of hers who was married briefly to a captain in the British Indian army. Now she had come to know — through old letters discovered and read by a cousin in England — that this great-aunt had visited Benares in 1945 and fallen under the spell of a famous Tantra practitioner. She had stayed with this man for a few months. It was an outrageous thing for a British woman of her time to do. Her marriage to the army captain had broken up soon afterward and she had returned to England to a series of lovers. She had finally died in Norfolk, alone, a few weeks ago.

"What a story!" Miss West said. "It's like *Passage to India* and *Jewel in the Crown* all jumbled up together. The letters are to her younger sister and they don't mention it, but I am quite sure she had an affair with the Tantrist. Those Tantrists are great experts on sex, aren't they? I am sure the men she slept with in England felt themselves blessed."

A few months ago, I would have been embarrassed to hear her say this. I only smiled this time.

I wondered if she was monitoring changes in my manner. I often made up an excuse when she offered to take me along on her social rounds through the city. I agreed to go with her to a party at Sarah's house, but then had to feign illness hastily after I came to know that a concert by Anand was scheduled later that evening.

"You look out of sorts. What's wrong?" she often asked as I went up to my room after a long, gloomy evening at the ghats. She was curious about my time in Mussoorie with Catherine: the maharajah, she said, hadn't mentioned me in his account of our lunch at his hotel. She was especially curious to know about the unscheduled day and night in Kalpi. Was there a hotel there? What kind of room was it? Single or double?

She had, I knew, put somewhat less probing questions to Catherine. Did she suspect something? I couldn't tell.

But there shortly came Shivratri, when I almost gave myself away.

In Benares's calendar, teeming with festivals, Shivratri occupies a special place. Millions of pilgrims visit the city that day to bathe in the river; and it was to witness their slow exuberant late-afternoon progress through the streets and alleys of the old city that I arranged to meet up with Catherine and Miss West on Dashashvamedh Ghat.

I reached the top of the broad flight of steps a bit before the appointed time. It was, I remember, a day of streaming refulgence, one of those perfect days of March, whose tingly mornings, tenderly azure skies, soft, sun-caressed afternoons, and long, indigo twilights are the last parting gifts from the gods of spring before they are abruptly deposed in April by the malevolent spirits of the Indian summer. All around me, and in the far distance, swarmed a crowd of pilgrims, with not a patch of uncovered ground to be seen anywhere, pilgrims surging into the main road from all directions, through narrow lanes and maze-like alleys, from between houses leaning into each other, pilgrims holding marigolds and red hibiscuses, brass and steel platters filled with lit diyas and sweets and vermilion powder, pilgrims wearing pink and purple saris, crimson and white turbans, glossy silk and threadbare cotton, pilgrims ocher-robed and naked — ash-smeared mattlocked Naga sadhus with gleaming tridents, their long penises slackly swinging as they walked toward the ghat — pilgrims everywhere, chanting slogans in praise of Shiva as they went down the steps, past the coconut and flower sellers, the anxious-eyed cows, and the fat priests under their tattered straw umbrellas, to the river, throwing rose petals over their heads, up toward where the monkeys balanced on electric poles, quiet and watchful.

It was from this crowd that Miss West suddenly emerged, sunglassed and straw-hatted, wearing a pale yellow kurta over blue jeans, her face flushed with excitement.

It wasn't just the excitement of the surroundings; she had experienced that too many times. She had more stories of Catherine's friends. Catherine was too protective of her friends to disclose to me anything more than what was strictly mentionable about their misadventures in India. She did confide them in Miss West, however, who thought them both deliciously funny and sad and wasn't slow in relating them to me in full detail.

This was the somewhat gossipy side of her. A strange fascination shone from her eyes as she quickly ran through a few of the stories, the crowd flowing past noisily all the time.

Claire, the woman with whom I had the argument about Evelyn Waugh, had returned from Orissa full of bitter complaints about young hooligans who accosted her at every street corner with obscene requests. She also had her camera and Swiss Army knife stolen by her honest-seeming host in Ahmedebad. Pierre — Miss West called him "a troubled young seeker" — found himself awakened in the middle of the night by his French-speaking Tamil host in Pondicherry and offered his nubile daughter's virginity as pre-marital dowry. Deirdre, an unhappily overweight woman Catherine knew through another friend, had unexpectedly got married to a young importer-exporter in Rajasthan; he could not pronounce her name and so called her Didi. And Danielle, an avowed Thervada Buddhist, had gotten involved with a Tibetan boy while on a "meditation retreat" at Bodh Gaya, but then fled the scene in some panic when the boy began to speak about the wonderful life they would lead together in France.

From where I was, I could see quite far into the distance. Catherine would, I knew, stand out even in the massive crowd, but there was no sign of her anywhere. As Miss West spoke on, I began mechanically noting things: the hastily erected telephone booth, freshly painted, but without its constitutive instrument; the mispellings and malapropisms on the bright little posters for Keo Karpin hair oil on lamp-posts and the vaguely fluttering banners between them; the paunchy constables lathi-cutting a narrow swath through the crowds for a VIP visitor.

More minutes ticked past, and I began to grow slightly impatient. The appointed time came and went. Four, four-ten, four-twenty, half past four. The second hand moved with agonizing sluggishness.

I interrupted Miss West to ask her if she knew why Catherine was late. But she didn't, and she didn't seem very concerned as she carried on with her stories.

I began to speculate about what had happened to her. Grotesque visions danced before my eyes: a rickshaw accident, mangled metal and rubber, the indifferent bystanders. All the repetitive horrors and trite headlines of the local papers sprang to mind: broad-daylight kidnapping, rape, murder, absconding criminals. *Where was she?*

At five the crowds were still coming in, and it was with a kind of choking despair that I watched every fresh wave of cheerful unfamiliar faces roll past.

Miss West still hadn't finished with Danielle's story. Her abandoned Tibetan lover had followed her to Kathmandu, along with a crudely carved wooden-handled knife, which he pressed against her neck one morning in her hotel room, demanding suitable recompense for the humiliation and ridicule he had suffered in the eyes of his Tibetan compatriots to whom he had already promised to send Disney T-shirts and Levi's jeans from Paris. She had to shell out a lot of money before the knife was removed.

Miss West said, "Catherine said there is still a scar on the poor girl's neck. She must be having a hard time explaining it to people in Paris."

And then in the same breath, she said, "Look! There she is! There's our Catherine."

She was pointing toward the river. Catherine had come by boat, not on foot as originally planned.

I saw her paying the boatman. There was the usual brief argument and then the boatman turned away, satisfied. Catherine now started in our direction.

Disappearing for a while behind the straw umbrellas, the billowing saris, she reappeared in the middle distance, tall, fair, distinctive, springily striding ahead of the returning throng of bathers, her white sleeveless kurta all shimmering folds and dimples.

She saw us and waved. Closer, closer, across and up the slushy flower-strewn steps, past the dazzle of the brassware stall, and I saw the pale skin aglow on her bare arms, her curly mop of hair gently bouncing behind her head, her mouth half open, as if in expectation of the apologies and explanations that would soon pour out. She came up the stairs in one last energetic spurt and now finally stood before me, panting and excitedly stuttering and gesticulating, and although I tried to listen I couldn't and only kept nodding weakly in response to her flow of words. It seemed as if somebody had switched off the sound, and the whole of the teeming ghat had dissolved in a watery blur.

As I stood there somewhat helplessly I suddenly noticed Miss West.

She was staring at me and had in fact been doing so for some time, her expression alternating between frank curiosity and puzzlement.

She turned away now as our glances met, and it was in profile that I saw the small lopsided smile on her lips: the then-unreadable smile that, in retrospect, appears as much bitter as benevolent.

5

Rajesh reappeared at the library one afternoon after an absence of ten days.

These recurring periods of absence from the university struck me as odd, but he never disclosed where he had gone. He had been away, he would say, on urgent work.

What kind of work, I wondered, but the question always stayed with me.

This afternoon, Rajesh said that he was on his way to visit his mother, who lived in a village forty miles west of Benares. He added that I could come with him if I wished to.

It wasn't like him to make such invitations; and he extended it to me with some shyness. His eyes were turned away as he spoke, and he looked as if he would be relieved if I said no as quickly as possible.

I almost did. I knew little of Rajesh's background, and in the past many weeks, I had been intermittently curious about it. But my interest in him, as in a lot of other things, had dwindled since my return from Kalpi. I was preoccupied with different matters altogether, and my first reaction was to decline his invitation.

It was when I was ready to present him with an excuse that the depressing thought came to me of another empty evening on the ghats.

We left one morning from Benares railway station, on the steam-engined and usually empty shuttle that in those days used to run on the narrow-gauge line between Benares and Allahabad. It was unusually cold and foggy for March. The newspaper I bought at the railway station spoke of fresh and unexpected snowfall in the Himalayas, and I thought immediately of Kalpi, imagining it snowbound, the chokidar drinking himself into a stupor in his outbuilding, the sadhu at the temple serenely going on with his small, restricted life.

A chilly wind, gritty with coal dust, blew in through the iron-barred windows as the train puffed and wheezed through an endless flat plain. The loud rattle of wheels made it impossible to talk for more than a few minutes, and we stretched ourselves on hard wooden bunks, wrapped from head to toe in coarse military blankets that Rajesh had brought with him, and gazed out the window, where stubbly fields stretched to tree-blurred horizons and coils of smoke stood torpid above ragged settlements of mud huts and half-built brick houses.

A tea vendor, wearing a monkey cap with flaps that covered his ears, kept walking up and down the corridors. He looked inquiringly at us every time he passed. Rajesh finally summoned him, speaking in a local dialect I had never heard before from him, but the cardamom-scented tea seemed to turn cold the moment he lifted the kettle off his tiny coal stove and poured it into glass tumblers.

Rajesh sat up and hurriedly put on his tennis sneakers as the train clanked and rattled to a stop at a station that resembled one of the many small stops we had passed. The platform was deserted; the station building had a red-tiled roof and, unexpectedly, bougainvillea curling out of hanging wood baskets. Outside, on a concourse littered with horse dung, three tongas stood waiting, a couple of emaciated, mangy dogs staggering around the still horses.

Rajesh said that it was another half hour's tonga ride from there.

The view cleared as soon as the tonga left the concourse, the horse's hooves clattering loudly against the cement surface, his long brushy tail swaying and flicking against his hind legs. On both sides sprawled mustard fields, divided into compact squares by muddy ledges on which peasants, diminished against the surrounding vast flatness, walked in orderly rows. Water gushed out in thick jets from tubewells, and raced and gurgled through narrow drains to the fields. The narrow tarmac road was corroded at the edges, as if infested by termites, and the tonga lurched ominously each time a bigger, faster vehicle — usually a snub-nosed tempo — forced it into the dusty rutted roadside. From under the hooded roof at the back, we watched as the tempo receded whimperingly down the tree-lined road and dust swirled up slowly from the ground, to be caught and illuminated in hundreds of crisscrossing sunbeams.

Mango groves appeared on both sides, the dust thick on the leaves of the trees closer to the road; then, in small clearings, a few buildings: box-shaped houses of naked brick and mud huts with large courtyards where men slumbered on string cots; cold-storage warehouses; tiny shuttered shops. Swarthy blouseless women squatted on the ground before thatched huts, slapping together cakes of cow dung, little igloos of which lined the road. A few half-naked children with distended bellies ran around screaming at the top of their voices.

Finally, at the end of a row of identical

buildings, there was Rajesh's mother's house, one room, the walls unpainted, with the brick showing through. The children went very quiet as the tonga slowed to a stop, and then as we got down from the tonga, they crowded around us in a little mob, their mouths open and eyes wide with frank curiosity.

Their hair had turned rust-blond from malnutrition. The mucus from their running noses was white against the dark skin. I looked at Rajesh for a reaction of some sort, but his face was expressionless as we walked up to the house. The children followed us. One of them reached out a hand and caressed my khadi kurta. I looked down to see curiosity and fear alternating wildly in his eyes.

The door, its wooden frame warped and chipped, was opened by Rajesh's mother, a tiny, shrunken, fair-skinned woman in a widow's white sari, one end of which she wore over her head as a kind of veil. There was a restless quality about her wizened face, which spoke of continuing struggles. In this first moment of meeting her, I didn't notice much resemblance between mother and son; it was a little while later that I saw that Rajesh had inherited her eyes, so full of uncertainty and now, on seeing me and the children behind us, puzzlement.

But when Rajesh introduced me as a friend

from the university she suddenly grew very welcoming, and invited me into the room with an old-fashioned gracious gesture with her hands.

After the early-morning light, it was dark and damp inside the high-ceilinged room. There was a solitary window, but it was closed. In one corner, partitioned off by a flimsy hand-loomed sari, was the kitchen. The wall there was a sooty black, and on the wet floor a few brass utensils gave off a dull gleam. In another corner lay a string cot, under which was a tin trunk, leprous with rust. On the walls were garishly colored religious calendars: a benign Shiva, Ram with lips painted bright red, and at his feet Hanuman, hands clasped and head bowed in his usual pose of devotion.

It was unsettling: the half-naked screaming children outside and the bareness of the room. I hadn't been prepared for this; the poverty these surroundings spoke of wasn't immediately apparent in Rajesh's life in Benares. I could have guessed previously that he wasn't well-off, but one could have said the same of almost all students at the university.

Rajesh, who since the morning had become increasingly silent, left the room as his mother busied herself with breakfast. I sat stiffly in a straight-backed wicker chair and tried to make some conversation. Both of us had to speak very loudly to make ourselves heard above the fierce hiss of the kerosene stove.

It wasn't easy to express sympathy in so strong a voice, and sympathy was what was required of me as she began to tell me stories from her past.

She had been widowed fifteen years ago when Rajesh was still a child, and soon afterward her weathy feudal in-laws had started to harass her. The house in which she had lived with her husband was taken away from her, and her in-laws also refused to return the little dowry she had brought with her. Her parents were dead; her brothers too poor to support her. There was only Rajesh, who'd had his own struggles: he had worked since he was thirteen, first in the maize fields, and then at a carpet factory in Benares, where he had gone to evening school and done well enough to enter the university.

The years had somehow passed in overcoming all these different obstacles. But now she was worried. Rajesh, she feared, had reached a dead end. There were no more openings for him. All the government jobs these days were going to low-caste people, and not only did Rajesh have the wrong caste, he had no connections anywhere. He also had too much self-respect to work for low-caste shopkeepers and businessmen.

Disdain entered her voice as she said this. I had encountered it before. It came from an exalted sense of being Brahmin, of being marked and set above people from other castes, races. Rajesh himself possessed some of that feeling, which in his case was also an awareness of not having lived up to old standards. "I am a Brahmin," I had heard him say, "but I have done things no Brahmin would ever do."

But I didn't think of this then. I was shocked by what Rajesh's mother had told me about his life. How little of his past I had known! Of the childhood spent in maize fields and carpet factories, I had known nothing at all. I did know a bit about those factories. They had been in the papers after some human rights organizations petitioned the government to prohibit them from using child labor. There had been pictures of large-eyed, frightened-looking children in dimly lit halls, framed against their exquisite handiworks. I had read the accompanying articles and then I had forgotten about them.

To think of Rajesh as one among the children was to shrink the usual distance I kept from these things — the cruelties of rural India, occasionally reported in the papers and then buried under reports of similar cruelties. It was to have, however briefly, a disturbing new sense of the harsh world around me.

Rajesh himself changed in my eyes when he came back to the room. Behind his unreadable handsome face, I now saw tormenting private memories of childhood. The instability I had noticed and feared on more than one occasion appeared a natural consequence of his past.

But the moment passed soon. Rajesh set out small wooden seats on the ground and his mother served out hot steaming parathas with mango pickles in large brass thalis.

She did not eat with us; it was too early for her, she said. She spread a sack on the floor, sat cross-legged on it, and then watched us alertly as we ate, quick to offer us more parathas and refill our steel tumblers with water.

She apologized all the time for the meagerness of what she was offering. Once she asked me about my plans for the future; she asked me if I was preparing to take the Civil Service exam.

She didn't say much to Rajesh. Most of her conversation was directed at me; and when after breakfast I said I was going for a walk, it was to give them some time together.

The children, whose noises had reached me inside the small room, had quieted down a bit when I walked out into the bright day outside. They stood in a small crowd, watching for oncoming vehicles on the road. They turned and stared as I approached, but averted their eyes and turned back swiftly to the road as soon as I met their gaze.

I walked back the way we had come and was soon past the row of box-shaped rooms. Mud huts lined the road after that, buffaloes tethered in front yards messy with hay, and women cooked midday meals on dung-cake fires, the hot foamy yellow dal trickling down from above the quivering pan.

The huts ended and the mango groves began. I was a few paces into the grove when the voices reached me, loud accusatory yelps rising from somewhere deep in the cluster of trees.

I walked farther and saw in a leveled clearing, screened off from the road, five or six children playing cricket. The ball was rubber and bouncy; a rectangle cleanly carved on the bark of a tree served as wickets; and the bat was equally improvised, somewhat akin to the wooden truncheon with which washermen beat clothes on the ghats in Benares.

The children were so absorbed in their game, they barely noticed me. Their voices receded as I penetrated farther into the grove on a narrow pebble-strewn path zigzagging between trees, and were reduced to a lone extra-loud yelp.

Soon, the grove was all silence, and the only sound came from my shoes crunching the pebbles on the dirt path. Overhead, the trees, fruitless, with the season still months away, formed a thick awning with their abundant leaves. A few sunbeams filtered through them to fall in bright patches on the ground, carpeted with dead leaves and wild grass.

I had been walking for some time when I stopped, and then stood still for a while. My thoughts, briefly disturbed by the unexpected disclosures about Rajesh, had returned to Catherine. The possibility that I had merely been for Catherine a source of comfort during her troubles with Anand had come to me repeatedly in the previous days. I had begun to wonder if my time with her had only served as a release for her anxieties about Anand.

And thinking about that now, facing the mute trees — old, with gnarled, coarsefibered roots — I felt again a heavy sluggishness in my heart.

I had been standing there for a few minutes, hearing only the slow regular rhythms of my breath, when I heard, faint at first, but growing clearer by the second, the tinkling of bells. I recognized the sound instantly. I had heard it countless times in the alleys of Benares; it was the sound of cows going past. The large number of wandering cows in the alleys made it blend into a kind of continuous ringing; and it was, along with conch shells and temple bells, one of the sounds of the old city.

Detached from the city, and in this mango grove, among the still trees, the bells had different associations. Coming closer all the time, they seemed deeper, melodious, almost meditative, an emanation as if from unknown ancient times.

Presently, I saw them, the herd of cows pressing closely against each other on the narrow path, a cloud of dust billowing softly behind them. They came closer and I stood aside as they passed me.

Sharp long horns were raised threateningly for an instant as they examined me with large limpid eyes. Then, they demurely dropped their gaze to the ground and moved on.

It was as the last of the column filed past me that I saw the boy.

He had been totally concealed by the cows, by their high, bobbing backs, but he had been there all the time I had been watching. He probably lived in one of the mud huts of the kind I had passed a few minutes ago where midday meals were being cooked on dung-cake fires. He didn't appear to be more than ten years old, even in his oversized shorts.

which hung down well below his knees. The half-sleeved vest he wore above the shorts showed his thin, tender arms. He held a small stick in one tight fist, and there was in his large brown eyes, below the unruly mop of hair, an expression of pure terror.

He stared at me for one fugitive instant, then quickly jerked his head away. He walked with his stick pressed stiffly to his thigh, his head turned, like the cows', toward the ground, and watching his retreating back, the twitching folds of his vest, which expressed fear and suspicion, watching him go, the cow bells slowly dying away in the distance, I was overcome by an inexplicable desolation.

I stood for a few more minutes on the spot where I had stopped to let the cows past.

It soon grew quiet again. But something didn't seem right; the spell had been broken.

I began to walk fast; I walked like someone in a hurry. Out on the road, I saw the herd of cows again, restored to ordinariness in plain daylight. I couldn't see the boy, but I didn't look long before starting back for Rajesh's mother's house, past the mud houses and the loitering, half-naked children, who on seeing me were stirred by curiosity yet again.

On the train back to Benares — after a bone-rattling tonga ride through empty fields

— Rajesh broke his silence to say that he had read *Sentimental Education*, and that it was a story he knew well. *"Yeh meri duniya ki kahani hai. Main in logo ko janta hoon,"* he said, in Hindi, in a louder voice than usual to make himself heard over the racket of the train.

"It is the story of my world. I know these people well." He gave me a hard look. "Your hero, Edmund Wilson," he added, in English, "he also knows them."

I had got used to his silence; I was thinking of other things, and I had almost forgotten that I had lent him *Sentimental Education* and Wilson's essay.

Rajesh was still looking at me. "Achha? Really?" I finally replied. I didn't know what else to say.

But with one part of my mind I puzzled over what Rajesh had told me. It didn't make sense. What could Rajesh, a student in a provincial Indian university in the late 1980s, possibly have in common with Frédéric Moreau or any of the doomed members of his generation in this novel of mid-nineteenth-century Paris?

Rajesh kept looking at me in a challenging way, as though wanting me to respond to what he had said, wanting me to ask him to explain his gnomic remark about *Sentimental Education*. But I didn't say anything. I already felt awkward over the unexpected disclosures about his past. I hadn't known how to respond to them, and the embarrassment over my lack of response obscured the admiration I might otherwise have felt for Rajesh, for his hard journey from the maize fields to the university. In any case, these thoughts about Rajesh existed in a separate and very small compartment. I didn't see how they could be related at all to the new doubts I had developed about my relationship with Catherine, which had been preoccupying me.

In the darkening fields there were beginning to appear little spots of yellow light. Coal embers glowing red flew past the window. Farther ahead, frequently obscured by the jet-black puffs of smoke from the engine, a golden glow on the horizon announced Benares.

6

The telegram was waiting for me at the house when I got back from the railway station. It read, simply: YOUR FATHER SERIOUSLY ILL. COME SOON. It had been sent two days before, and it was signed by a woman named Deepa.

I had been looking forward to some kind of message from Catherine. We had planned to meet the next day; it was what I had been thinking about during the rickshaw ride to the house. But she hadn't come to the house all day. Miss West told me this, her eyes as always inquisitive and searching my face for a drastic change of expression, and after this piercing disappointment my first reaction to the telegram was to keep it aside, as I had kept aside, and eventually failed to act on, the first letter informing me of my father's illness.

But later that night, I woke up seized with guilt and fear. Had something irrevocable happened? Were the words "seriously ill" a deliberate euphemism, as they often were, on the part of a cautious sender? Was he already dead? I stayed awake for quite some time, assailed by grim possibilities, thinking of that other death, of my mother, when I had arrived too late.

It wasn't an easy decision. I wasn't sure how long I'd have to stay in Pondicherry. It seemed likely that I wouldn't be able to return for a very long time to Benares and the life I had found there.

But in the morning, my mind was made up. I could no longer postpone leaving Benares, which, I now told myself, would in any case have lost much of its attraction for me after Catherine's departure. It was time to go, and in my self-reproaching mood, I now told myself that it had been time to go when I received my father's letter on the day I returned from Kalpi.

A sympathetic Miss West arranged rail tickets for the next day through her travel agent. There were no second-class tickets available. I had to go first-class air-conditioned. I hadn't any money for it, and I had to make an awkward request to Miss West for a loan.

She was quick to oblige. "Don't worry about it," she said. "Send it back whenever you can."

There weren't any last-minute urgencies. I took down the books from the niches, where once little clay vermilion-splattered idols of Ram and Krishna had rested, and wrapped them in newspaper and string; I brought in the clothes I had left to dry out on the roof. I swept the floor with a broom. I settled all outstanding accounts with Panditji's wife. I packed all my possessions in two bags, and although I was ready to leave, I still had almost a whole day and night to kill.

I walked to the library, and sat for a while at my desk, looking out over the patch of lawn and the dark luxuriant trees beyond it. Voices echoed loudly in the cavernous halls, which were full of wall painters in stained blue overalls. The students in the reading room quietly played gin rummy, elbows planted on the table, eyes fixed unwaveringly on the cards. The women were still leaning their cheeks on open palms and tracing their initials with long, painted fingernails on the wooden desktop.

I went walking on the ghats. I was in a strange mood. The thought — and it recurred very frequently now — of parting from Catherine caused a fresh wound each time, but a part of me also felt relieved to be going away, to be putting an end to a time of futility and unhappiness. I told myself that something new would now have to begin, and these mixed emotions of sadness and a somewhat forced optimism now obscured everything I saw around myself. The gossiping boatmen the children playing hopscotch, the chess players, the old men gazing at the sparkling river, and Benares looming in the misty distance with its palaces, temples, and funeral pyres — I was already remote from them.

Later in the afternoon, I went back to the house. "No," Miss West said, as soon as she saw me, "Catherine hasn't been here."

Emptiness building up again, I took a rickshaw to Catherine's house. On the way, I imagined running into Anand and worried about what I'd say to him. I wondered if I could ask Catherine in his presence for some time in private before I left.

But there was no one at the house. A rusty iron padlock hung over the door to the staircase. The sadhu with mattlocks gazed indifferently at me as I scribbled a message about my impending departure.

I walked back home through the ghats and unexpectedly saw Rajesh. I had seen him only the day before, but the visit to his house, and the peculiar memories from that day, already seemed to belong to a very old past. I hadn't thought about him even once after reading the telegram from Pondicherry.

I saw him from the top of the stone steps leading to the river. He was wearing white kurta pajamas; there was a vermilion tika on his forehead. I was wondering what he was doing here when I suddenly remembered that it was Tuesday, the day on which he fasted and offered prayers at a nearby Hanuman temple. He was with a young student, who looked familiar. He might have been one of the many who hung around him constantly.

I could overhear him from where I stood: it was one of the odd pedagogic monologues he offered to these students. I saw him pointing to the empty expanses of sand and scrubland across the river. "That," he was saying, bringing out each Sanskrit and Hindi syllable precisely, "is *sunyata,* the void. And this" — he pointed at the teeming conglomeration of temples and houses toward the north of the city — "is *maya,* illusion. Do you know what our task is?" The student shook his head. Rajesh continued, "Our task is to live somewhere in between."

The student looked alternately bewildered and terrified. I thought of going up to them and then decided against it. Rajesh had always been an exacting companion, and I was in a state of mind where every encounter becomes a tremendous strain.

Back home, Panditji had just finished his evening lessons. After the room emptied, and the European and American students made their way to the roof to smoke opium, I told him that I was leaving. He was surprised and overwhelmed when I bent down to touch his feet. He blessed me by placing his hand over my head and reciting a Sanskrit hymn, and then I went upstairs to eat with Mrs. Pandey and Shyam for the last time.

That evening they watched my face with unusual alertness, searching for signs of worry or grief. They lived without words, and felt only the most basic emotions; the watchfulness was their attempt at sympathy. As I realized that, I grew more self-consciously grave.

Catherine arrived as I went up to my room. She had just got my message, she said, and had come straight from her house to see me. Her face was flushed red from running up the stairs; she said she had been running around the cantonment with Anand all day, arranging for air tickets. They were to leave in a week's time: another hasty departure.

She didn't offer any excuses for not having arranged a meeting earlier in the day as promised. She said she was very sorry to hear about my father. Her eyes and manner indicated that she wanted to say more, but we were with Miss West, who had come over from her room to say hello to her. Catherine didn't stay long; she said she had to rush back to meet the travel agent at her home. She said she would come to the station to see me off.

I spent another sleepless night with the same thoughts and feelings I had known since the arrival of the telegram from Pondicherry — thoughts and feelings that formed no pattern, led to no resolutions, and simply seethed within me.

In the morning I said goodbye to Miss West. It was too early for her but she had insisted on seeing me off. She was still in her nightclothes, her hair tousled, and she didn't come down to the rickshaw, where my two bags had been placed by Shyam. "We'll miss you," she said, hugging me, and I felt close to tears.

She slipped a present into my hand as I came down the stairs: it was a gift-wrapped CD, useless for me as I didn't own a CD player.

Mrs. Pandey and Shyam looked up and nodded as I passed them. Panditji was lying on his bed, eyes closed, an expression of pure serenity on his face, when I went into his room. I left without waking him.

And then only one more goodbye remained to be said.

At the railway station, the train was late and all was disorder as usual: piles of lumpy luggage scattered across the dusty floor of the platform, incomprehensible echoing announcements from the loudspeaker, food stalls with their stacks of oily bread pakoras and swarms of flies, a stench of drying excrement from the exposed tracks, perspiring harried faces everywhere, below frenziedly spinning fans.

From this chaos, Catherine emerged, without warning. I had been searching for her in the crowd flowing down the overbridge stairs, but she crossed on another overbridge, and the moment I had been anticipating since I left my house, the moment of her arrival on the platform, felt oddly flat.

She was dressed a little too elaborately for the occasion: looped silver earrings, long flared black ankle-length skirt, and sparkling white cambric blouse. Her hair was brushed back from her forehead and wound in a coiled mass above her head, revealing a long stretch of delicate pale neck. Men turned to stare at her; women considered her from the corner of their eyes with faint hostility.

The train was to arrive at the same platform on which Anand had made his dispirited goodbyes as we left for Mussoorie. The thought must have struck Catherine, for her first words to me were: "Anand is jealous of you, of my friendship with you. He said he was worried that I might fall in love with you when we went to Mussoorie. He suffered a lot when we were away. . . . He did nothing all day. He could do nothing. He didn't even practice; he just lay in bed and smoked a lot of cigarettes."

I was taken aback and I could not say anything. I remembered well Anand's run-down appearance as we arrived from Kalpi and found him in the house. But I wasn't expecting to hear about Anand at this time. It broke into my mood; it briefly cooled the emotion that had been working up inside me on the rickshaw ride to the station, the pangs of grief that I had felt over and above my anxiety regarding my father.

Some of my optimism about the future had already begun to leak away; it seemed more and more a consoling lie, and the sadness I now felt came as much from the fact of leaving Benares, and with it, Catherine, as from the undeniable truth of our separation, its unknown length, the uncertainties we were both traveling to in different ways.

I knew that no matter what happened to Anand, I was going back to the same old uncertain life. Anand was the lucky man, moving on to a new life, with its own assurances and securities and even luxuries; I couldn't think of him as a sufferer.

We stood there for some time in a dull, estranging silence.

It was Catherine who finally spoke, "I am sorry to see you leave," she began, slowly, her voice low. "Everything happened so fast between us. There was no time to think. But you must promise me this . . ."

The last sentence was drowned out in yet another droning announcement from the loudspeaker. I asked her to repeat it. She did, with a sudden fit of shyness. She appeared to have prepared the words for the occasion; she hadn't expected to be interrupted.

Her eyes were turned away from my face and fixed on the ground as she spoke again: "You must promise me that you will never regret anything. No matter how painful it is for you. . . ."

She jerked her head up to look at me. I saw her eyes were wet; her lips quivered as she repeated, "Will you promise me this?"

I said, my voice hoarse, "Yes, I promise."

"What do you promise?" She was now gazing at me with a ghost of a forced smile hovering over her face.

I was about to reply and then just nodded. It was hard for me to join her mock-cheerful banter.

A tremor of excitement suddenly moved across the crowd: the train was approaching and when it came, the engine softly blowing at the banks of dust arrayed on the platform, the passing faces at the windows were weary but expectant.

Fighting our way through noisy, agitated crowds, we went straight to the air-conditioned coaches. A strong smell of phenol filled my empty compartment. We had just finished storing my bags under the seats when Catherine was in my arms, sobbing softly in the way I had seen her all through the long journey from Kalpi to Benares.

But the moment was brief this time. We could stay like that only for a few seconds, Catherine's head resting on my chest, before the world began to trickle in.

The sliding door to the compartment was yanked back open once, twice; curious gazes rested on us and were then withdrawn.

The third time, a uniformed colonel came in, his batman tottering under a heavy iron trunk. His family followed: first, his plump, bespectacled wife, and then their teenage, sullenly pretty daughter, who was holding a sheaf of *Archie* comics.

Their presence and voices shrank the compartment; new perfume and deodorant smells filled the air. An awkward silence grew between Catherine and me; we waited for them to leave the compartment.

But, their luggage stored after loud, urgent exhortations to the batman, they settled themselves in a row, the colonel, wife, and daughter, on the seat before us and shot appraising glances at Catherine as she wiped her tears, and then at me.

Catherine at last said, her voice choked, "You must write. I'll wait for your letters," and before she could even finish her sentence she burst into fresh tears.

The colonel and his family stared even harder.

Finally, it was Catherine who suggested, in a whisper, "We must go out. It's really awful, the way they are staring."

We had been out in the corridor for barely a second when the warning whistle blew. Catherine groped in her skirt pocket for something and brought out a cream-colored envelope. "This is for you," she said, and leaned forward and kissed me on the cheek.

She seemed more composed now. "You are a treasure trove," she said. It was what she had told me in Kalpi. "We'll write each other and then one day we'll meet. Soon," she said, and then added with extra emphasis, "*Very* soon."

I felt tears welling up inside me. The train lurched forward; Catherine hurried to the open door of the coach, her skirt swishing, and stepped down agilely onto the platform.

I stood stunned for an instant, clutching the

envelope, and then dashed toward the door, almost colliding with a mystified coach attendant coming in with a bundle of towels and sheets.

As I leaned out of the open door, I saw her standing behind a magazine stall, her hand raised in a still wave. I waved back with one hand, holding on to the cold steel door rail with the other.

The train lurched a few more times and then began to slide quickly off the platform. As it picked up speed, large sackcloth bundles lying at the end of the platform blocked my sight of Catherine. When the view cleared after some agonizing seconds she was walking away, with that brisk steady gait of hers, receding serenely into the background confusion of spinning fans, bundles, men, magazine and food stalls, and I thought, as I had so many times before, of the rest of the journey that took her away from me — up the footbridge to the exit and a waiting rickshaw, through the streets and alleys I had just passed, past the sadhu with the mattlocks, up the staircase with the Ram-Sita mural — the short journey that took her to the faraway place where her real life existed.

7

It was raining in Pondicherry when I arrived, and it continued to rain with brief interruptions for the few weeks I was there.

After all my anxiety about him, it turned out that my father had had a minor stroke. And in the time that elapsed since the telegram was sent to me his condition had improved dramatically. He had been discharged from the hospital; he was home now, attended by a full-time nurse and Deepa, the woman who had sent the telegram to me, and who I discovered had become my father's constant companion.

I came to know all this from Deepa herself in the very first moment of my arrival late in the evening from Benares after nearly twenty-four hours of continuous travel. She was a middle-aged woman with a bob of gray hair and a severe expression on her sharp-featured face. She smiled easily, though, and then an appealing shyness would emerge. Her first words to me were: "Your father is sleeping. You can see him tomorrow. He is all right. There is no cause for worry. He hasn't been well looked after. That's all."

I wondered if she was alluding to my mother, and her decision to leave my father and live in Benares. But I didn't ask her to elaborate. I was too exhausted, and eager to get to the hotel where my father had arranged for me to stay.

Deepa told me that the hotel was run by the Aurobindo ashram, and after I arrived, scampering through the rain, at a big whitewashed building at one end of the sea-facing promenade, my weary senses could register only the middle-aged ashram inmates in khaki shorts and white cotton saris who staffed the reception; and the garlanded portraits of Sri Aurobindo and his French companion, the Mother, that hung in my austerely furnished room.

I dropped straightaway into sleep after checking in, and when I awoke many hours later, it was to a world of pure emptiness. The sea before my window was a broad sparkling band of silver foil — blinding after a long spell in my curtained room — which, later that afternoon, as dark clouds gathered, shaded into restless gray. The rain, when it came, briefly pockmarked the sea and then obliterated all sight in a steamy white mist. The long asphalt promenade was deserted now; but on some humid, rainless afternoons that followed, I would see a couple of toy sellers, their bright red and yellow balloons straining upward against the silently heaving sea.

I saw my father the evening after I arrived. He looked frailer than when I had first noticed his advancing age, years ago at the ashram in Benares where my mother died, and where he disclosed to me his intention of retiring to Pondicherry.

But an unfamiliar peace had settled on his lined face underneath the shock of thick gray hair. The life of the ashram suited him; he surprisingly said as much to me — he who had never talked about anything except the most practical matters.

I saw him every day for dinner at the communal dining room run by the ashram. He was invariably escorted by Deepa, leaning on her shoulder in an intimate way that I found slightly embarrassing. We didn't discuss his illness after the first time I asked him about it. He said he had been in a bad way, but he was much better now. It was a symptom of old age, he said, and his tone indicated that he didn't want to talk more about his infirmities.

He was curious about my time in Benares. But I could tell him little. I told him about the house I had lived in; I told him about my visits to the library. To speak of Miss West or

253

Catherine would have meant drawing upon a store of ease and frankness that had never existed in our relationship, and to my relief the subject of Benares soon dropped out of sight. Instead, on each evening he punctiliously asked me about my activities during the day.

I replied as best as I could. There wasn't much to report. The rain and the heat kept me indoors for most of the day, in bed, unwilling to stir from under the fan. To walk for just a few minutes away from my room was enough to bring rivulets of sweat coursing down my body. The hotel was empty except for a few aging Germans, whom I saw each evening contorted in yoga postures on the smooth green lawn of the landscaped garden below, and the restaurant was closed. For lunch I had to go to a nearby café for South Indian food, where restless flies collided head-on with the windowpanes and drowsy waiters sat slumped below furiously revolving fans.

Then, each afternoon at three o'clock I would venture out of my room after a failed attempt at a siesta. I would walk through the blazing forecourt to reception, where a stern-faced woman sitting behind a long, glass-topped desk would inform me every day in the same measured, gravelly tone that there were no letters for me.

But there must be! I would remonstrate to myself as I walked back to my room, past the forecourt and up three flights of stairs, and threw myself on my bed, picking up again from the side table the card Catherine had slipped into my hands at the Benares railway station.

All three sides of the card were scribbled over with her tiny curly handwriting, the shape of each letter familiar to me by now.

Dear Samar,

Perhaps this card will only make you more emotional, but I couldn't resist the temptation to keep the line of communication still alive for a few moments, even after we have parted. I tell myself "detachment is the key" and then even a few more minutes of unbroken attention means so much to me! It has been such a joy to first see our proximity grow and then open up entire new fields of understanding, of affection, and of ourselves as we are. I don't express myself very precisely — English is only my second language as you know — but it is in itself such an impalpable feeling, this sense of communication with each other. It is such a relief to know that you have seen me naked, dejected and in moments of despair, because thanks to this I am not afraid now to tell you anything;

there is just no need at all to pretend. What a freedom you have given me, a great gift indeed. I promise my next letters will be more factual and consequential, but I just wanted to say how much you mean to me. Such a friendship is a benediction, one of the things for which you feel worthy of living. And to think of the part I have played in your once secure life — what a mystery love is! Indeed, it will be exciting to tell each other the manifold meaning it shall acquire for both of us. For me you have already been something of an earthquake, compelling me to rethink about my relationship with Anand. How can I thank you if only for this. Let's promise each other that this friendship will continue to be a source of help for each other, so that I can enrich you and you can, out of your loneliness, enlarge and protect our solitudes. I'll write again soon and send you an address once we have one. A long kiss,

Catherine

I had read the letter for the first time on the train to Madras, Benares sliding past the window. I had read it in a hurried disconnected way, jumping from middle to end and back, and I had raised my wet eyes to meet the unblinking stares of the colonel and his family. I had read it several times since then, waiting for the bus to Pondicherry at Madras bus station, in the jolting bus to Pondicherry, in the taxi to my dark, curtained room at the hotel, and the growing exhilaration I felt then had tinged everything on my journey — the night-light in its rattling cage as well as the colonel's daughter reading *Archie* comics on the train to Madras; the pinpoints of yellow light in the dark night outside the window; the bright paddy fields and coastal mountains in the morning; the bustle of Madras bus station; the muddy country road through dense coconut groves to Pondicherry; the schoolchildren in neat school uniforms at village stops — with the kind of all-suffusing private joy that could redeem even the grimy interiors and surly waiters of the South Indian café where I usually had lunch.

In recent days, I had come to read the letter more carefully, pausing over each word and sentence, turning them over, examining them for deeper sentiment and larger implications. I paused longest at the last sentence: "I'll write again soon and send you an address once we have one."

Such promise lay in those words, and it was why I felt so keenly the stab of disappointment every afternoon. I had gone to the local post office and inquired about the time it took for letters between France and Pondicherry.

By my calculations, Catherine would have written by now, but the days slipped past and no letter came. She was supposed to have left for France six days after my own departure from Benares; I had more than once imagined her — Anand always absent from these mental pictures that came to me from films and books — at the airport in Delhi, where I had been once as a child, the brightly lit chaos of the terminal pressing on her from all sides, counters with Closed signs over them, empty telephone booths, shabbily dressed tourists squatting on luggage trolleys, forlorn bales of merchandise, and anxious-looking Sikhs traveling to a better life in the West. I imagined the takeoff into darkness, the brisk solicitude of remote, self-possessed air hostesses, the long stupor of stopovers and duty-free shops, and then the arrival next morning in another world. I wondered if her parents came to the airport to receive her. What were her thoughts during the moment of arrival? What kind of house did she spend her first night in? Why hadn't she written?

I imagined her letter as answering all these questions. I imagined it full of memories of our time together, of the kind of heartening messages I had found in the letter she had handed me in Benares, the few handwritten words on paper that had possessed such power as to cancel out the days of disquieting doubts and gloom I knew in Benares after my return from Kalpi. I no longer thought of those days, and the separation from Catherine felt less painful when I set it against the hopes for the future I now had, a future in which a quick and lasting reunion seemed a possibility.

There was no doubt in my mind that something of great significance had occurred in my life, and I was filled with a sense of wonder again at how the vague longings and expectations of childhood and adolescence had crystallized into a clear, sharp feeling for someone who was a stranger to me in so many ways, a foreigner I wouldn't ever have known had I not gone to Benares. I had a growing conviction that I had all along been marked in some mysterious way, that after the dull, pointless years of drift, the long years of childhood and adolescence, the time during which I had increasingly felt myself homeless and unprotected and lost, I had been predestined for the moment when I met Catherine — the encounter in which some of the richness of life and the world were revealed to me.

I felt blessed and fortunate and the desire to share this private certainty often came over me. But whom could I have shared it with? No one I knew could have followed me in my new life. Nevertheless, the desire to give it some public form made me start a letter. I had already written to Miss West, describing my days in Pondicherry and returning her the money I had borrowed for the rail ticket. I now began a letter to Catherine.

I wrote with some awkwardness; the peculiar vocabulary of intimacy that Catherine possessed so naturally and employed so fluently felt heavy in my hands. I wrote several drafts and threw away all of them. In the end I decided to wait for her own letter before writing about more personal things, and instead described Pondicherry's French colonial connections at some length.

I also wrote about my father. She had been curious about him, and my own curiosity about him — which had not been aroused before, when all I knew was the world he had brought me into, where he was an aloof, reticent parent — was provoked by his proximity to Deepa, who was rarely away from him. He turned to her very often for advice and support; he listened with great care to everything she said, his slightly droopy eyes alert and apprehensive. I remembered him as an aloof and self-contained father and husband. The softness in his manner when Deepa was around was odd and disconcerting.

He had changed considerably in the las

year. I hadn't forgotten what he told me soon after my mother died, one evening on the ghats in Benares. Freedom from all bonds was what he had desired: this harsh ascetic resolve had brought him to Pondicherry. The intimacy with Deepa now made me wonder about the life he had shared with my mother, the deprivations he had come to know in it, the special needs which Deepa appeared to fulfill.

Deepa herself was aware of this. She often dropped hints about her dissatisfaction with the way my father had led his life so far. These remarks, and the proprietary claim they appeared to make on my father, made me uncomfortable. I didn't know how to respond, but hopeful thoughts of Catherine would usually banish the anxieties I felt about my father.

The days drifted past, and I began to feel a bit bored and restless. The hotel didn't cost much and food in Pondicherry was cheap. But there was little reason to stay on. The heat, for one, was an extremely discouraging factor. All that had once struck me as somewhat interesting for its newness — the dazzling sea, the blinding white light, the geometrically straight boulevards stretching emptily into a trembling haze, the high gray walls of secluded houses and their knife-edged shadows — all that now seemed stale, and as I awakened every morning to the curtains fading slowly in the harsh light from the sea, I told myself: Let Catherine's letter arrive today and I'll pack my bags and leave tomorrow.

It was not possible to think beyond tomorrow. The future seemed such a large blank, and it seemed even larger when my father, in his new solicitous mood, wanted to know about my plans for the year ahead.

His health had improved hugely. He had resumed his normal routine. He no longer appeared on Deepa's arm when he went into the dining room and he often lectured me in the way he had in the past. He spoke of the need for a design in one's life; he spoke of ancestral obligations; he spoke of *samskara*. "We all have something in us of our forebears; we must act true to their legacy." It was something I, as a child, had often heard him say, and it didn't make clearer sense to me now.

But I did feel myself on the spot when he asked specific questions. Among other things, he wanted to know if I had been preparing for the Civil Service exam during my time in Benares.

These probings of my father always jolted me out of my distraction. I couldn't think of much to say and I gave vague replies to him

But once I was frank and focused enough to say that I was more interested in an academic career than in the Civil Service. I said I wanted to study at a university in Delhi for a Ph.D. degree. It surprised me to see how receptive he was to the idea.

He added that it would be a good idea for me to get some teaching experience in the months that remained before I could apply for admission to a university. He suggested I talk to Deepa; she had friends in Dharamshala who ran a primary school for Tibetan children.

Deepa was in fact present on the occasion we had this discussion. She was wearing her usual uniform of white cotton sari, and walking alongside my father in her slow graceful manner. We had gone for a stroll along the promenade. It had just stopped drizzling and the sea looked lazily replete. The strong salty breeze billowed and fluttered the white shirt of the ice-cream vendor in the deserted distance; gusts of steam rose from the drying asphalt and immediately vanished.

Deepa said, in her slightly high-pitched anxious voice, "If you want I'll call my friends and ask them if they have a vacancy. They are always looking for new people. The salary isn't much but you'll like Dharamshala."

The idea attracted me, not for the reason

my father had mentioned but for the proximity to the Himalayas it offered. Even as Deepa spoke, I felt a great longing to be back in the mountains, to know again some of the drama that, after Kalpi, had come to be attached to them in my imagination.

Images from my previous travels there occurred often in my daydreams. I remembered in particular my time in Darjeeling, the rain steadily drumming on the corrugated-iron roof while I sat myself before a vivacious log fire, and watched through large French windows the steam-engined toy train scuttling out of a thick wall of fog, triumphantly hooting, its greasy elbows frantically working. I remembered, too, the clear days, when I could see far in the distance where low arching clouds formed elegant awnings over the rumpled green silk of tea estates. There were many other mental pictures, and their suggestions of travel and new sights came as a release from the anxiety and restlessness I had come to feel in Pondicherry.

Deepa called her friends. As it happened, they did need an English teacher for the school semester beginning in three months' time, and they were happy to accept me; they weren't discouraged by my lack of formal qualifications. Working with remarkable speed

Deepa arranged my job in just two more phone calls.

I was asked to reach Dharamshala two weeks before school started in mid-July. In the meantime, there still remained many more weeks to kill. On the idle afternoons I spent in my darkened room, I daydreamed of traveling around India, as I had done the previous summer. Walking past the Alliance Française, I toyed with the idea of learning French: I imagined Catherine's delighted response to my secret proficiency in the language. The day came to be broken up into these separate daydreams and reveries. I didn't read much. I found my attention quickly drifting from even the newspapers and magazines I picked up at the reception. The bag full of books I had brought from Benares remained unopened in one corner of my room.

I lay in my bed for most of the morning, eyes never averted for too long from the wall clock under the portraits of Sri Aurobindo and Mother. Punctually, at three o'clock every afternoon, I went down to the reception, where the stern-faced woman no longer said anything but simply shook her head on meeting my nervous gaze, and I would trudge back to my room, through the forecourt and up the stairs, in an agony of dejection, which would slowly subside through the rest of the day and night, only to turn into fresh expectancy the next morning.

Then one day Deepa said, "You must meet my niece, Priya. She is staying at your hotel and is also bored with Pondicherry. Maybe you two could spend some time together."

I at once knew whom she meant. I had seen her almost every evening as I came out of my room and stood on the balcony. She sat facing the sea, with her back to the exercising Germans, on the edge of a wooden bench, her hands in her lap. She couldn't have been more than seventeen, touchingly thin and flat-chested in her ill-fitting kurta, her coarse frizzy hair massed over her narrow shoulders. I often saw her at the hotel laundry, and seen from up close her elongated face was pretty, with small delicate features and large black melancholy eyes.

Deepa said, "She has just finished school. She went to an exclusive Christian boarding school and came out completely westernized. Her parents are very devoted to the ashram and feel very alienated from her. They sent her here to get some Indian culture. But I can't do much with her. I hardly have any time."

Time wasn't so much a problem as the appropriateness of being with a girl who was only three years younger than me. But when I looked at my father, whom I expected to be alert to this aspect, he was nodding his head in agreement. Deepa herself seemed quite keen and arranged a meeting the very next day.

I had no experience of girls like Priya, and I was apprehensive at first. There was something confusing about such simplicity as she seemed to possess. I responded with caution to her eager and open ways. It took me time to realize that she was what she appeared to be, and as the days passed, I came to be grateful for her company.

The childlike enthusiasm with which she talked about her school, the nuns and friends she idolized, the books she read, all this was so remote from my own preoccupations that I could not but welcome the different associations and thoughts they created in my mind.

We went for walks on the promenade and often ran into my father and Deepa on their evening stroll. These encounters had a subduing effect on Priya. She had little to say to my father, who in turn had never been easy in the company of younger people. She held Deepa in great awe and was tongue-tied before her: the reason lay in the family story she had heard from childhood, the story she once repeated to me, of how Deepa, as the sole owner of a vast business, had renounced everything in order to be at the ashram and work as a minor administrator.

Things improved when Deepa lent me a ramshackle but still operative moped and Pondicherry and its environs opened up for me as places that could be explored and even enjoyed. Every day now, I went on the moped to Auroville, the international village a few miles outside Pondicherry. Most of the sprawling area was forested, with clusters of elegant buildings in small clearings. Its residents were mostly middle-aged or elderly Europeans and Indians who had been living there for a decade or more; something calm and contented lay behind their reserved demeanor and unhurried gait. They were part of the soothing bucolic nature of the place: the bullock carts trundling down long, somnolent roads, their passengers, colorfully dressed peasant women, solemnly staring as you attempted to pass them; the dirt paths meandering through dense woods of banyan trees; the crickets crepitating through long, smoky twilights.

Priya often came with me to Auroville, riding behind me on the moped, her hair frequently flying into my face as she turned her head, one arm draped around my abdomen. There, in a café set in a shaded clearing between thick bamboo groves, we lingered for hours, drinking tea or nibbling at the walnut cake the place specialized in. I listened to Priya as she recounted the plot of *The Scapegoat* and *Rebecca* — she was devoted to Daphne du Maurier — in her vivacious sing-song voice, her head childishly drooping leftward, large eyes flickering to take in the fresh arrivals at the café, one hand habitually smoothing her unruly hair.

She often brought her notebooks and wrote little haiku in them, wetting the tip of the pencil as she ruminated over a word. She never showed the poems to me.

"You would laugh. Grown-ups are so cruel," she said.

I idly wondered about her life on the occasions she spoke about it. The schoolgirlish intimacies with other students, the crushes on male teachers and pop stars, the starry-eyed anticipation of the future — all of this seemed so remote from my own life and so embalmed in innocence.

It rained a lot in Auroville, especially in the afternoons; these monsoon showers, so heavy and furious, were consoling to me as we sat in the café, dry and safe. A light breeze carrying a fresh aroma of moist earth would be the first sign of approaching rain. Then the scattered black clouds would steadily blend into a vast, smooth canopy. A few outsized drops fell randomly at first and were immediately soaked up by the parched red earth. After a few minutes began a firm, regular pattering on the tarpaulin roof of the café's verandah; the ground in front softened and then in few seconds was scored with crisscrossing channels of water. Outlined against the dark foliage of mango trees and the brown corrugated-iron roof of the lavatory, the rain was all thick ropes at first and then, as it thinned, delicately fibrous.

Long after the rain stopped there would remain the flushing sounds of overflowing drains, the burble of tiny rivulets busily furrowing the pliant earth, and, finally, the steady plop-plop of water sloping down the tarpaulin roof into a rusty Ovaltine jar.

The sun was quick to reappear and soon dried everything. Red dust swirled through the bars of sun below giant ancient banyan trees, and naked bronze-bodied children frolicked noisily in shaded ponds as we returned each sunset to Pondicherry.

As we neared the city, the traffic growing thicker all the time, the clouds on the horizon gloriously crimson and pink, a familiar disquiet would gnaw at me.

Once when the reception woman bluntly shook her head, Priya, who was standing next to me, said, "Why does that woman always shake her head when she sees you and why do

270

you suddenly turn so grim and silent?"

She was alert to my moods now; she had started questioning me about my own life. Her questions were bold and intrusive; they could exasperate me, but I could also sense, and was moved by, the simple curiosity that I thought lay behind them.

I told her nothing on that occasion. I said I hadn't ever noticed the woman shaking her head at me; I denied being "grim or silent."

I lay awake until late that night, suddenly full of self-recriminations and trying to work up a new resolve.

8

Priya was sitting behind me on the moped, on our way to Mahabalipuram — the last of our excursions together — when I told her that I was leaving the next day. I told her I was planning to travel around the country for a few weeks before heading off to Dharamshala to take up my job there.

She didn't say anything, but I felt her arm wrapped around my abdomen suddenly slacken. She was sullen and withdrawn and disheveled, her hair tousled after the long, windy ride, as I parked the moped and walked down the sandy paths with her to the shore temples.

All through the morning I had known a familiar heaviness of heart: the special feeling before departure, which in this case was mixed up with the ever-present anxiety of not having heard from Catherine, and a sense of the unresolved things I would be traveling with.

I was expecting a day of small quiet distractions at the shore temples. But it was not to be: loudspeakers blaring Tamil film music followed us from temple to temple. Guides holding plastic-sheathed certificates and speaking pidgin Hindi lurked behind every sculpted column. Noisy school tour groups thronged the forecourts, and tourist coaches disgorged squinting Europeans in straw hats who were immediately set upon by a small army of half-naked beggars lying in wait outside temple gates.

After an hour of this, Priya said she was bored. She asked me if she could go for a swim, and when I agreed, the undercurrent of delight that always lay in her voice seemed to return. As we trudged through wildernesses of thick burning sand, she pointed and laughed at the corpulent Russian tourists slumped beneath faded beach umbrellas, the fleshy folds around their torsos glossy with suntan oil; she bantered with the ragged coconut vendors and drug pushers and masseurs that pursued us for a while before giving up.

She finally found a secluded place in a clump of coconut trees, and reappeared in a white swimsuit that set off the swarthy complexion of her thin arms and legs. She dropped her kurta and jeans by my side and then in a sudden burst of energy, sprinted away, a tangle of brown limbs. She waded and splashed through a timid wavelet and then, with a squeal of girlish delight, dived headlong into a nascent breaker, only to emerge a few seconds later, shaking her head from side to side, wiping away wet sticky hair from her face.

She swam farther out than my half-shut eyes could see in the silver-blue blinding glare. A couple of coconut vendors came over, lingered a few feet away, and shot hopeful glances at me. After them there came a long procession of young boys in dhotis, with caste marks on their foreheads, supervised by a short, stocky man in a silk lungi, their cautious steps leaving a trail of footprints on the wet sand. I had seen them filing out of their bus at the temples; they looked incongruous here.

After the boys went back, the beach remained empty. I occasionally saw Priya's bobbing head in the far distance. A small breeze occasionally blew in from the sea, and when it did, the serrated shadow of a coconut leaf swayed over the unread page of the book I held open in my hand. The sun climbed higher in the hot white sky.

At some point I noticed Priya coming back. She was dripping with water; grains of sand stuck to the soles of her feet; there was a warm shy smile on her face as she collapsed on her stomach beside me.

We lay there silently for some time, th

trees behind us swaying and crackling in the breeze, the surf hissing up the gentle slope to the beach and abruptly shimmying back, unveiling a glittering mirror of watery sand.

I had become so used to the silence that it startled me to hear Priya speak.

"What were you thinking about?" she said.

I turned to look at her face freckled with tiny drops of water, and she repeated her question, abruptly flicking back curly strips of wet hair from her face. "What were you thinking about when I was swimming?"

I quickly lied. "Nothing, nothing important," I said.

What were you thinking about? From Priya, it was now a recurring question, and it irritated me with the offhand way it unraveled the complicated web of thoughts within my mind.

I could tell her nothing: it would have shocked her to glimpse even a hint of thoughts and memories set so far away from this flat bright seascape: the white glowing peaks straining defiantly against a star-spangled sky and the damp chill of the room in the rest house at Kalpi, the swaying shadows, the sound of falling water outside, the desultory intimate talk, the long, melancholy silences during which I had suddenly realized that Catherine was watching me, an expression of tender expectancy playing around her soft moody eyes and enigmatically smiling mouth.

I had been thinking about all that again, and in a much more complicated way. I was hoping, as I always did, to coax out more meaning from remembered moods and gestures. At the same time, I could not avoid a creeping sense of exhaustion. In recent days, these forced memories had come to have some of the monotony and boredom of a too frequently observed routine, and I was often surprised, while in the midst of them, by a great urge to break away, to read, to travel, to engross myself in the great world, in an endeavor so exalted and consuming that I would forget about everything else, most of all my own welfare and happiness.

I would have found it impossible to explain any of this to Priya, and, as always, I told her nothing.

It was close to dusk when we returned to Pondicherry. There were a few strolling families and ice-cream vendors on the promenade. At the bandstand, aging policemen wearing French-style red helmets played "Halcyon Days" to a small indifferent audience of Hindu pilgrims. Invisible behind the bright sodium lamps, the sea heaved and broke on the rocks.

At the hotel, Priya went off to buy some incense sticks from a nearby store. I went straight to my room; I no longer stopped at the reception.

Later that evening, I was in my room, packing for the next day's journey, when Priya came in through the open door, freshly bathed, and bearing a whiff of talcum powder.

I thought she had come for a walk on the promenade, and I didn't look up from the crammed suitcase I was pressing down in an attempt to lock it.

I struggled with the suitcase for some time, half-expecting her to help me. When the two ends of the lock finally met in a click, I looked up. She was sitting in the only chair provided in the room, facing the sea, but with her hands over her face, her thin shoulders jerking spasmodically with ever deeper sobs.

Her sobs intensified as I walked over and squatted beside her chair. I asked her what was wrong, but she wouldn't reply.

I watched her helplessly, waiting for her to speak. But when she did, her speech was so blurred and indistinct that I had to strain hard to hear each individual word.

"You . . . are . . . going away, you . . . are . . . going . . . away," she said, "and I . . . and . . . "

Before she could complete the sentence, a fresh wave of emotion convulsed her.

The piteous sight released something in me, in that heart which ached with its own secret burden. Tears sprang to my eyes, and as I was trying to control them she removed her tiny hands from her face.

Her eyes were swollen red, her cheeks drenched. But now as she looked at me, she noticed the wetness in my own eyes which I was trying to hide, and a strangely beatific expression came over her face.

Once again my mind was somewhere else, but she was not to know this as, looking up at me, her sobs receding, she began to speak, once, twice, choking and sniffling between words, her voice pleading and anxious, "Will you . . . miss . . . me? . . . Will . . . you . . . miss . . ."

As if in a farce, I heard a muffled cough behind me.

It was Deepa, framed against the open door, her face dark and unreadable. She wasn't unexpected. We were to have our last dinner together that evening. Deepa was to accompany us to the dining room.

She walked toward us. Her face appeared in the light. She looked as severe and composed as always. She asked, "What's wrong? What happened to you, Priya? Why are you crying?"

Priya said nothing, and kept sniffling, her head hung low. Deepa said, "Please go to your room now and wash up. We are going to the dining room in five minutes." Stern authority now resonated in her voice.

Priya got up reluctantly, knocking against the leg of the chair, her eyes downcast, with tear trails scored all over her cheeks. Slowly, with almost imperceptible movements, she shuffled out of the room, fear and shame written large in the curve of her back.

Deepa turned to me. I had been trying surreptitiously to wipe my eyes with my shirtsleeve. She said, the sternness in her voice abruptly gone, "I feared that this might happen. You should have been more careful. She is an impressionable girl. God knows what kind of romantic rubbish they give her to read in that awful school of hers."

These were her only words on the subject. Priya didn't join us for dinner. Deepa went to her room when she failed to emerge after ten minutes and came back saying, "She wants to rest, poor girl. I don't blame her."

She made no reference to Priya during the dinner. She joined my father in asking me about the traveling I proposed to do. She told me about her friends in Dharamshala.

These dinners in the communal dining

room had always been brief; it was still early in the evening when I came back to the hotel, after tepid, somewhat formal goodbyes to my father and Deepa.

All through dinner, I had kept worrying about Priya. I had no idea of what I would say to her, but I felt it imperative to go up to her room.

I was striding past the reception when I heard the stern-faced woman calling out my name.

"There was a letter for you this afternoon," she said, in her clear gravelly voice. "The chokidar has slipped it into your room."

"Where . . . where?" I stuttered stupidly.

"In your room," she repeated, a slight edge of irritation in her voice.

Suppressing the impulse to run, I briskly strode across the dimly lit forecourt with its throng of gleaming bicycles and scooters; then, once out of sight of the reception, I bounded up the steps two at a time, startling an old German with thick white hair coming down with bundles of laundry.

With a pounding heart I reached my room, fumblingly took out the key from my pocket, rammed it into the lock, turned, and entered; as always, the curtain on the far, sea-facing window of the room billowed toward me and then, as I shut the door and killed the draft was sucked back into outlining the iron bars of the window.

The light switch was a few meters away from the door, but I didn't bother with it. I looked down; the letter would be on the floor if it had been slipped underneath the door.

As my eyes adjusted to the dark, I saw a faint glow on the floor and realized I was standing on part of it.

I picked it up. It was a white envelope, imprinted now with dust from the sole of my shoe and — a mild twinge of disappointment there — oddly lightweight.

Still standing in the dark, I tore it open with trembling hands and then realized that while doing so I might have rendered illegible the return address on the back of the envelope.

I finally reached out and pressed the light switch. But I forgot to turn on the ceiling fan and it was many hours later in that humid airless room that I discovered that my throat was dry and my body drenched from head to foot in sweat.

Catherine's spidery handwriting covered the entire length of the one small page of thin airmail paper. *"Samar,"* it read,

Two weeks ago, Anand found a letter I was writing to you and everything between us came very suddenly and painfully to the

281

surface. We still haven't recovered, maybe we will never recover, and this might give you an idea of the violence I did to Anand by having an affair with you. The question before me is: why did I do it? And why did you do it? What was the meaning of this affair in the total economy of our lives, apart from giving me a sense of mischievous adventure and providing instant gratification to both of us. It was a perversion of human emotions, of our humanity. I now see that perversion within myself and feel ashamed. I feel ashamed of your role also. You only encouraged the development of harmful ideas and notions inside me. You told me to detach myself from Anand. What were you aiming for? In all this process, I have destroyed the trust Anand had in me — the trust of the person I love most in my life. I don't know what you can do to save the situation. Perhaps, nothing. Please don't write or try to get in touch in any other manner. Please accept this break with dignity and grace if it is possible for you.

Catherine

PART III

1

The world is *maya*, illusion: it was one of the very first things my father told me. But it is a meaningless idea to a child, and the peculiar ordeals of adulthood take you even further away from true comprehension. New deprivations and desires continually open up within you, you keep learning new ways of experiencing pain and happiness, and the idea of illusion, never quite grasped, fades.

The world you find yourself in then becomes the supreme reality — the world you have to go on living in, with or without your private griefs.

I left Pondicherry the next day and traveled around the country for several weeks. I had little money; and I traveled cheaply, mostly by bus and train. The plan and itinerary I had postponed drawing up while in Pondicherry, hoping to do it in a calmer state of mind, never came into being. My travels came to be ruled by whim and chance; the map traced by them, if I were to draw it today, would resemble the aimless drifting of one of those sadhus you still find traveling in second-class train compartments, people with gaunt blank faces and depthless eyes fixed on the passing scenery.

In some sense, I traveled everywhere and nowhere. The miles clocked up, and there came a point when I could no longer distinguish between the settlements clattering randomly past my jaded eyes — the over-populated slums with their tottering houses, fetid alleys, and exposed gutters, their cooped-up frustrations and festering violence, their hardened ugliness; the small and big towns where I often spent a sleepless night in a tiny bare hotel room, kept awake by the varied cacophony emanating from the other rooms, where young men of distinctly criminalish appearance drank rum and watched jaunty Hindi musicals.

Something in me longed intensely for unfamiliar sights. But unfamilarity couldn't have, and didn't, last long on the peculiar trails I took. In the weeks that followed my departure from Pondicherry, I came to know all too well the plangent cry of the speeding train in the night; the whine of the overused pneumatic door to an overcrowded waiting room where sleeping bodies lay swaddled in white sheets on the floor. It all came to be very predictable after so many journeys — the heat, the dust, the noise, the anxiety, the fatigue, and the cold bucket-bath in a dismal flophouse at the end. Thrown into the the chaos of a railway platform I could already anticipate the eerie silence that would descend after the train had gone. A sense of futility hovered above the long hours spent waiting at desolate mice-infested bus stops in the middle of nowhere, over the greasy late suppers amid the colored neon lights and throbbing speakers of all-night dhabas.

And as it turned out, the unfamiliar world I longed for proved to be disturbing in an un-suspected way. It was nowhere more so than in the towns I passed through that had experi-enced Hindu-Muslim rioting over the then-still-standing Babri Masjid. In these places, I couldn't walk a few yards away from my ref-uge for the night without encountering some conspicuous trace of recent violence: burned or scorched buildings, charred cars, buses and scooters, upturned carts with missing rubber tires that, I would read in the papers, had been used as "flaming garlands," looted shops showing the wretched brick behind the now-destroyed paneling, shards of broken windows on empty roads and, here and there on the ground, faint gray stains of unwashed blood.

I saw all this — the clumsy brutality, the rage, the dereliction, the damage I had so far read about in the papers — I saw all this and the great grief I felt was reduced gradually to wordless fear. I kept telling myself as consolation: this isn't my world, I'll soon be out of it.

Yet it was hard to deny that something in it matched my own state of mind. I knew I couldn't get away from it by simply taking the next train out.

At this time of pain, and in the numb years that followed, there would often come to me the memory of the boy I had seen near Rajesh's mother's house: the boy with the cows whose sad melodious jingling I had heard that vacant afternoon in the mango grove, amid the mute trees, the golden dust, the gnarled, humped roots.

The image came to me as if from a recurring dream, and it was always as unexpected, and had the same effect, as that sudden rent in the wall of rock streaking past train windows which reveals, for one brief second, sheep grazing quietly on a grassy meadow, around a pond whose still surface mirrors the clean blue sky.

The image with its perfect configuration of solitude, contentment, and beauty was a kind of balm in those days of exhausting travel; it revived me by throwing me into daydreams of a simplified life and world — the kind of world where children herded cows all morning and returned home late in the afternoon to meals cooked on dung-cake fires.

It was pure fantasy, and I now recognize it as such. But we live by fantasies, and this one did then what, in retrospect, was a necessary thing: it created new hopes in order to offset the destruction of old ones. It diminished, however briefly, the feeling I had known after Pondicherry that I had been contaminated in some profound way. It made bearable my random travels and made it possible for me to think that I had another chance.

And when that chance came — by luck much sooner than I could have expected — the fantasy not only survived but filled what appeared to me as the large and ominous void of the future.

In Dharamshala, where I arrived at the end of my travels to take up the job Deepa had arranged for me, I found new ways of being that weren't far from my daydreams of that simple life.

Dharamshala was then, and has remained to a great extent, an unambitious little town. Its small population consisted mainly of Tibetans who had arrived in the 1960s as refugees from their homeland, and something of the private and incommunicable melancholy of permanent exile hung over its huddled houses and pinched streets. This effect impressed me deeply when I arrived early one monsoon evening.

Stocky monks with tonsured heads, swirling robes, and oddly garish socks scurried in and out of the fog swaddling the mountaintop town in gray vapor. Hollow television voices and pressure-cooker hisses escaped through curtained doors of tiny houses leaning into each other. Open iron-barred windows revealed cramped fluorescent-lit rooms where Tibetan women sat sewing, and in dimly lit shops, aging men with broad, lined faces sat still and pensive behind jars of sticky sweets. They looked remote and abstracted even while talking to you, and you wondered what memories of lost homelands were decaying behind the piercing sadness of their stoic Tibetan faces.

Part of my luck lay in finding the right house, and it began the very first night, when I saw a handwritten notice behind the receptionist's desk at the hotel I was staying in. "Vacant," it said, "a two-bedroom house. Long-term tenants welcome. Contact Uma Devi at Harry's Restaurant."

I remember well going next morning to Harry's Restaurant, and my first glimpse of the house I was to live in. I felt relatively calm that day; it was part of the minor satisfaction of traveling as I did, cheaply and randomly. To arrive at an unknown town after a long, exhausting bus ride; to squat under a vigorously flowing tap; to change into a freshly laundered shirt and pair of trousers and then step out, renewed, into the garish bustle of a bazaar — every one of these minor acts contained a brief but precious moment of well-being.

An aroma of ground coffee, and earnest, cigarette-punctuated conversations, hung in the small room that served as Harry's Restaurant. In one corner, an auburn-robed young Tibetan monk kept erupting into head-turning shrieks of delight in response to whatever his companions, a middle-aged American couple, told him.

I asked for Uma Devi. I was expecting a local shopkeeping woman drowsing below framed pictures of the Dalai Lama. But Uma Devi turned out to be a slightly talkative, tonsured woman in her late thirties, from Bavaria, Germany; she had adopted the name after converting to Buddhism.

"That was ten years ago," she said. "Now I feel like I was born with this name. It's *beautiful*, isn't it?" she asked, suddenly turning a liquid gaze upon me. "Anyway, did you say you wanted to see the house?"

Agilely she led me through first a litter of back alleys, where ruddy-cheeked Tibetan children in those days played hopscotch, their exuberant cries borne aloft by the moist air and left to linger above the town, and then up a steep rock-strewn trail into a dense cluster of pine trees. She complained all the time of pot-smoking tenants who had recently destroyed the peace of her house. I listened only fitfully, panting to keep up with her unrelenting pace.

We passed the debris of a large picnic on a sunny glade — green plastic bags, pickle-stained paper plates, bits of eggshell, apple peels, and crumpled packets of Uncle Chipps and Frooti — to which Uma gestured and said: "These yuppies from Chandigarh. They think they own the fucking universe and can do whatever they feel like doing. By the way, what do *you* do?"

"That's *great*," she said when I told her I was going to teach at the primary school.

We kept walking up the steep slope. Patches of sunlight trembled on the mossy ground littered with pine needles. A low lichened stone wall joined us on the left, petered out and then recovered. The trail looked as if it would level out soon, but didn't. We kept going until Uma turned and pushed a wicket gate in the stone wall; she entered and then paused to wait for me, arresting the gate in mid-arc.

Quite out of breath by now, I clambered up the last of the rocky steps, went past the gate, and looked up and had, at the very moment the gate creakingly swung back on its rusty hinges, the first of many invigorating sights of what was to be my home for the next seven years.

It stood in the middle of a grassy clearing on which the surrounding pine trees spread slender interlaced shadows, a one-story red-roofed cottage, shyly hiding itself behind baskets streaming with bougainvillea. Inside, there were two large parquet-floored rooms whose clean-cut teak furniture gleamed in the austere white light filtered through muslin-curtained windows. There was a living room with a disused fireplace, a large picture of the Dalai Lama on the mantel, and a faded flower-patterned carpet between wicker arm-chairs. A fly whined somewhere in the dank depths of the bathroom. The narrow kitchen-ette had a foggy window that looked out onto a tiny back yard, where one exotically colored bird pecked at the muddy puddle left behind by the previous night's rains.

It took little time to settle things with Uma Devi. She arranged for a maidservant to clean the house every week; she arranged for a boy to deliver dinner from her restaurant; she also helped in many other aspects of housekeeping. The only favor she wanted in return was for me not to take down the framed and garlanded picture of the Dalai Lama on the living-room mantel.

It didn't take me long to adjust to my new surroundings. I moved into the house and spread my few possessions around. I let the house retain its bareness and equipped it with only the few items of furniture that were strictly necessary. I liked walking through its large empty rooms and listening to the echo of my footsteps on the wooden floor.

After many mornings of waking up in strange rooms to homesickness and heartache, I now opened my eyes to the white light coming through the muslin curtains, behind which I knew was the dewy lawn sparkling in the morning sun.

The days filled up once school started. My duties weren't onerous: three classes a day, and occasionally a private session with a student. I wished for more responsibilities, but the school had its own peculiar ways of functioning.

It had been inaugurated some years back; the marble plaque marking the event mentioned the Dalai Lama and some other local dignitaries. But lackluster management had led to swift decay. The principal — Mrs. Sharma, Deepa's friend, a high-strung woman in her mid-thirties — was hardly ever there; the sarcastic explanation offered by other teachers was that she was away "junketing" around the world at various seminars on education and refugee problems. Her younger sister, Gita, a pretty, plump woman with something unstable and fragile in her personality, looked after the day-to day administration. But she wasn't very efficient, and the results of her inefficiency were visible all across the small compound. The hall with the corrugated-iron roof, where all five grades were accommodated, was littered with metal filing cupboards and expensive-looking projectors. New furniture still lay under plastic wraps months after arrival; sports equipment covered with dust stood in another corner. The electric voltage was too low for even ordinary heaters to work, and teachers had to resort to illegal log fires when the cold became unbearable.

I felt sympathy for Gita. She was resented by the other teachers, many of whom were much older than she was. Her own sister, on the few occasions she was present at the school, treated her with startling rudeness in public.

But I kept my distance from her problems. I did what was required of me — reciting the English alphabet three times a day, conducting spelling tests, prescribing homework — and went home. I exchanged little more than small talk with the other teachers, several of whom were people like myself, academic aspirants hoping to pick up some teaching experience. They stuck close together and thought me peculiar for keeping to myself; murmurs to this effect reached me at times, and I came to sense both curiosity and mockery in the excessive cordiality they displayed toward me.

With the children themselves, I had a working rapport. They came mostly from Tibetan homes, the first from their families to be sent to school, and they were eager and intelligent learners, particularly of my subject, English, which was their passport to the larger world. Among their parents, who ran the small businesses and shops in the town, there were many who constantly worried about the progress of my wards. They were the ones who stood outside school as I came out, tightly grasping their slightly embarrassed child by the hand, accosted me with simple, often naïve, questions, and touchingly offered me special discounts at their shops.

There was still a lot of time left over from

my teaching duties, and I filled that first semester with reading and long walks in the surrounding forests. In the market, I discovered a Tibetan bookseller. New kinds of books now appeared on the living-room mantel next to the picture of the Dalai Lama, where there had mostly been Penguin and Picador paperbacks. My reading tastes changed. I lost my passion for literature, and in fact developed a kind of fear about novels and the sprawling shapeless human lives they seemed to contain. Instead, I read books on wildlife and the environment; I learned to identify all the trees and birds and flowers in the area. I followed all the latest advances in science and astronomy. I also acquired a stereo system, and from a tiny shack tucked away in the back alleys I bought tapes of music that Miss West had once introduced me to: Schubert, Brahms, Mendelssohn, Beethoven, Sibelius. I made other good discoveries in the town: cheap restaurants, shops that sold good bread and cheese.

I grew to like the variety of people passing through Dharamshala, the artificial bustle they created in the town's winding and narrow alleys. The town received a disproportionate number of visitors. Some were Indians, young affluent men in packed Marutis, the "yuppies" Uma Devi disliked, and honeymooners who posed for pictures, gingerly perched on horseback, in heavy ethnic costumes and jewelry. But most of the visitors were Tibetophiles from the West. There were aging hippies with ponytails and beer bellies; European and American dowagers in crimson robes and necklaces with big brown beads; German tourists clutching paperback copies of *Siddhartha*. One dusky evening the Tibetan man at the shop where I bought my provisions pointed out to me a famous Hollywood actor and his equally famous wife, a fashion model. In more conspicuous numbers, however, were the tourists without spiritual ambitions, the American teenagers and bronzed Israeli young men on leave from compulsory military service, who, late in the evening, crowded into dingy video shacks run by a foppish Tibetan youth in fluorescent anoraks and earrings.

The liveliness of the bazaar was a welcome contrast to the peace and seclusion of my house, which I appreciated afresh every time I pushed the creaky wicket gate and went in after an unusually long and exhausting day at school. The natural serenity of the surroundings — the lawn in front, the shaded paths through the forest, the oaks and pines, beyond which slumbered the Kangra valley — brought me closer to the inner composure I so keenly sought in those early days. I'd never had a place I could call my own home, and as time went on I came to feel something close to a homemaker's possessiveness and love for this house, which had given me, I felt, a new chance.

At the end of three months, my time at the school came to an end. But I wanted to stay on, and as I expected, the school was only too happy to grant me an extension. I wrote to my father, explaining my decision. He wrote back a short note saying I could do whatever I felt comfortable with at the present moment. He encouraged me to keep the "bigger picture" in sight. He once again talked of *samskara*.

The monsoons turned into autumn. More visitors from the plains arrived. Dead leaves carpeted the path to my house. Then one night, fresh snow fell on the Dhauladhar ranges; the wind turned chilly; charcoal braziers and men with fur caps appeared in the alleys, and the crowds of visitors abruptly thinned.

Winter came, and one night, as I slept, it snowed in Dharamshala. The light through the curtains when I woke up the next morning was dazzling; I parted them to find the world startlingly white. Icy breezes blew across the lawn, and on the verandah, under the dripping corrugated-iron roof, a stray cat lay curled up on my cane rocking chair.

The school closed for two months, but I stayed in Dharamshala and walked every morning through alleys slushy with melting snow to give special tuition to a Tibetan child. In the evening, the yearning melodies of Sibelius's symphonies flowed through the bare rooms while clean rectangles of pale yellow light from the windows stretched across the snow-carpeted lawn outside.

Spring came, the school reopened, and I fell back into the old routine.

When school closed again for the summer, I locked up the house and took a bus to the Lahaul valley, where I spent the next two months, trekking through vast landscapes of bleached snow-splattered rock, milky blue lakes, and clear shallow streams.

The sun was hot, with scarcely a cloud in the sky. My skin quickly turned very dark; my lips were chapped; tiny spots danced before my unshaded eyes, and I had to refresh myself every hour from the cool streams where trout flicked over smooth pebbles. At the end of each day of walking, I would make for the nearest village, visible by the coils of smoke loitering above it, and find food and shelter for the night at the house of a potato farmer.

In the morning I would start again, with no

trace of exhaustion at all. I felt renewed, and reaching a small summit after a day of clambering up steep rocky slopes, I would be suffused by a sense of well-being I had never known before. This was to me the new and exhilarating discovery of that time, during those long walks through the endless valley: the discovery that health lay not only with the whole mind but with the robust body.

When school started again that monsoon, I put in an application for a long-term extension. I wrote to my father, saying I wished to continue indefinitely at the school. There was no reply from him for some weeks, and when the letter came, it was full of reproaches. He said that being a teacher in a primary school in a small town was justified only if you saw it as a step toward something much bigger. He said he had wanted to see me in a more prestigious academic position. He once again spoke of a sense of obligation to ancestors; he spoke of *samskara*. His exasperation came through clearly in his concluding remarks: "It is your life," he said, "and you know best."

I didn't reply immediately, and when I did, I talked of other things. I wrote about the mythological significance of a nearby temple. I spoke insincerely about my wish to visit Pondicherry soon.

In the meantime, my application was accepted by Mrs. Sharma, back from one of her foreign tours. She also gave me an unexpected bonus. She had arranged Gita's marriage to a Delhi-based businessman, and she now, in her brisk fidgety manner, promoted me to deputy principal. I was to remain a teacher but have additional administrative duties.

The result was that my days at the school lengthened. The number of Tibetan parents waiting outside the school gate increased. I was greeted in the town's alleys with new respect, and gifts of sweetboxes in shiny yellow cellophane wrappings appeared outside my door on Diwali morning.

That summer I went to the Spiti valley. I walked through flat gray plains of snow and rock, and into verdant valleys. I stayed in an ocher-colored monastery to which a shopkeeper in the bazaar had recommended me. It was perched high on a treeless hill, and from my bare room I watched silvery-gray twilights in the snow-muffled valley, oaks with scrawny limbs silhouetted silently against the white ground, the first lights cautiously appearing in the distant haze, while the still air quivered with the sound of tinkling bells.

The following summer I traveled to Kinnaur, and every summer for the next seven years I went walking in some part or other of the Himalayas.

I made no other travels. The thought of the big world beyond the mountains filled me with apprehension. My father often wrote to renew his invitation to Pondicherry and I had to find a fresh excuse each time.

2

When you are in your twenties, seven years can seem like a long time — especially if you live a secluded life, if you know neither ambition nor love nor any of the other preoccupations of that age.

However, my time in Dharamshala passed swiftly, divided between unchanging routine and solitude; there were hardly any periods of restlessness or torpor. I did my work — reciting the alphabet and maintaining petty-cash accounts — without feeling greatly committed to the school or the children. I read many books out of an old reflex. I listened to music for long hours. I went for walks. The years passed.

When, in later years, I watched the people in the bazaar — the honeymooning couples, the high-spirited youth, the sober spiritually minded Europeans — I watched them with a sense of strangeness and dread. The gratifications and torments of their personal lives, their desires, fears, and insecurities, their interconnected roles in the large world they came from — I didn't wish to know more about them than what I saw.

I still sensed something raw and incoherent within my own personality; and I remained vulnerable to those large vague longings, the urge to throw oneself into a grand and noble venture, into whatever could give coherence and shape to my own life. But these moments went by quickly, much to my relief. I did not resist the self-pity that inevitably followed them. I was more conscious than ever of how absurdly romantic and incongruous these longings were for me.

In the first few years in Dharamshala, I was still vulnerable to many memories from my time in Benares and Pondicherry — I had to train myself to see that past as dead. It became important, as a kind of mental discipline, not to think about it, or attempt to ferret out any meaning from it. It had taken much time and willpower before that past could settle in my mind as a time of confusion and loss, to which I no longer needed to return.

But then all of a sudden, and in quick succession, people from that very past appeared in Dharamshala, and I was forced to think about it again.

The first visitor was Priya, who showed up

at my school at the end of a taxing day. The peon told me that a girl from Chandigarh had come to see me. I went out into the dusk and saw a diminutive figure standing under the crescent-shaped rusty signboard that had the school's name painted on it.

She was as thin as I remembered her, with shorter hair and eyebrows whose earlier thickness had been stylishly plucked. She wasn't alone; there was a tall young man with her, with smooth-shaven cheeks, blackheads around his sharp-edged nose, and straight long hair that he kept wiping across his forehead in short nervous gestures.

I had been in touch with her after leaving Pondicherry. I had written her a brief note apologizing for the misunderstanding I had caused. She had written back a surprisingly mature letter, in whose tone and vocabulary I saw the hand of an elder person, probably Deepa. She berated herself for her "childish impetuosity" and proffered her own apologies.

From another, later postcard I had learned that she was living in nearby Chandigarh, attending the local university. And now she was here in Dharamshala, on an excursion, I soon recognized, with her first "boyfriend," to a hill station.

It was a big adventure for her; and she was

306

awkward before me. I took her and her boy-friend to Harry's Restaurant, where we had an uncomfortable tea, none of us saying much. The vulnerability she revealed in Pondicherry was even more pronounced now; so were the contradictory ambitions. She now told me that she wanted to be a social worker, but wanted to do an MBA first, in the United States. Then, changing her mind, she said she wanted to write poetry and be a writer.

An inquisitive Uma Devi sat behind the counter and gazed at us, trying to figure out my connection to the young couple.

Later, walking through the market, I spotted them at the video shack, laughing and joking with the foppish Tibetan youth who ran it. They looked relaxed, restored to their natural everyday selves.

And then one day in August, the school semester yet to begin, I was browsing through a shelf of expensive new arrivals at the book-shop and chatting about the pound-rupee exchange rate with the owner, a kindly old bespectacled Tibetan called Tenzing with a big black bump on his forehead, when I heard someone behind me say, "Guess what! A voice from the past!"

I turned back to see Mark, looming over me, grinning, his abundant hair falling over his ears. He had seen me come in just as he was about to go out; he said he had hung around and eavesdropped on my conversation with the bookseller in order to make sure that he wasn't mistaken.

A slight paunch bulged out above the broad scruffed belt of his khakis, but he hadn't lost his handyman's tough good looks and friendly manner. He held in his hand a new book on Ayurvedic medicine. But it turned out that he had given up his research. He had a new grant from some foundation but had turned it down. He had gone back to America for a few months in the summer and then had come straight up to Dharamshala, where he planned to spend a few weeks before returning to Benares. He said he had been coming to Dharamshala for the summer and monsoon months almost every year. He couldn't stay away from India; it had become a routine that he couldn't do without.

When I told him that I had been in Dharamshala for seven years, he gave a small whistle of disbelief. "It's weird, you know," he said. "We should have bumped into each other by now."

He was in a hurry, he said, but lingered on, talking about the Kangra valley, where he had just done a long trek.

And then he added, apropos of nothing.

"Have you heard about Panditji? He and his wife died suddenly, within days of each other. People said there was something fishy about it; apparently they weren't on great terms with their son, Arjun . . ."

He was still speaking as he moved toward the door. "I've got to tell you about Miss West," he said, pushing out the door, "but it'll have to wait until next time. Anyway, now that we are connected, let's keep in touch. Drop in sometime. I'll tell you where my house is. You go two blocks to the left . . ."

A few days later, I found myself walking down the quiet cobblestone alley Mark had described. Hanging baskets of bougainvillea framed the front doors of the small houses and white prayer flags fluttered from the clotheslines stretched between roofs.

It had taken me some time to decide whether I should visit Mark, and I still wasn't sure if it was a good idea. I had been surprised at first by the coldness with which I heard about the death of Panditji and his wife: the event seemed so distant, with so little relation to anything in my present life; it was like the events in the newspapers I occasionally picked up at the bookshop. But then, later, the news had worked on me in my solitude, had loosened another kind of memory of Benares: the memory of the serene days I had spent there, the afternoons at the library, the evenings at the ghats, the smoky blue twilights, all the eventless days with their restful vacancies. Something within me kept going back to it, wanted to stay with the pictures in my mind; it was what took me to Mark's house that afternoon.

A bespectacled Indian girl wearing a chikan kurta opened the door, and for one moment I thought I had come to the wrong house. But then she said something with an unmistakably American accent, the sun sparkling on her glasses, about Mark's having gone out to the bazaar, and I knew I hadn't.

She said, "You are welcome to hang out here if you want."

Inside, there was the same assortment of ethnic knickknacks I had once seen in Mark's house by the river in Benares: Azamgarh dhurries, Himachali wall hangings, Gujarati lampshades, Tibetan tankas, and various kinds of pots and pans.

The woman extended a small warm hand, introduced herself, and then sat down before me on the dhurrie. Her name was Rekha and she was in her final undergraduate year at Berkeley, California. That made her someone in her late teens. But she looked older; her glasses gave her a severe, studious look, and she spoke fast, with a kind of flatly emphatic tone and accent that sat oddly with her Indian face.

She said she was "working" as an intern for the rights of single-mother minority women in San Francisco. After graduation, she planned to get into law school and work permanently as a lawyer for the rights of single-mother minority women.

The conversation floundered on my side. She asked me no questions, and I wasn't sure how to respond to her disclosures, which she seemed to make with complete sincerity and frankness; when she got up to make some tea, I half wondered if I ought to offer to help her.

It was as she puttered about the kitchen, blindly reaching out for shelved jars and cups, that I remembered Debbie. Where was she now? I wondered, and sitting in the narrow, dimly lit room, surrounded by the clutter of Mark's days in Benares, I had a sudden melancholy awareness of the large store of unrecalled and unreflected-upon memories I carried within myself.

Mark came in soon after we finished our tea. He looked delighted to see me, and his news came out in a rush.

He said he had recently reached a momentous decision in his life; it was something he had agonized over for years now. He was going back to America. He was going back next year, and planned to settle down with Rekha in California. Yes, the time had come. He loved India deeply, particularly Benares, and it hurt simply to think about leaving it. But it had to be done. It was a now-or-never thing.

I kept waiting for him to move on to Miss West. I didn't dare ask about her myself, for fear of being confronted with unsettling subjects. It was why I hadn't had any news of Miss West for a long time. I had written to her from Pondicherry; she had replied with a postcard, one of whose innocuous sentences had leapt out and startled me: it said she was going to Paris for the summer to see some friends, including our mutual ones. I had received the postcard soon after I arrived in Dharamshala, and a sudden attack of dread had made me tear it up. I hadn't written her again.

Now, according to Mark, she, too, had made a "momentous" decision in her life. She was still in Benares, but planning to leave soon.

Mark said, "She has broken off her long-standing relationship with the guy in England. It wasn't going to work out. It took her twenty-seven years to realize that and I think she's pretty devastated by it all, but she's so

English, she wouldn't let on anything to anyone. All I know is that she has bought a house in East Anglia, somewhere in the country, and plans to live in it for the rest of her life. I've been there once; it's very flat and damp. I can't imagine why she wants to go there — I mean she could move to California, or someplace less depressing — but I think she has basically given up on the idea of waiting for this guy. She has to go somewhere, and I think she's leaving Benares and India because it wasn't going to work out for her. Too many memories, I guess. I guess she wants to be in some place she can call home."

And now Mark went on to make a long speech. He said, "I don't know if she'll be happy again. I was talking to my Hindi teacher the other day and he was giving me his usual line about how everyone in the West thinks about nothing except pleasure and happiness. I was trying to make him realize that there is a different kind of pain attached to this kind of life. It comes with adulthood, like hair on your chest, a pain in the gut like the one your father probably had and it'll stay with you the rest of your life. Maybe drugs and alcohol and art would relieve it for a little while but it always returns. You could win the academic lottery, get tenure or whatever, but even that won't knock that pain out. And what I was trying to tell him was just this: that it's a different kind of pain no more or no less than what you see here. People are people all over the world, in America or anywhere else, and they really all want one thing and little else: love, which is really lacking in life as we live it today."

This monologue, halfway through which I remembered that I had heard similar things from him before, turned out be the prologue to the plans Mark now disclosed to me, plans for, as he put it, "feeling and conveying love," "expressing our common humanity." He had already given up his research on Ayurvedic medicine; he was now also going to give up his interest in Indian classical music. He was going back to work for a rehabilitation center for AIDS victims in Berkeley. In the time left over from this demanding work he would serve as a volunteer for an environmental organization.

All this had been arranged by Rekha, he said, turning back to where she was sitting. But, unnoticed by him, she had quietly left the room some time earlier. As he turned back toward me, he mumbled something about getting married to her later in the year.

He continued, "I find it hard to believe that I was once a fanatical scholar who cared for nothing apart from his work. But Rekha really has given me the courage to face up to my real self and cut through the bullshit. And made me see what I really want. It was so simple. Like everyone else I also want to love and be loved. Just that."

And then, looking up at me with clear confident eyes, he grew unexpectedly wild. "There is another thing I realize. It's that we are made of flesh and bone and this flesh is the most important thing we have. You know, you realize after some time what a load of bullshit" — he raised his arm and pointed toward the jute bookstand, which I had examined when Rekha was in the kitchen: it was full of books published by presses called Shambhala and Tricycle and Wisdom — "all these great religions and philosophies are, this thing about solitude and loneliness being good for your spiritual and artistic growth. So you end up starving yourself in every way, waiting and hoping for this truly awesome spiritual jackpot that never comes, and then one day you are down there all alone on Manikarnika Ghat turning to ashes with not a single soul on the fucking planet who feels sorry for you . . ."

I left Mark's house feeling a bit disoriented. It was dark outside; I had forgotten to bring my flashlight, and after stumbling once or twice on the cobblestone path, I began to walk very slowly.

Mark's words were still ringing in my head, and I couldn't but feel their alienness. I hadn't heard anyone speak like that for years now; the vocabulary, the concerns, the themes, and the passion all came from another world.

As he spoke, I had begun to recall something Miss West had told me: "He wants to get home . . . insecure . . ." As he went on, more memories came to me, including one of the conversation I had overheard the evening of Miss West's party; and I felt that Mark's words were meant as much for himself as for me. He needed to convince himself through other people's approbation; he needed to measure himself in other people's eyes.

It was how I sought to place Mark. But his words, particularly the second part of his monologue, kept coming back to me, and I couldn't but be aware of the odd resonance they had. There was also something vaguely threatening about them, about the way in which they forced me to reassess my own life.

For years now, I had lived neutrally, on the surface. I had learned to live without the feeling I'd had for all of my childhood and early adulthood, the quiet certainty that had existed over and above the fear and pain of those years, that something good and precious was growing within me. I no longer felt that way, and now that that sense of inner growth had faded, I didn't have the same self-doubts. I didn't miss the old intensity of contradictory hopes and fears, the hopeful blind striving I knew in the days I came to live in Benares, which I often felt was leading me nowhere. Instead, I saw its fading away as a good thing. I thought it meant that I had reached the end of a time of bewilderment.

This placid life I had in Dharamshala was severely judged by many people: my father, my colleagues at the school, whose slightly malicious gossip often reached my ears. But it was all I had. I had tried hard to build it up, using all the means at my disposal, and on more optimistic days I could even think that this detached, eventless life wasn't very far from matching the old Brahmin idea of retreat, from fulfilling those ancestral obligations my father still wrote me about.

Mark had asked me to visit them again, but I stayed away. I had gone the first time out of curiosity, but now I was fearful — so much so that once, seeing him hunched over a shelf at the bookshop, I turned and quickly ran down the steps, much to the puzzlement of the boy at the counter.

I now wonder at my extreme reaction. But Mark's insecurity and self-aggrandizement weren't what I, after years of my own private struggles, wanted to be involved with when my own equanimity, the balance I had arrived at in Dharamshala, was so fragile. I did not want it to be threatened — particularly by something that was an echo from my time in Benares.

3

But when a parcel from Miss West came one cold autumn morning, I thought of Benares again, and the feeling came over me of having left something incomplete and unresolved.

Inside the parcel there was a brown-paper-wrapped packet that looked like a book; there was also a postcard with a picture of Benares, a badly printed generic picture of the ghats, with a few lines scrawled on the back.

It was a very brief letter. But it had something of her bantering manner and it broke into my placid routine with unexpected power.

I read the lines over and over until they became a meaningless jingle in my head.

Dear Friend,

Just found out from Mark where you have been hiding all this time. Benares isn't the same without you. Do come for a visit sometime, I'd love to see you again and catch up with your news.

Love, Diana

PS: Lots of new CDs here!
PPS: I enclose something for you that someone left here for you ages ago.

Before the postcard came, I had been thinking of what Mark had told me about Miss West. I had once envied her for her great luck, for living her life, as I saw it, in ever-new glamorous settings. But what I had seen as luck had come with its own special burden, its own store of disappointments and frustrations, and now that burden, which Miss West was to carry for the rest of her life, made the luck seem tainted.

I hadn't realized this, and I wondered again at how much in other people's lives I had either missed or not been equipped to see at all. While in Benares, I had remained busy with monitoring the many different registers of my own feeling and thinking self, and later, when that phase of my life ended, I became preoccupied with the next one. Other people were reduced to minor figures in this large drama of the self; they ceased to exist in themselves. My vision of them kept shrinking, and some of them, like Rajesh, for instance, had dropped altogether out of memory.

I had last seen Rajesh on the ghats on my last day, speaking to the terrified young student about the illusion and the void. I was full of other things that day; I had kept my distance from him.

I now unwrapped the packet inside Miss West's parcel to find the Penguin Classics paperback of *Sentimental Education* and the xerox copy of Wilson's essay on Flaubert that I had once loaned Rajesh.

That moment was the first time in years I had thought of Rajesh. I imagined he waited for me at the library, and then, after I failed to appear for several weeks, he must have gone to Panditji's house to return the book and the essay. I wondered if he had met Miss West, and if he had, was he puzzled by her in the way I was years ago, when I saw her sitting out on the roof in the evening listening to music.

I put the book next to the framed and garlanded picture of the Dalai Lama with the row of novels that I no longer read. I almost threw away the essay after it had been lying on a side table for some time; it ended up in a file of xeroxed pages I rarely looked at.

Then one evening in the town, I went to a travel agency to arrange for a school excursion and ran into Pratap. He was one of Rajesh's hangers-on from a nearby village, one of those students who used to sit under the giant banyan tree outside the university and gossip about prohibitive dowries and corrupt civil servants. Pratap had completed his several attempts at the Civil Service examination and was now a tour guide for Indian tourists. He traveled with them on buses across several states: a hard and poorly paid job and very remote from the dreams of power and affluence that he, along with many others, would have had in Benares.

He was wearing a floppy white cricket cap over a bright red windbreaker; his imitation blue Levi's sat loose on his thin frame and his thick sneakers in fluorescent colors seemed too big on his feet. He was embarrassed when I recognized him, and it was out of this embarrassment that he began to speak of Rajesh. He hadn't seen him for many months now, but he had news of him from other people. Rajesh was now more notorious than ever.

Why notorious? I wondered. I had always known about his connection to Vijay, the Allahabad student politician who had sent me to see him. I had seen the pistols in his room and wondered about his connection to the rioters and the strange people who came to visit him in the Ambassador with tinted windows. But I hadn't thought of him as notorious.

Pratap looked at me with some puzzlement. He said he thought I knew all about Rajesh. I said I didn't. The miscomprehension was soon cleared.

Pratap had seen me as an intimate friend of Rajesh's, and now, as he spoke, he grew increasingly surprised at how little I knew of his life. He was surprised that I didn't know while in Benares that Rajesh was a member of a criminal gang specializing in debt collection on behalf of a group of local moneylenders and businessmen.

Although I was taken aback, I realized that it did explain his long, mysterious absences from Benares, the pistols in his room. I had attributed the absences to a secret mistress hidden away somewhere, but the pistols had unnerved me. I remembered, too, the sinister-looking Ambassador with tinted windows, and from this sudden rush of memories emerged one of Arjun, Panditji's errant son, whom I had once seen badly injured. Rajesh had said that Arjun was trying to mortgage a house that didn't belong to him, and he had asked me lots of questions about him. How did he know all this? Was Rajesh involved in beating Arjun?

I asked Pratap. He couldn't remember at first, and then as his memory returned he looked amazed at my ignorance. He said that Rajesh had taken on the commission of roughing up Arjun basically to keep him from troubling me.

These commissions, Pratap went on, were

a good steady business. Once confronted with the possibility of violence, people paid up very quickly, or did whatever you asked them to, without involving the police.

But then Rajesh had graduated to something riskier — and at this point, although shocked and bewildered by what I had already been told, I was not prepared for what I heard next.

Pratap saw the disbelief on my face. He seemed to be enjoying it as his voice grew more dramatic. At some stage, he said, pausing after every word, Rajesh had turned himself into a contract killer. It was an extremely well-paid profession, also a well-connected one. You worked for small-time contractors, who in turn worked for wealthy industrialists. These businessmen also did favors for local political bosses, who did not always rely on their own private armies — he used the Hindi word.

Pratap went on, excitement glistening on his face. You got to know everyone well after a few years in the business. But there were problems. You worked for all these important people, yet you were always on your own. The chances of survival weren't very high. Sooner or later, the police came to hear of you. Fierce loyalties of caste and clan ensured that every murder would be avenged.

It was what would happen to Rajesh, he said. He could see now an ambush of the kind often reported in the local papers: Rajesh would be on his motorcycle when four men would surround him at a busy intersection in the old city and shoot him dead.

I was suddenly appalled by this turn to our conversation, by the prurient way in which Pratap imagined Rajesh's fate.

He wanted to talk more, and was moving toward a tea stall, when I realized that I needed to be alone. Pratap couldn't have told me anything significantly more about Rajesh, and given his overly excitable mood, I didn't want to encourage him further.

I said I had to attend to some urgent work at the school and slipped away so quickly that there was no time for Pratap even to suggest, as I knew he wished to, another meeting. He did appear a bit hurt by my suddenly great desire to part from him, and I thought later that perhaps I had been unfair. There was nothing premeditated about his malice toward Rajesh. He was speaking out of his own frustrations, the sense of having reached a dead end in his own life.

It also occurred to me afterward that I should have asked him about Rajesh's current whereabouts, and I thought at the same time of the futility of the request, had I indeed made it.

That part of my life was over. I did not plan to return to Benares.

I wondered if I should write to Rajesh, but simultaneously felt the incongruity of such a correspondence. What would I say? It was hard for me to think about Rajesh in a focused way even though he had been a major presence in the other life I lived at the university. It was hard, too, to disentangle him from the mass of suppressed memories.

Instead, I kept thinking about what Pratap had told me. My mind was filled with banal images I knew well from those Benares papers: they formed the usual pattern of daylight murder in the city. I kept seeing Rajesh at that busy crossing, trapped in the dense swarm of scooters, cycle rickshaws, bullock carts, cars, buses, trucks, and bicycles, the four men converging upon him, producing pistols from their pockets . . .

A few weeks passed. I kept thinking about Rajesh and then one day wrote to Pratap to ask him about Rajesh's whereabouts. He replied almost immediately: a short note saying that he had just met Rajesh after many years. He had told Rajesh about his unexpected meeting with me in Dharamshala; he had also passed on my address to him and mentioned my desire to be in touch again.

And then one day a letter came from Rajesh himself. The envelope was postmarked Mirzapur and did not have a return address. Inside there were a few sentences on a piece of lined paper.

Dear brother,

    It is one of the great mysteries of life that I should hear about you again after so many years. Pratap told me about you, the special path you have chosen, in which you appear to be content. I knew when I first met you that you'd somehow break out of the world we knew, that you would go on to do different things. That you have done so makes me very happy. Pratap said you asked about my mother. I have sad news to offer. She passed away three years ago. I was with her during the last days of her life. The final rites were in Benares. She often asked me about you. She didn't have too many visitors at her house, and whenever someone showed up she would remember for years afterward. After her death, I moved from Benares to Mirzapur. But I am rarely there. I travel a lot and I don't stay in any place for too long. Pratap said that you would like to meet me. This is awkward. Do not misunderstand me when I say that any meeting between us, even if practically possible, would put you in a very

327

difficult position. I wish it was otherwise, but the life I have chosen has shut me off from many things I valued in the past. You, who liked reading so much, would be unhappy to know that I don't read anything apart from newspapers. I have no friends left from my time in Benares. The city is a foreign place for me now. But I can't write or think too much about this. After all these years, life is no more than a habit, it is not a subject for reflection. I simply go on. I do not think much about what I do or what I have become. On certain days I remember those lines of Faiz: "This is not that long-looked-for break of day / Not that clear dawn in quest of which those comrades / set out . . ." But how many of us can say they have reached that dawn — so, I am not alone, there are millions of us, and this is a source of consolation. I hope you'll understand and forgive me.

Your elder brother, Rajesh

I had never seen his handwriting before. He wrote a beautiful Devanagari script, and there was an elegant formality in his prose which I thought would have come to him from the Urdu poetry he read. And that wasn't the only unexpected thing about the letter. I had imagined him as someone cut off from his old life

328

of ruminative reading, someone inevitably undermined by rough times, by the brutalities of his trade, and I had expected a more direct statement about the unsuitability of our meeting. Such a considered response made me wonder if I had ever really known him.

The bigger revelation still lay in the future. The letter had confirmed what I already suspected: that no further contact with Rajesh was possible. And it had begun to fade from memory until a few weeks later.

One day I was looking through old files for a missing receipt from the school when I came across the xeroxed copy of Wilson's essay on Flaubert. I was casually flipping through the pages when I saw some passages underlined in red. I could never bring myself to mark up printed text, out of an old and automatic reverence I had for the printed word. It could only have been Rajesh.

I read the underlined sentences:

> Frédéric is only the more refined as well as the more incompetent side of the middle-class mediocrity of which the dubious promoter represents the more flashy and active aspect. And so in the case of the other characters, the journalists and the artists, the members of the

nobility, Frédéric finds the same shoddiness and lack of principle which are gradually revealed in himself.

The passage went on. But I was struck more by the underlining. What had the words said to Rajesh? I wondered.

On another page of the essay, the underlined passage read:

Flaubert's novel plants deep in our mind an idea which we never quite get rid of: the suspicion that our middle-class society of manufacturers, businessmen, and bankers, of people who live on or deal in investments, so far from being redeemed by its culture, has ended by cheapening and invalidating all the departments of culture, political, scientific, artistic, and religious, as well as corrupting and weakening the ordinary human relations: love, friendship and loyalty to cause — till the whole civilization seems to dwindle.

Wilson's denunciation of capitalism here had an old-fashioned Marxist ring. Nevertheless, it was a good passage in that it offered a small glimpse of Wilson's way of finding connections between life and literature. But why had Rajesh underlined it? Again, how had he interpreted it?

I thought of the day I went to visit Rajesh's village; I had remembered from it only the boy I saw in the mango grove, the boy who came to symbolize my aspirations for a quiet, restful life. Some other memories bubbled up now: the steam-engined train chugging away through stubbly fields, coils of smoke torpid above little huts; his mother's tiny room, with its calendars of Shiva and Krishna; her conversation about Rajesh's past; and Rajesh's own words about *Sentimental Education* on the journey back to Benares, the coal embers darting past us in the dark, words I had dismissed as exaggeration, the hard, determined look on his face as he said, "It is the story of my life. I know these people well. Your hero, Edmund Wilson, he also knows them."

What had he meant by that?

It took some time to decipher these remarks. My mind kept probing them in idle moments, but it was only when, overcoming my fear of novels, I decided to reread *Sentimental Education* that I began to arrive at some kind of answer.

I eventually saw that there had been purpose behind Rajesh's invitation to his home, his decision to reveal his life so frankly to me.

Even the remarks about *Sentimental Education* and Wilson on the train: he wanted me to know that not only had he read the novel, he had drawn, with Wilson's help, his own conclusions from it.

In the hard and mean world he had lived in, first as a child laborer and then as a hired criminal for politicians and businessmen, Rajesh would have come to know well the grimy underside of middle-class society. What became clearer to me now was how quick he had been to recognize that the society Flaubert and Wilson wrote about wasn't very different from the one he inhabited in Benares.

"It's the story of my life," he had said. I couldn't see it then, but in Benares I had been among people who, like Frédéric and his friends, had either disowned or, in many cases, moved away from their provincial origins in order to realize their dreams of success in the bourgeois world. Rajesh was one of them. So was Pratap, and so, in a different way, was I, with all the confused longings I had for a true awakening to the world, for everything I felt lay out of my reach.

But only a handful of these students were able to get anywhere near realizing their dreams of joining the Civil Service. Most of them saw their ambitions dwindle away over the years in successive disappointments, and they knew not only failure but also the degradation of living in a world where self-deception, falsehood, sycophancy, and bribery were the rule.

The small, unnoticed tragedies of thwarted hopes and ideals Flaubert wrote about in *Sentimental Education* were all around us. And this awareness — which, given the meagerness of my means and prospects, was also mine but which I tried to evade all through my time in Benares — this awareness had been Rajesh's private key to the book. Reading it during the tormented days that followed my return from Kalpi, I had seen only the reflection of a personal neurosis in it; the character of Frédéric seemed to embody perfectly my sense of inadequacy, my severe self-image.

Reading the same book but bringing another kind of experience to it, Rajesh had discovered something else; he had discovered a social and psychological environment similar to the one he lived in. He shared with Flaubert and Wilson — so far away from us in every way — a true, if bitter, awareness of its peculiar human ordeals and futility.

"To fully appreciate the book," Wilson had written of *Sentimental Education,* "one must have had time to see something of life."

Rajesh had exemplified this truth even as he moved into a world where he couldn't be followed.

It had taken me much time to realize the simple fact that Rajesh had been struggling to make sense of his life, to connect the disparate elements that existed in it: his self-consciousness about his Brahmin identity, the pistols in his room, the talk of illusion and the void.

And now, whenever I recalled my time in Benares, I felt that it was a task I had shirked, that I had understood very little and misunderstood much during those months there. I was haunted by the sense of having left something incomplete, and with it came a quiet yearning to go back, to gaze with a fresher eye at things grown so dim in memory.

I struggled for some time with this growing desire. Then one evening I came home, my mind miraculously made up, and without even pausing to switch on the geyser in the bathroom, I sat down at the unused dining table and wrote to Miss West.

Miss West took her time in replying, and when she did, made no mention of her own plans.

Her letter came as school was about to close for winter. Dark clouds every day threatened snow and sleet. Dull gray light came out each morning from under the curtain in my bedroom; the day appeared stale even before it had begun. The town wore a deserted look after the tourist invasions of autumn; the day died early in colorless sunsets.

But I couldn't leave straightaway. Events at the school kept me busy. We received a high-level visit from the state education minister. His approval was necessary in acquiring official recognition from the government, and Mrs. Sharma, the principal, came back from another long foreign sojourn to take personal charge of the visit. Her sister, Gita, came up from Delhi, bejeweled and plumper than before; she came ostensibly to help but created more problems by quarreling constantly with her sister.

The winter holidays had leaked away, and the school was scheduled to reopen after just a few days, when I finally left for Benares.

4

Taxi to Pathankot, the railhead of the British Raj, and from there the old train that once took vacationers back to Calcutta from the Kashmir valley. The taxi was a luxury, and it was with the same lightheaded extravagance that I canceled my earlier reservations and upgraded my ticket to second-class air-conditioned.

We left at night, and for a very long time I was unable to sleep. Shadowy figures moved silently outside on the poorly lit platforms; a luggage cart would trundle past, with a muffled drone; and in the silence that descended upon the compartment after it had gone, the soft rhythmic snoring of the overweight man on the berth next to mine would become audible.

A strange agitation in the mind, a kind of noise created by random thoughts and memories, kept me awake. At one point, I gave up all attempts to sleep and instead lay still on my berth, listening to the rattle and roll of the wheels, and waited for the morning, which seemed to hold something of great significance.

It was in that position that I drifted back to sleep.

I woke up early. The flimsy curtains on the window promised light, but when I parted them, the world outside, seen through the murky window of my compartment, the world I had feared and was seeing for the first time in seven years — flat fields, ramshackle sheds at level crossings, battered trucks with bundles of hay, bullock carts inching forward on rutted dirt tracks, buffaloes splattered with mud, children playing outside low huts — the world with big skies and wide flat horizons that held millions of competing lives, that world appeared empty and lackluster.

The train swayed and clattered ahead through tangles of gleaming tracks. Benares appeared at last after a series of small deserted stations, and the view contracted: it was now naked brick houses and messy electric wires and algae-covered ponds around which sat early-morning defecators, gazing up meekly at the passing train.

The monotonous silence of the compartment that I had got so used to was finally shattered at the railway station. Chaos erupted as the train slid to a stop along the congested platform: emaciated coolies in threadbare woolen jumpers muscled into compartments; hysterical parents shouted at their children as they unloaded their luggage; ragged urchins shrilly hawked chai, and loudspeakers high above on the roof of the platform kept indifferently booming out the bad news of long delays and cancellations.

Outside, giant hoardings of new Bombay films loomed over the concourse, the pictures of soft-cheeked men gnashing and grinding their teeth and pointing outsized guns at each other; the dhaba shacks blared loud devotional music; the big colored trucks revved out dense clouds of diesel smoke; urchins leaning from tempos thumped the battered sides in a bid to attract arriving passengers; and rickshaw drivers with thin, unshaven, hostile faces seethed in small mobs everywhere.

I surrendered my bag to the first rickshaw driver who approached me: a small, dark young man with a thick curled mustache.

I had no place to stay; I was hoping to find an inexpensive hotel somewhere along the ghats. But when the rickshaw driver suggested, the veins in his swarthy legs puffing out as he pushed at the pedals, a new "ultra-modern hotel" near the station, I let him take me there.

It was a white building, strikingly clean behind brick walls garish with film posters. The bright deserted lobby smelled of floor wax; the sofas were upholstered with shiny brown leather; and the place appeared empty, the keyboard at the reception desk full. The receptionist, a gawky young man with glasses, kept fumbling with the registration ledger, scribbling and then striking out an erroneous entry. Behind him, in a glass cubicle adorned with a Mickey Mouse clock and framed calendar-art pictures of Shiva, sat the owner of the hotel, a thickset man in a gray safari suit, carefully counting a wad of hundred-rupee notes.

I filled in the sheaf of duplicate forms brought by the receptionist, who kept calling me sir with exaggerated courtesy. I then waited as he examined them.

Suddenly, at the far end of the lobby, the elevator doors slid open to reveal two young paunchy khadi-clad men — minor politicians, I immediately thought. Their steps echoing across the lobby, they strode with brisk assurance to a white Ambassador, waiting with open doors under the portico. They got into the car but the doors with the tinted windows remained open; they appeared to be expecting someone else. The man in the driver's seat kept looking straight ahead.

Soon I heard the elevator doors open again. They now revealed two slim, swarthy young women, wearing almost identical salwar-kurtas of some shiny synthetic material, with sequinned chunnis draped around thick gold necklaces. Crimson lipstick almost blotted out their small mouths; gold bangles flashed on their wrists; silver anklets jingled softly as they strutted past me on very high pencil-thin heels.

They joined the politicians in the car; the doors slammed shut in the void of the fore-court; the car slunk off.

As I turned away, I saw the receptionist looking at me with concern.

He attempted to smile. He said, in English, "Special guests, sir."

But it wasn't what he wished to say; his weak English had let him down, and he knew that almost instantly.

He turned his head to glance at the man in the cubicle, who was still counting the notes, and when he looked back at me his face showed fear.

It was an odd return to Benares; it wasn't what I had been expecting. I had imagined the moment of arrival would be calm. I had imagined it would be infused with gentle memories. But the spell had been broken at the railway station itself, facing the truculent coolies and the rickshaw drivers.

Nothing in that scene was unfamiliar to me, but during the tranquil years in Dharamshala I had lost the old instinctive ways of dealing with it. I could no longer summon the casual self-possession required to bargain out a correct rate with the aggressive rickshaw driver. I lacked the indifference, the unseeing blank gaze of the hardened traveler.

Then the hotel, revealed in the first few minutes as an assignation spot for local politicians, and the nervous receptionist, the man in the cubicle counting the rupee notes — that wasn't anything I had expected.

I was alert, almost preternaturally so. I felt my senses on edge, but they had registered only strangeness as the rickshaw strained past the "fast-food" parlors with dark glass windows, the white-painted hotels with multicolored flags listless on their roofs, the banners advertising computer courses swaying across the roads, and now this hotel room, described by the receptionist as a "honeymoon suite," all done in pink, the walls cluttered with framed posters of tender-faced white children and garish Swiss landscapes with Christian homilies.

This wasn't the city I knew; what I knew and remembered lay farther down the road, closer to the river and the ghats, the decaying palaces, the half-submerged temples. I began to feel I had made a mistake in allowing the rickshaw driver to take me to this hotel.

The moment of calm came later, when I woke up after a short nap. Light flooded the small room and created a radiant glow against the pink walls and upholstery and bedcovers; snatches of music and talk came in through the open windows.

The morning and the anxiety of my arrival seemed far away as I stood at the window that opened out on the forecourt. From this elevation the street appeared different. Brightly painted rickshaws stood in a queue before the hotel's gates; a little boy pushed a vegetable stall on the empty road, hawking his wares in a surprisingly deep voice; a man in white flapping pajamas hurled up the shutters of one of the grocery stores, and the Coca-Cola logo vanished with a brief rattle.

As I watched, a rickshaw suddenly swerved in from around the corner and thudded and jolted across a small pothole. The driver rang his jingling bells as if to protest against the shock, and the sound unfastened an old memory: the cold foggy mornings I woke up to during my first days in Benares, which I spent in bed, huddled under Panditji's thin quilts, trying to read *The World as Will and Idea* as rickshaws overloaded with children lurched down the potholed alleys and old

Hindi melodies wafted out of unseen radios and jets of water from municipal taps cannonaded into plastic buckets, and a woman whom I could never see towel-dried her hair with that peculiar sneezing sound.

I showered, put on fresh clothes, and went down to the empty restaurant in the lobby for a late and heavy lunch of parathas and pickle. Miss West wasn't expecting me until later in the afternoon; there was nothing to do until then, and after lunch I went back to my room and played with the television set, switching channels randomly, moving swiftly from MTV to Santa Barbara to CNN and back.

It was the first time in seven years that I had sat before a television screen, and to confront the unfamiliar faces and speech — the anorexic MTV VJs with their bare midriffs and eyebrow rings and rapid-fire banter — was to feel as if I had arrived in an alien city.

I switched off the TV; I went and stood at the window and watched the street. I switched on the TV again, and immediately turned it off as a long, wailing sound filled the room. I lay on the bed for a while. I felt a gentle restlessness. I wanted to go out; I wanted to be away from the hotel.

When I eventually went out into the mellow winter sunshine, things appeared to happen in an effortless daze.

I did not have to think before telling the rickshaw driver the name of the area where Panditji's house stood; the words slipped out of my mouth as instinctively as they once had. Sitting on the rickshaw, feeling a cool breeze upon my face, passing through streets and alleys so familiar — the tattered kites trapped between power cables, the house with the tiny door that opened toward a large sunny loggia-like space where on crisp winter afternoons women sat on charpoys and oiled their thick black tresses, the men staring out vacantly from dark chai shops — I had the sensation of reentering a dream.

It was damp as always in the alleys leading to Panditji's house. But a small surprise awaited me at the house itself.

In my memory the main door leading in from the alley had always been open, revealing a small dark courtyard beyond which were the room where Panditji lay under layers of blankets and a bathroom with scars of green slime on the lower end of the walls. The door was now locked from inside.

I knocked; I heard people talking: a man's voice and then a woman's.

Waiting for the door to be opened, I looked up at a strip of blue sky and noticed a woman staring down at me from the roof terrace of the adjoining house. Her face beneath her sari veil was fleshy and expressionless, and I wondered, with a pang of disappointment, if she was the one I had heard drying her hair.

The voices inside grew louder and stranger and then the door was yanked open.

A tall and skinny white man in a lungi and khadi waistcoat stood before me, his head and shoulders hunched under the short door frame. His hair was long and stringy; the skin on his long face was stretched tight over his cheekbones; on his bare pale forearms there were identical tattoos of the goddess Kali, her bright crimson tongue a dab of startling color in the surrounding blackness.

His body filled the entire frame of the door, and he seemed to be concealing someone behind him. He stared at me with his mouth slightly open, and then said, "What do you want?" His voice was gruff, and the accent was Israeli; I had come across it many times before in the alleys and shops of Dharamshala.

His manner softened when I mentioned Miss West.

"Oh, I see. You want to talk to the English lady?"

I nodded.

"She's upstairs, on the roof," he said, and

stepped away from the door.

I went in. I heard a shuffle of slippered feet, and the door to Panditji's room banged shut immediately. I caught a flash of bare brown legs — a woman's legs — and coils of cigarette smoke inside.

The Israeli man looked at me and smiled — a sheepish smile.

I trudged up the steep stairs, remembering how I used the brief exacting climb to prepare myself for the blank gazes of Mrs. Pandey and Shyam sitting outside the kitchen.

But there was no one in the courtyard, which had been extensively renovated. The walls had been painted a bright yellow; the door leading to Mrs. Pandey's bedroom had new Diwali floral decorations on it; the place close to the kitchen door where she and Shyam once sat was now occupied by a sparkling white washbasin with a welter of exposed red rubber pipes underneath it.

But the room with the iron-barred door beside the kitchen still brimmed with darkness, and here, as my eyes adjusted to the dark, I thought I saw someone stir inside.

I went closer. It was a man. He was sitting on the floor, his legs drawn up against his torso, leaning against the wall facing the stairway; he would have seen me come up.

At first, I saw only his eyes, then the rest of

his swarthy, stubbly face, and then the grimy khaki shorts from which his dark hairy legs stuck out; I realized that it was Shyam.

I was too shocked and unsettled to speak. I stared at him for a moment, and when I eventually managed to get the words out, I spoke my name. I asked him if he recognized me. I tried to speak in the local Hindi dialect I used with him and Mrs. Pandey.

I could see his eyes clearly now; I felt something flicker in them. But no words came out.

I came closer and now held the smooth iron bars with my hands. A faint smell of urine met my nostrils.

I spoke my name again, a little louder this time. I told him that I had once lived in the room on the roof.

"He doesn't hear anything," a voice said behind me.

I turned back to see a tall woman in a sari; she had silently appeared out of Mrs. Pandey's room.

It was Sita, Arjun's wife. She nodded and said Namaste, inaudibly moving her lips. My presence didn't seem to surprise her a bit. I would have recognized her immediately if she had been wearing the sari over her head in the way she used to when I passed her on the stairs.

She hadn't changed much: she was as thin

as I remembered her; her upper teeth slightly jutted out; frank curiosity lay in her round dark eyes and there was a soft solicitude in her voice.

"He doesn't hear anything," she repeated.

"What happened?"

"We had to take him to a mental asylum after Mataji died," she said, in Hindi, using the word *Pagalkhana.* "He got into a fight there; someone hit him on the ear with a hammer."

I looked back at Shyam. He hadn't moved; and now his eyes met mine: something dead now lay in them.

"Will you have some tea?" Sita was asking, half-gesturing, as I turned to look at her, toward the kitchen.

I was beginning to decline politely when I heard a sound behind me. It was a low mumble. But a few words came through somewhat clearly; I didn't have to listen to all of them to know what he was saying.

"Greed," he was saying, "greed is the biggest evil. It divides families, sunders husband from wife, son from parents . . ."

I saw Sita throw a quick impatient glance at Shyam before saying, "Have some tea. It'll only take two minutes to make. We have a gas stove now."

As she spoke, the door opened behind her,

and Arjun came out, thick-lipped, with thinning hair, but startlingly cleanshaven. He scowled at me for an instant and then his face broke into a smile.

"Hello, boss," he said. "How are you? Come to see Miss West?"

It was the bantering manner of college-educated youth. "Yes, yes," I stammered, suddenly remembering what Pratap had told me, and still held by his face, the lips that appeared thicker without the beard.

"Have some tea," Arjun said. "You must be tired. You have come a long way."

I heard Shyam's monotonous drone behind me. ". . . divides families, sunders husband from wife, son from parents . . ."

"See the kitchen, at least," Sita was saying. "You will not recognize it. It's all modern now."

"It'll take two minutes only," Arjun said, in English. He added, a smile on his face, "Miss West is not going to run away in that time."

Inside the kitchen, Sita flicked on the naked lightbulb hanging from the ceiling. The sooty black walls and the cow-dung-paved hearth were gone. White tiles gleamed on the walls, and on a raised cement platform squatted a gas stove, its metal frame painted a garish green. In one corner was a small fridge, with a large Dennis the Menace sticker on the door.

5

As I came up to the roof from the constricted courtyard, the sky suddenly lay open once again, but darkening now, the sun muffled behind a thick bank of dark clouds on the western side, the river gray and placid, a few black boats scattered around the deserted ghat.

The riverfront was unchanged, but the view on the other side of the house had altered. A new shed of corrugated iron stood in the temple courtyard. The roof of the facing house had higher balustrades, stubs of iron girders sticking out of the uncemented brick wall. An unfamiliar lock with a round combination dial hung on the door to my room. Two tie-dyed lungis with batik patterns hung down from the clothesline. I had to push them out of my way in order to reach Miss West's room.

The door was open. She was standing over the table with the piled-up CDs, in the way I had often seen her, her gaze downcast, surveying the discs, her hair falling in a thick blond veil around her face, and for one disorienting instant I almost expected her to say, "So what shall we listen to next?"

She turned and in another familiar gesture shook back her head a bit and nimbly tucked stray locks of hair behind her ears. "Oh, hello there," she said, smiling. "Come on in. I was sort of expecting you early. You have come too late for tea, I am afraid."

There was affection in her smile, but her alert eyes looked at me intently.

She said, "You have changed, you know. You look taller and broader — or is it just my eyes?"

She had changed, too. It was dark inside the room and the light through the door highlighted the wrinkles on her face and the loose skin on her neck in contrast with the black turtleneck sweater; her eyes, though still vigilant, had lost their old luster; they looked tired when not focused on something. She would have been past fifty now, and her face, its fine balanced features, held a kind of resignation, which enhanced its natural serenity — the serenity that had struck me in the days I used to see her sit out on the roof, watching the river.

I was full of what I had seen downstairs. Shyam in a cage of sorts; Arjun and Sita, their voices so calm, their manner so full of solicitude.

After what I had heard, I was expecting them to be strained and nervous with me, with someone who had lived in the house when Panditji and his wife were still alive, and who had heard about the quarrels and the conspiracies Mrs. Pandey suspected her son of hatching against her. But with almost effortless ease, they had assumed the role of the house's owners, with the casual confidence that went with it, a confidence unfazed by the presence of Shyam, another witness from the past.

I mentioned some of this to Miss West.

"People talk," she said, "but there is no evidence. Nothing that points to their involvement. Of course there were no postmortems — the funerals were held very quickly. People got suspicious about that. I wasn't here, you know. But we all know what happens during the summer rush at the funeral ghats. All those poor villagers dying like flies in the heat. You either bribe your way through or wait your turn behind a thousand corpses rotting away by the riverside. So they had to do it quickly. Anyway, they have been good to me. I was worrying that they might ask me to leave or ask for some ridiculous rent after Panditji and Mrs. Pandey died. But they didn't. I only wish they hadn't let the downstairs room to those wretched sex-maniac Israelis. Did you see them on the way up? They never leave the house; they go at it like little rabbits."

It was the voice and manner I remembered, unambiguous, matter-of-fact, and with a sharp edge; and I had now a somewhat absurd retrospective sense of having missed them all these years.

"Did you get the packet I sent you?" she said, abruptly changing the subject. "Someone left it outside your door just after you left. I didn't see who it was. No one saw him."

"Yes," I said, thinking of Rajesh walking up the stairs to my room. Had he met Arjun then?

"Who was it? Who?" Miss West was saying.

"It was someone I knew at the university," I said, and then found myself adding, "I recently found out that he was a criminal."

"Was he? How interesting," she said. "But the university is full of them!"

I wished suddenly to change the subject.

I told her about the prostitutes at my hotel; I told her about my all-pink room, how the receptionist had called it the honeymoon suite.

"I am not surprised," she said. She paused and suddenly shivered and wrapped her arms around her chest. "It's the new mafia people talk about. They are going to transform the city. You see that happening already. Those ghastly fast-food places and beauty parlors and so-called Italian restaurants and the hotels with discotheques — the money for all this comes from the mafia."

As my eyes adjusted to the dark, I saw more of her room, which looked much the same as before. An earthen pot damp with water sat beneath her bed; behind the flimsy curtain of the wardrobe lay the stacks of clothes; a row of paperbacks leaned on the windowsill; the clunky music system still perched on the narrow wooden shelf nailed to the wall; her straw hat clung to the wall, hanging from an invisible nail.

The only new item appeared to be a glossy poster advertising performances of Mozart's *Marriage of Figaro* at the Royal Opera House. The year on it was 1995 — which meant that she had been to England recently.

But the pictures on the wall were gone — the photographs from Miss West's past, among others, of Christopher, the pictures that had once given me such a wounding sense of faraway unattainable worlds, that had stirred so many inadequacies and yearnings in me.

Miss West said, "I can't give you tea, I'm afraid. But let's go out. Let's go for a boat ride. Let's do the touristy thing. You would like that, wouldn't you?"

"Yes," I said, "yes."

She snatched her straw hat from the wall; and then placed it back on the nail, which had suddenly looked exposed and vulnerable. "The weather looks dodgy out there, doesn't it?" she said, squinting into the gray day outside. "It might rain."

We went out, down the stairs, through the gloomy shadowless alleys, past the little shrine to Hanuman, to the ghats. The gray placid river was pierced here and there by scimitar-like flashes of light. The birds on the ancient banyan tree chattered loudly. The sun still shone on the massive stone ramparts of Ramnagar Palace, but the city to the north cowered under an enormous pile of woolly dark clouds.

The stone steps on the ghat were slippery with wet mud. As we went down to the river, Miss West once swayed a bit and seemed about to fall before recovering quickly. There were a few boatmen closer to the river, squatting on the ground in a circle, quietly smoking beedis and talking. They saw us, and one of them immediately detached himself from the group and began to walk toward where we were.

The man came closer; his hair was white as snow above his dark-complexioned face.

"Is that Ramchand?" I asked, suddenly

remembering the exceptionally handsome boatman who had come up to us the first time I went with Miss West on a boat ride.

"No," Miss West said, her voice neutral, "Ramchand is back in his village; he has tuberculosis. This is his father."

It was in the same indifferent tone — the boat freed from the bank, the ropes tossed off, and the old boatman straining at the oars with small grimaces upon his bony face — that she began speaking of events and personalities from the past.

She spoke of the breakup between Mark and Debbie, who was now a graduate student at Indiana University. She also spoke of people I hadn't known but she assumed I did. None of this was unfamiliar to me; it matched my memory of her. So much of her time in that room on the roof used to go into these extensive analyses of people she knew.

She barely noticed the city sliding past us, the ghats with their isolated groups of people and solitaries, the tattered beach umbrellas, the melancholy widows in white saris, the stray coils of smoke from funeral pyres at Harishchandra Ghat.

She spoke of a courtesan she had known for a long time.

"In her time, when she was beautiful and attractive and all that, this woman had known

356

practically every rich person in town. That's what makes it so shocking and depressing. I heard this just today. She died recently in great poverty and her neighbor had to go around to collect money to buy wood for her funeral pyre."

A long boat appeared in the middle distance; it seemed to be approaching fast in our direction.

Miss West had appeared to stop but now she added, with a vehemence that made her voice sound cracked with emotion: "It's all such a waste. Such a *bloody* waste."

She was silent for a while, and in the silence I thought of the morning I had awakened to find her sitting on the roof and crying over something I couldn't then understand. "Such a waste, such a bloody waste": that's what she had said then — the exact words — and she had bemused me by sounding so different, her tone so far from the assured intimacy and confidence that had made such an impression on me.

I used to think then that her solitude committed her to puzzling out the characters and lives of people she knew. It came to me now that her curiosity was all along dictated by her own complicated life, by the setbacks and disappointments she suffered in it.

Yellow flames flickered and glowered

through the gray haze at Manikarnika Ghat. The peal of temple bells traveled in light wispy echoes across the river. The sky above was heavy and expectant with thick dark clouds.

It grieved me to look at the despair that had passed over Miss West's face as she spoke, to have the sense, as I once had, of the density of memories, wounds, ambitions, and regrets seething inside her.

And I was looking away, at the looming city, when I heard her saying, her voice abruptly bright: "But you would remember her, wouldn't you?"

"Who?" I asked.

"The courtesan I was talking about," Miss West replied. "The woman with the kohl-rimmed eyes. She sang that beautiful song about Krishna and Radha at that party we had when you first arrived in Benares, where Anand played the sitar and Catherine did her bit with the tanpura. You remember that, don't you?"

The moment was inevitable. I knew it would come from the time I ran into Mark in Dharamshala. With such dread and curiosity had I anticipated it, and now, as an old suppressed vision arose before me, I knew again the familiar horrible clamor of memories, memories of that evening on the roof, the night at Kalpi, the evening in Pondicherry, and so many other days — the poisoned past that for many years never left my side, that first clung to me on those aimless travels across the country, during sleepless nights in creaking, crackling train compartments, as relentless and futile as the circling shadows around me, the past that scratched old wounds on serene mornings in high mountain valleys and amid the sullen ruins of remote monasteries, the past that, long after I settled in Dharamshala and began to heal, pursued me into innumerable exhausting dreams.

Miss West was saying, "I suppose you haven't heard about Catherine and Anand."

The boat coming in from the opposite direction moved closer. Its four or five rowers frantically pushed at the oars, sending little ripples coursing through the water; their frenzy enhanced the stillness of the women with long sari veils and men in white kurtas, one of them holding a large gleaming brass urn.

Miss West said, "The whole thing collapsed not long after they got to Paris."

The boat appeared to be heading directly toward us, and in the end passed us barely inches away. It was at that very moment a strong wind suddenly came over the water. The veils of the women fluttered and were immediately tugged back into position. Little clouds of dust and sand loomed up on the other, empty side of the river and rolled for a little distance before abruptly fading.

Miss West said, "It collapsed once it became clear that Anand was no Ravi Shankar. I sort of knew it wouldn't last long, but I was surprised by how quickly it folded up. I remember just before she left Benares, Catherine was neurotic about him; she would go on about him to everyone she met. I thought she was totally insecure, almost pathetic in her insecurity. But she was right to be so, because when they got to Paris no one would give Anand a job, even those Indians who are in the cultural business in such places and do things for European consumption. Catherine's parents were horrible to him, in their own subtle manner. Catherine defended him; she was good at that. She still went on about him, but in a different way."

We were halfway to Dashashvamedh Ghat, its throng of bathing devotees partly visible behind the plume of black diesel smoke that one of the empty anchored boats breathed into the air. The boat slid forward in smoother bursts now. A small breeze blew in from the other side, ruffling the water and making Miss West, as she spoke, draw her shawl around her even tighter.

She said, "I saw them together once in Paris. She had a little party; all her friends were there; she kept talking about Anand to her friends; he was her little trophy from India. Anand this, Anand that. Oh, look at him, isn't he wonderful. But when I next went to Paris, he was gone. He had gone back to India. Catherine wouldn't speak much about him; her mother, a rather tedious middle-class woman, complained to me about the water he spilled on her bathroom floor. Catherine was living with a new boyfriend, an Algerian, some sort of filmmaker. I didn't see her again.

"She wrote a few times. Her boyfriends kept changing. The last time she wrote she was with some stockbroker; she said she was planning to marry him, raise a family. She felt secure with him. It was all very odd: she sounded so much like her mother; she wanted children, security, stability, all those middle-class things. All that bohemianism had gone.

"I saw Anand in Delhi a couple of years ago. He plays for some studio orchestra in Delhi and lives in some dreadful slum east of the river — probably not a slum, most of Delhi, even the middle-class suburbs, looks like a slum to me. He looked completely wasted, even thinner. His sisters are still unmarried; his parents have almost disowned him. When I met him, it was four years after he came back from Paris and the poor man was still devastated, still pining for Catherine, hoping for some sort of miracle, writing long letters to her and getting shorter and shorter notes in return.

"I had to be tough with him. I told him to stop thinking about her. I told him to move on, get married, work hard, lose himself in something. But I thought later that I was probably too harsh with him.

"His love for Catherine, his time in Paris: this was the greatest thing that could ever happen to him. He had only this past and he was trapped by it. Catherine could move on, but he was stuck. She is drifting, too, poor girl, but she is supported by her father's money, her culture, her background; they give her at least an idea of what she owes to herself.

"Anand, people like him, they can't afford such ideas; they don't know who they are; they don't know what they want; they are simply trying hard not to sink into the misery and wretchedness they are born into. That's what he is doing now.

"But he was young when he first met Catherine. And when you are young you have these desires like everyone else; you're greedy for love, you feel then that the world owes you your happiness; you feel you are entitled to it simply by being alive."

She stopped suddenly. We were about to reach Dashashvamedh Ghat. It was dark over the river now; a tangle of sounds from the city reached us. Broken reflections of the sodium lights on the ghat glimmered and trembled in the black water.

I couldn't see Miss West's face, and her voice seemed to come from the same faraway world she had been talking of. She said: "I have been going on for far too long. Now tell me about your own life. It's been such a long time since you were here."

Until now, as she was speaking, I had felt an old bitterness and anguish surge up within me. I had suddenly felt myself full of things to say. I had longed to speak, to somehow or other express the great turmoil in my heart.

But now the moment was dead, and Miss West's question left me feeling drained. What could I have told her about my life? There were the broad details, and I tried to list them: the school, the job, the travels in the Himalayas. But the things that really mattered in it were all so private; they were like the events in Miss West's own life. Where would I have started? How could I have confessed to her the circumstances that had driven me to a life so different from any I could have expected to lead when I first knew her in Benares? How could I have confessed that the larger world that I had once longed to enter had become a fearful place to me?

A thin drizzle had started by the time we got out of the boat. A stronger wind now blew in from the other shore; the anchored boats rocked and thudded into each other.

The glare of the sodium lamps outlined the slanting threads of rain as we went up the long, wide steps to the top of the ghat. The concourse ahead was a sea of agitated black umbrellas and glistening plastic sheets, people everywhere running for cover, past the bright blurred gleams of the brassware and gift shops.

"What a dreadful time to rain," Miss West said. "We'll all get pneumonia."

She added, "But look! There's a rickshaw!"

She skipped and flounced toward it, the hand she had raised to point at the rickshaw still held up, and then jumped in.

I followed her to the rickshaw and stood before it.

Miss West wiped the rickshaw seat with her handkerchief, and then in one swift movement pulled the tarpaulin hood over her head. There was a moment of uncertainty before she realized that I was not going to join her.

She extended a hand; it was cold and clammy to the touch.

She said, "I am going away in a couple of weeks. Back to England."

I nodded, and she said nothing more. She hadn't talked about leaving Benares to me. But she knew that I knew.

She kept her hand in mine for a few more wordless moments.

"Goodbye," she said at last.

And then added: "Come and visit me in England. We shall . . ."

She appeared to pause in midsentence, but then said nothing more.

The rickshaw driver mounted his seat. I felt Miss West withdraw her hand. The roving headlight of a scooter illuminated her pale serene face for a brief instant and then darkness moved in.

The rickshaw moved off with a brief jerk. I felt something well up inside me.

As I watched, the rickshaw lurched away and soon melted into the tumultuous traffic ahead. I was turning to go when I suddenly remembered that this was where I had once stood with Miss West in the middle of a festive afternoon, waiting anxiously for Catherine. I remembered how flustered I had been when Catherine finally appeared, how the freshness and grace of her face came to me as a little shock each time. I turned back and there, between two white temples, was the entrance to the lane with the mattlocked sadhu and the house with the Ram-Sita mural, and I remembered how I would walk through the bustling ghats and alleys to Catherine's home, with that anticipatory thrill in my heart, and it all came back to me in a rush: the empty days, the long smoky-blue twilights, the flickering fluorescent light and the pigeons in their neat rows, the voices from the alley floating up to the small room with the gleaming sitar in one corner, all that slow leisurely life of old Benares, and the furtive tender growth inside me; and I felt sad, and full of mourning for the past, for that pure time of desires and dreams I knew when I first came to Benares and lived in a crumbling old house by the river.

The rain suddenly grew intense. Heavy hard drops fell on the back of my neck. I turned around to look for another rickshaw; there was none in sight.

I ran toward an autorickshaw I saw standing in one corner, and then sat back, panting slightly, as the driver plunged, weaving and pirouetting, into the swarming chaos of running pedestrians, rickshaws, cycles, and scooters.

The rain flowed down the frontshield,

which the driver kept wiping with a rag that lay on the dashboard. Gleamingly vivid for one moment, the streets dissolved into smudgy fluorescent colors the next. Passing scooters and autorickshaws kept spraying thick jets of muddy water from the water-logged road into the back seat.

We finally arrived at the hotel, after lurching and splashing through an unknown maze of potholed dark back alleys. There was no power in the area, and the big white concrete block of the hotel stood brooding dumbly over its waterlogged forecourt. Inside, all was chaos: the weak light from petromax lanterns fell on rolled-up carpets and hectic men with pails and mops. The receptionist said that I would have to wait in the lobby; the roof had leaked and some of the rooms had been flooded. He went on to describe the rest of the evening's disasters. I only half-listened. Water ran down my back; my socks were wet; my feet cold. But I was feeling oddly calm.

ABOUT THE AUTHOR

PANKAJ MISHRA, born in 1969, lives in New Delhi and Simla. He writes for *The New York Review of Books*, *The Times Literary Supplement*, and other journals.